JUNE TATE was born in Southampton and spent the early years of her childhood in the Cotswolds. After leaving school she became a hairdresser on cruise ships the *Queen Mary* and the *Mauretania*, meeting many Hollywood film stars and VIPs on her travels. After her marriage to an airline pilot, she lived in Sussex and Hampshire before moving to Estoril in Portugal. June, who has two adult daughters, now lives in Sussex.

The Docklands Girls

June Tate

Allison & Busby Limited
12 Fitzroy Mews
London W1T 6DW
allisonandbusby.com

First published in Great Britain by Allison & Busby in 2016.
This paperback edition published by Allison & Busby in 2016.

A CIP catalogue record for this book is available from
the British Library.

10 9 8 7 6 5 4 3 2 1

ISBN 978-0-7490-2061-3

Typeset in 10.55/15.55 pt Sabon by
Allison & Busby Ltd.

The paper used for this Allison & Busby publication
has been produced from trees that have been legally sourced
from well-managed and credibly certified forests.

Printed and bound by
CPI Group (UK) Ltd, Croydon, CR0 4YY

To my lovely son-in-law, Ron Phillips.
He's one of the good guys!

Chapter One

Spring, 1944

Hildy Dickson pushed back a stray hair under the turban on her head. She was working at what used to be the Sunlight Laundry, but had exchanged sheets and shirts for making parts for Spitfires. The men and women who were employed worked in shifts to enable them to keep up the production of the vitally important work.

Hildy was a supervisor and it was her job not only to work on the assembly line but to keep an eye on the female workers, making sure that there were no shirkers. She was a dedicated worker which didn't make her popular, but it didn't bother her a jot. She was there to do a job and that was what she did. She was relentless with those girls who after a night out on the town would complain to her they were unwell.

'Then take more water with it!' she'd say. 'Think of those poor devils who have to fly the planes we supply. They don't complain. Now get back to your bench.'

She had thought of joining one of the women's services. The WRENS or the ATS, but her mother had begged her not to leave home and as her drunken father had walked out on them when she was a child, she had taken his place as head of the household and felt duty-bound to stay put. But deep down, she resented the position in which her father had placed her. She felt life was passing her by and her mother clung to her like a leach, which didn't help. Consequently, she was a frustrated young woman. But she did insist on either going to the pictures or dances, once or twice a week. There at least she could forget her cares and relax. It was the only thing that saved her from completely losing her freedom and she relished those moments.

The bell rang for the end of the shift and she breathed a sigh of relief, took off her turban and shook her hair free. It had been an early morning shift and she thought she'd walk through the park, sit and have a quiet cigarette before going home.

Despite the havoc that the bombing had caused, the Southampton parks were still well cared for and now, in April, there was blossom on the trees, daffodils showing their trumpet-shaped blooms and after the decimation of much of the town in the Blitz, the parks were a thing of peace and calm in the uncertain world at war.

Hildy sat down on a bench and took out a cigarette, lit it and leant back taking in her surroundings. She'd been up at the crack of dawn and now it was lunchtime. She took a packet of sandwiches out of her pocket to eat after she'd enjoyed the welcome hit of nicotine. Fish paste on wartime bread wasn't much to get excited about, but when you were hungry, it didn't matter too much. She sat and watched the passers-by. Mothers pushing prams, office workers taking a break as she was and the usual mixture of troops from different parts of the world, wandering aimlessly, trying to fill time in a strange country.

Rumours were rife and talk now was of an impending invasion. With the troops lining the streets, sitting on their tanks, others in camps, it certainly seemed likely and there was almost a hint of desperation in the chat-up lines aimed at the girls. Soldiers, afraid of what was ahead of them were determined to live what life they had to the full knowing that the possibility of death awaited them.

To alleviate the strain on the waiting troops, the Americans arranged dances for their men, inviting certain females to their camps, transporting them there and back in trucks. The female staff of Tyrrell & Green, one of the main stores in Southampton, had been issued invites and Hildy was going with a friend of hers who worked there and had managed to get an extra ticket. She loved to dance and it was another night of freedom from her mother. She sat eating her sandwich wondering what to wear to the dance.

Olive Dickson was not best pleased when her daughter told her of her plans for the evening.

'Going where?' she demanded.

'Stony Cross.'

'But how on earth will you get there in the blackout?'

'The Americans collect us in trucks from the Civic Centre and bring us home.'

Olive looked appalled. 'In trucks . . . like cattle! Well really, I don't know what the world is coming to, really I don't!'

'Oh, for goodness' sake, Mother, it is only a form of transportation. They could hardly take us all there in cars. Anyway, I'm going whether you like it or not!'

Olive changed her tactics immediately; she began to simper.

'You know how I hate to be on my own at night. You know how nervous I get and, what's more, I'm not feeling very well.'

Hildy was used to the emotional blackmail and didn't respond in the way her mother hoped. '*It's That Man Again* is on the radio tonight. You know how much you like Tommy Handley. You can listen to that! I'm off to have a bath.'

When she was alone, Olive quietly fumed, telling herself she didn't deserve such a selfish daughter. She went into the bedroom, got undressed and climbed into bed, placing a bottle of aspirin beside her. She lay in wait.

Hildy crumbled a bath cube in the required five inches of bath water before climbing in and relaxing. After a quick soak, she eventually climbed out, dried herself, went to her bedroom and put on a dress she'd chosen. She pulled on a pair of Lisle stockings wishing they were nylons, but these were in very short supply, unless you had a GI boyfriend.

When she was ready, she walked out of her room and saw a light on in her mother's bedroom as the door was ajar.

Tapping on the door, she asked, 'Mum. Are you there?'

'Come in,' was the reply in a wan voice.

As soon as she entered she saw her mother laid against the pillow and saw the bottle of aspirin. Her eyes narrowed.

'Let me look at you for the last time,' said her mother.

Hildy just glared at her. 'You really should be on the

stage, you know. Sarah Bernhardt has nothing on you! I'm off.' She walked out, her cheeks flushed with anger.

She was still angry as she walked to the Civic Centre. She was twenty-three, for God's sake! Not a child. She did have a life of her own. She was a daughter, not a slave! Oh, how she longed to walk away from her mother – the heavy chain around her neck, but how could she? She felt duty-bound to stay. At the back of her mind was always the small doubt, would her mother cope or would she do something stupid? That was the hold that Olive had over her and it was killing her.

There was a crowd of chatting, giggling young women outside the Civic Centre waiting to be collected. Hildy found Joan, her friend among the melee.

'There you are!' Joan rushed over to her. 'I wondered if your mum had stopped you coming.' Joan was aware of her friend's difficulties.

With a tight grin, Hildy said, 'No, but she did her best to do so. Anyway, let's forget her and have a good night.'

Two trucks duly arrived and the girls were helped on by cheerful GIs who were delighted with their cargo. Inside, a bench seat was either side of the vehicle and everyone squeezed in. The air was alive with happy expectation. Wafts of Evening in Paris perfume and Californian Poppy filled the interior. Some wore stockings, others had put tan on their legs and drawn a seam down the back with an eyebrow pencil. Everyone had made a great effort. An invite to an American army camp was to be relished.

* * *

11

Eventually the trucks arrived at their destination and the girls were lifted down with enthusiasm by the soldiers who flirted outrageously and they were led over to a hall. Inside, it was lit brightly; an American flag was at the back of the bandstand and a band was playing as they entered. Each girl was given a beautiful buttonhole and pin as she handed over her coat which was a delightful surprise. And without hesitation, soldiers stepped forward to claim a partner.

Hildy forgot her cares and let herself go. She loved to jive and the Americans were good at it. The band was playing Glenn Miller's '*In the Mood*' and she was turned and twisted to the music by her partner. As the dance finished, he grinned at her.

'You're quite a mover, lady!'

'Yes, she sure is and this dance is mine, buddy!' Another soldier took Hildy by the arm and danced her away from her partner.

She laughed at him. 'That was pretty slick,' she said.

He winked. 'Don't pay to hang about these days, honey. Time isn't on our side,' and with his hand firmly on her back, he led her through the quickstep faultlessly.

Finally, just when Hildy thought she couldn't dance another step, a sergeant approached her and said, 'Lady, I really think you deserve a break! Come and have a well-earned drink.'

She gratefully followed him to the bar.

'What's your poison?' he asked.

'Gin and tonic, please.'

Pointing to an empty table and chairs, he said, 'I suggest you sit there and I'll bring over the drinks. It'll give you time to rest your feet.' His eyes twinkled as he spoke.

'You must be my guardian angel,' she said with some feeling.

'Who knows,' he replied.

Eventually he came over and placed her drink in front of her and a Coke for himself.

'Don't you drink?' she asked with some surprise.

'Sure I do, but I'm on duty tonight, keeping an eye on things, making sure you ladies all have a good time without any hassle.'

'And you are?'

'Sergeant Milt Miller, at your service.'

'Milt?'

'Short for Milton. And you?'

'Hildy, short for Hilda, Dickson. Supervisor at a factory building engines and parts for Spitfires.'

'A worthy occupation,' he said smiling at her.

Sipping her drink, Hildy looked around at the dancing figures on the floor.

'How long before you will all be shipped across the Channel?'

Grinning, he said, 'If I knew I couldn't tell you, you know that. But the fact is I don't know. All I do know is if and when we leave, it's my duty to keep my men alive.'

'That's some responsibility,' she remarked.

'One I don't want to think about tonight. You hungry, Hildy?'

She nodded.

'Then you come with me,' and he led her to the other end of the hall where a table was laid, packed with food.

Hildy's eyes lit up as she looked at the spread. There were sandwiches made with real ham as opposed to the usual Spam. The bread was white, unlike the grey of the National loaf. Sausage rolls and something called hot dogs, long sausages in a roll, were on offer as well as small cakes. She looked at her escort.

'Blimey! It's like Christmas has come early!'

Laughing, Milt filled a couple of plates with this manna from heaven and led her over to a small table. 'Go for it!' he said. And she did, savouring every mouthful.

At the end of their picnic, Milt left and returned with two cups of real coffee. When Hildy smelt the aroma of coffee beans instead of the usual camp coffee, she couldn't believe her luck.

'You have no idea just how great this tastes,' she told him. 'I don't remember when I last enjoyed a cup of proper coffee. How lucky you Yanks are.'

'Yes, I guess we take these things for granted. The Post Exchange store is pretty well stocked. In the States we haven't suffered the shortages you have. But at least we've been able to share our good fortune with others.' He opened a pack of Camel cigarettes and offered her one. After they lit them, he handed her the pack.

'Here, take these I have more.'

Hildy studied the man sitting opposite. He was tall, broad-shouldered with twinkling blue eyes and looked extremely fit, a little older than most of the other GIs. His dark hair was cut short just like all the other military, but there was something very solid about this man, she decided. Someone to be relied upon. She thought the soldiers that would be fighting alongside him would be in good hands.

'So, Hildy, what's going through your mind right now?'

She looked startled. 'Whatever do you mean?'

'Well, you've been staring at me for a while and I wondered what you were thinking.'

Her cheeks flushed with embarrassment. 'I was thinking that you looked as if you would know what you're doing on a battlefront.'

'Well I'm a regular soldier not a conscript so I guess I'm more trained than most of my boys. It's good to see them letting off steam tonight because in the future, they'll have to face the enemy and that ain't a great deal of fun.'

'Have you got a girl back home, Milt?'

'Lordy no! I've had girl friends, of course, but no one special. How about you?'

She shook her head. 'No, no one.'

'A good-looking chick like you, I find that hard to believe.'

Shrugging she said, 'Well you know how it is. Life and the war got in the way.' *And my mother* she thought to herself.

Milt studied the girl sitting opposite him. She had a certain air about her. A confidence yet at the same time there was sadness in her eyes and he wondered what the story was behind it. He thought he'd like to learn more about her.

'Well, Hildy, as it seems we are both free agents, how about we get together until we ship out? We could have some fun, no strings attached. How about it?'

She started to laugh. 'That's just about the nicest thing

15

anyone has ever said to me. Most men have an agenda, you know!'

This amused the American. 'You are so right. However, in wartime things are so uncertain, you have to seize the moment. What do you say?'

'I'd like that very much is what I say, Sergeant!'

'Then let's take to the floor and celebrate.' He held out his hand and she took it.

The band was playing a waltz and Milt drew her into his arms, holding her close as they danced to the music. She could feel his taught body against hers and could smell the scent of his aftershave. Somehow she felt at home within his hold and all the stress of her situation at home seemed to drift away as the music played.

They stayed together until the end of the evening and as he walked her to the truck waiting to carry the girls back to Southampton he said, 'I've got tomorrow evening off, fancy going to a movie?'

'I'd like that very much,' she replied.

'Great. I'll meet you outside the Empire cinema at six-thirty. Is that alright with you?'

'I'll be there.'

He lifted her into the truck with ease. 'See you tomorrow, Hildy, and thanks for a great evening.'

Joan overheard the conversation as she sat beside Hildy.

'Looks like you made a killing girl. Nice-looking fellow. Lucky you!'

'He's really nice, not fast like most of the Yanks. You know oversexed and over here.'

'All genitals and jeeps, I always say!' Joan retorted.

'These bloody men are like an overheated octopus. Hands everywhere given the chance.'

'He's taking me to the pictures tomorrow.'

'Huh! Your mother won't like that!'

'She'll bloody well have to lump it!' was Hildy's snappy reply. She spent the drive home going over the events of the evening and anticipating the enjoyment of the following one. She hadn't had a steady boyfriend for ages; it would be great to enjoy male company again and the idea of no strings attached suited her. It would give her something to look forward to and that would be a change. At the moment, her life seemed to be all work – and her mother.

The following evening, Hildy met her GI outside the Empire cinema and was delighted when they took their seats in the balcony and he handed her a bar of Hershey's chocolate.

'Oh my goodness!' she exclaimed. 'You have no idea just how much of a treat this is.'

Milt looked pleased. 'Happy to oblige ma'am,' he said with a grin and put his arm around her shoulders as they settled down to watch *Cover Girl* with Rita Hayworth and Gene Kelly.

Hildy was relieved that Milt didn't try to kiss her during the film. She'd have been disappointed had he done so and during the interval, he bought two tubs of ice cream for them. They sat chatting about the dancing in the film whilst they ate.

'I think Rita Hayworth is so beautiful and to see Gene Kelly dance is always terrific. No one makes a musical like the Americans!'

'I'm glad you think so. It's just the sort of movie that

makes you forget what's going on in the world and we all need to escape reality these days.'

Eventually at the end of the film, they stood for the national anthem and left the cinema. Milt led her into a nearby bar for a nightcap before closing time. As they sat talking, his gaze was penetrating.

'I can't help feeling that there is some sadness in your life, Hildy. Am I right?'

She was completely taken aback at his perception. 'Whatever makes you say that?' she asked.

He took her hand. 'Even when you're happy, there's a sort of melancholy behind your eyes. I've seen it in many of my young soldiers.'

'You're too bright for your own good!' she retorted, a sudden brittleness in her voice.

'I see I've touched on a nerve. I'm sorry; I don't wish to pry. But you know what they say, a problem shared . . .'

She gazed back at him. This was a man she felt she could trust.

'My father walked out on us, my mum and me, since then I've taken his place running the household. My mother is a demanding woman who tries to run my life. It's as simple as that.'

'That's not simple, Hildy. That can be like something that slowly sucks you dry. But you're a strong woman, how do you cope with the situation?'

She gave a wry smile. 'The best way I can. Now you know, can we leave it at that?'

'Of course, but now I understand you a little better. Come on, let's drink up and I'll walk you home.'

Outside, he tucked her arm through his and they walked in comfortable silence until they reached her front door.

Holding her face gently, Milt kissed her. 'I so enjoyed this evening, Hildy, and we'll do this often. When can I see you again?'

She smiled softly. 'Whenever you like.'

'I hoped you'd say that. What shift are you on tomorrow?'

'Early. I finish at one o'clock.'

'Tell me where you work and I'll meet you; we'll go for a coffee and a sandwich somewhere.'

She burst out laughing. 'I'll be in my work clothes!'

'So?'

'Well if you don't mind, why should I?' She gave him the address of the factory.

He kissed her again. 'Just remember I have broad shoulders. Enough to carry your troubles any time you want to offload them.'

'You are a lovely man, Milt, but I'm a big girl. I can manage.'

He laughed as he said, 'Fine. See you tomorrow!'

She smiled to herself as he walked away. She didn't know when she'd felt quite so happy. Putting her key in the front door, she hoped that her mother was in bed so that nothing could spoil this feeling.

Chapter Two

The streets around Southampton's docklands were teeming with military as well as the local inhabitants. There was an American military base camp on the common, which was now a restricted area. Sherman tanks lined the side streets around the town and there was a feeling of unrest in the air.

Southampton was slowly recovering from the Blitz in 1940 which had decimated the town centre as well as houses around the docks. The clearing of the debris to build one-storey shops in Above Bar Street had gone someway to restore normality and the relentless air raids had ceased at last.

The 14th Major Port Transport Corps had made camp to organise the handling of incoming cargo and ensure that the army was well supplied, as an influx of GIs had arrived in Southampton. Their arrival added some excitement around the battered town, mainly among the young women who were fascinated by the brash Americans and tempted by the offer of candy and nylon stockings. Many of the locals were not so pleased, especially when a company of black soldiers were also moved in. They were aghast when they saw girls walking in the town arm in arm with the 'darkies', as they referred to them. For many, it was the first time they'd seen a black man and so these boys were a topic of many a conversation.

There was also friction among the white American troops, especially those who hailed from the southern states where a black man had to sit in the back of the bus, where schools were segregated and where any black man risked being lynched if caught with a white woman. Yet here, they were free to walk arm in arm with the local girls.

In Canal Walk, where sex was for sale, business boomed. Canal Walk was a narrow, dark pedestrian street with shops either side. The pub at the end of the road, the Horse and Groom, had the reputation as the roughest pub in town with its huge one-room bar with smoke-stained walls, tables and chairs and dark brown paint, giving it a decidedly run down feel. At the far end were two enormous life-size stuffed brown bears, standing proud and somewhat menacing. Halfway down Canal Walk was another pub, the Lord Roberts: smaller, cleaner, fresher, with a cosy atmosphere and a less volatile clientele. It was a vibrant area in many ways. There were a couple of Jewish tailor's shops, a second-hand shop for clothing, a barbers, a butchers with meat hanging up in the window – and when available, rabbits and chicken, displayed outside – a shop for fishing tackle, the pawn shop which always seemed busy and a greengrocer's as well as a hotchpotch of others, all run by colourful characters.

It was here that the local brasses plied their trade, these days, either in the Horse and Groom or in the street, where they would stand, waiting for customers – and punters were aplenty. But nevertheless, like all docklands, these were mean streets. Black market deals were done in the pubs, pimps ruled some of the prostitutes, the town criminals gathered in the surrounding area and, sometimes, blood was spilt.

It was early evening when Cora Barnes entered the bar of the Lord Roberts and ordered a half of bitter. She preferred this pub to the noisy Horse and Groom and liked to sit alone for an hour before she began work. She was a pretty girl with her blonde hair and blue eyes. Her parents had both been killed in an air raid during the Blitz so now she was an orphan.

It had been a struggle to recover from her loss. She'd not only lost her parents, but like so many others, her home had been destroyed too. She had been working in a munitions factory and had rented a room near The Ditches, but one night she'd met a GI and they'd ended up at her place in a drunken state and gone to bed. After she woke in the morning, the Yank had left money on the side and returned to his barracks. She then realised he'd thought she was on the game and discovered she could make more money this way, so she quit her job at the factory. She intended to make as much money as possible so she could make a fresh start in another town where she was unknown and her past a secret.

The bar door opened and an American soldier walked in. He ordered a beer and looked around. Seeing her sitting alone, he wandered over.

'Hi there! Do you mind if I join you?'

She wasn't very enthusiastic as she considered this her private time and hesitated.

Seeing her reluctance, he said, 'Forgive me for intruding,

ma'am, but I'm feeling a bit homesick and would just like someone to talk to.'

There was something in his voice that made her change her mind. 'No, that's fine. Please, sit down.'

With a look of relief he did so. Holding out his hand, he said, 'I'm Hank Mason, from Detroit, Michigan.'

Shaking hands, she replied, 'Cora Barnes from Southampton.'

'Cora, that's unusual.'

'My mother named me after an aunt. Hank is a strange name, if you don't mind my saying?'

He laughed. 'It's short for Henry which I hate. My dad's name . . . he doesn't mind the Henry!'

For the next hour, he sat telling her about his home, his family and how he couldn't wait to get back there after the war. Then he asked after her family.

Her smile faded. 'They were killed in the bombing a while ago. I'm alone now.'

'Geez! That's really tough. I'm sorry for your loss. Do you live with some relations?'

Shaking her head, she said, 'No. I'm quite alone.' Looking at her watch she said, 'I'm sorry, Hank, but I've got to go to work.'

He looked surprised. 'It's almost seven o'clock. What work do you do at this hour?'

She gave a wry smile. 'I suppose you could say it's war work. Doing my bit as best I can.'

In the Horse and Groom, the patrons had started to arrive. All nations gathered here in the evening. British Tommies,

French sailors with their red pom poms on their hats, American GIs and the locals. A few of the local spivs were dealing in stolen petrol coupons, clothing coupons and any other goods collected in nefarious ways. There was always an underlying air of menace in the bar, even when it was quiet. Most Saturday nights there were fights; the police were always ready for the call, but sometimes an ambulance was needed.

Cora entered, bought her beer and joined a couple of colleagues sitting at a table.

'What's up, love?' Belle Newman asked.

'I've just met a really nice Yank, we were chatting and he was telling me about his family. He was just lonely, you know. He wasn't looking for business, probably didn't realise I was on the game.'

'And for a minute you wished you weren't, right?'

'Something like that.'

Belle shrugged. 'Don't, love. I was married once. Thought I could put all this behind me but when my old man found out about my past he only wanted me to go back on the streets so he could live off my money. Bastard!'

Cora looked shocked at the revelation. 'What happened?'

'I kicked the bugger out, went back on the game and kept the money for myself. No man lives off me, that's why I've never had a pimp.'

'I know what you mean,' Cora agreed. 'Cairo Fred tried to run me. I told him to take a hike!'

'Oh that slimy sod! Three of the girls work for him, I think they're nuts, but he caught them at the start of their career when they didn't know better.'

Cora started laughing. 'Career? Is that what you call it?'

'Yes, I bloody do! We don't lay down with a man for fun, love. We earn our wages. It's just as much a job as working in an office.'

'Hardly!'

'Well, you know what I mean.' Belle started to chuckle. 'Mind you, I'd rather work office hours, wouldn't you?'

Shrugging, Cora said, 'It would be nice, but the money isn't as good.'

Cora and Belle were good friends. Cora, quiet, Belle, older, outgoing and outrageous, with her dark hair and voluptuous body, but Cora was still well liked and popular. The bar began to fill up and soon a couple of GIs came over to the table and offered to buy Cora and Belle a drink. And so their work began.

In between punters, Belle would stand beside the pianist and sing one of The Andrews Sister's songs, to the enjoyment of the American GIs. Tonight, it was, 'Don't Sit Under the Apple Tree'. She sat down grinning at the applause.

It was almost closing time and Belle was sitting alone, tired after her night's work. She was looking forward to going home alone for a good night's sleep but as she drank up and walked out of the bar, she was followed by one of the American Negro soldiers.

'Excuse me, ma'am,' he said, 'But you busy or have you finished for the night?'

She was about to send him on his way, but as she gazed at him, she could see he was looking nervous and his hands were trembling.

'What's the matter, soldier?'

He looked down at his feet then slowly raised his head and said, 'I ain't never had a woman. I just would like the experience afore I'm posted to France, that's all.'

'How old are you?' she asked.

'Nineteen, ma'am. To be honest, I don't want to die wondering, that's all.'

How could she refuse such a plea, she asked herself. 'You come with me, soldier, and we'll put that right. Okay?'

He beamed at her, his teeth white against the ebony of his skin. 'That's mighty fine. Thanks.'

'What time do you have to be back at camp?'

'I have an all-night pass. I have to report back by nine in the morning.'

Taking his arm, she asked, 'What's your name?'

'Jackson Butler.'

'Then Jackson, let's go and have us some fun!'

As they walked towards her bedsitting room, she could feel the lad still shaking. He wasn't the first virgin she'd educated but certainly the first who wasn't gung-ho about the new experience. Most novices couldn't wait to grab at a bit of bare flesh and Belle was well covered.

Eventually she put the key into her front door and led Jackson inside. It was a large room with a single bed at one end, an easy chair, a small foldaway table and a couple of hard back chairs. There was a small sink, a kettle and a kitchen cabinet from where she took out a couple of glasses.

'Would you like a drink, Jackson?' she asked after making him sit down.

He frowned. 'Do you have any coffee, ma'am?'

She laughed. 'Well, that's a first and please call me Belle.' From the kitchen cabinet she took a bottle of camp coffee, filled the kettle and said, 'This won't be like any coffee you've ever had, love. But it's all we can get due to the war.'

'I can bring you some proper coffee,' he said. 'I'll buy some from the PX stores tomorrow, if you'd like?'

She looked delighted. 'Would I? I'd sell my soul to the devil for some!'

He began to relax and grinned broadly at her. 'Ain't no need to go that far, Belle!'

She smiled softly at him and cupped his chin in her hand. 'I can see you and me are going to get along famously.'

They chatted whilst they drank and he told her a little of his home life in Alabama and the restrictions on him and his ilk. She was appalled to hear the facts of being a black man in the south.

'If at home I was caught like now, sitting drinking coffee with a white woman, I'd end up dangling from a rope!'

This was too much for Belle. 'Well here, darling, you're as good as any man.' She took him by the hand and led him over to the bed. She felt him tense.

'Now just you relax,' she said as she kissed him, long and hard. Then she slowly removed his clothes, talked softly to him, sat him on the bed whilst she undressed in front of him, watching him all the time, seeing the expression of wonder on his face, the longing in his eyes – and his eventual erection.

She climbed onto the bed and took him into her arms. 'Come to Belle, darling,' she said softly, placing his hand on her breast, running her nimble fingers over his taut, muscular body.

'My but you're a fine figure of a man. You are black and beautiful, Jackson Butler!'

He gazed at her body in awe. 'Jeez, Belle, your skin is so pale, just like milk. I ain't never seen a woman naked like this before and certainly never a white one!'

An hour later, she gazed at the sleeping figure beside her and smiled. That was the most satisfying lay she'd had in a long time. She stretched out, set the alarm clock for seven in the morning, yawned and, cuddling up to the man beside her, she fell asleep.

The following morning, the alarm woke both of them. Jackson sat up suddenly, confused for a moment as to his whereabouts, then he looked at Belle beside him and he smiled.

'Oh, Belle, honey. That was a night I'll never forget as long as I live.'

Putting a hand behind his head, she pulled him down and kissed him gently. 'Me too, Jackson, love. Come here, we still have time.'

He eventually climbed off the bed, ran some water in the sink, swilled his face, stroked the stubble on his chin and asked, 'Don't suppose you've got a razor?'

Belle got out of bed, went to a drawer and gave him one and a bar of soap.

'Sorry, I don't keep shaving cream, will this do?'

He nodded and lathered his face.

She watched him shave and dress but when he made to pay her for her services, she declined. 'No, Jackson, this one's on me. It was my pleasure and I don't say that often. Just bring me some decent coffee and we'll call it quits.'

He took her into his arms. 'You are quite a woman, Belle. I'll be in the Horse and Groom again soon. I'll see you then but I gotta go now.'

She kissed him, opened the door and saw him on his way with a smile.

Slipping into a dressing gown, she made herself a cup of tea and, sitting on the bed, sipped the hot liquid. Black or not, he was a sweet boy, more polite than many of her clients and for her it had been a pleasure. What's more, she was looking forward to seeing him again. It was his vulnerability which had touched her. Despite the fact she was a few years older than Jackson and a prostitute, he'd treated her like a precious piece of china. Something to be cherished – and that hadn't happened to her for a very long time.

She'd become hardened to the life she led. With some men, all they needed was a bit of comfort, a chat and good sex. Others just used her, some didn't even undress but would sit and drink, smoke cigarettes and talk about their families. On occasion, she'd been in dangerous situations, but had managed to talk and charm her way out of most of them. Men came to her through frustration, a need to hold a woman, to be made to feel like an ordinary man and not a soldier, a number, with a fear of impending death across the water, facing an enemy, gunfire and mutilation. In the arms of a woman, they could put all this behind them for a short time. And Belle would do her best to leave them satisfied.

Chapter Three

Cora was window shopping in Above Bar Street wishing she had enough clothing coupons to buy a new jacket as she loved the red one on the mannequin in the window.

'Well, hi there! That'd look good on you, Cora!'

She turned in surprise to see, Hank, the GI she'd met in the Lord Roberts, standing beside her. 'Hello,' she said, 'what are you doing here?'

'Just killing time. I'm off duty for a few hours, how about you?'

'Window shopping, but I haven't any spare clothing coupons to buy anything.' She saw the look of puzzlement on his face and explained the necessity of such things here in wartime.

'Gee, that's real tough. I had no idea. To make up for your disappointment, how about I take you for lunch?'

'Really? Why I'd like that very much.'

They walked to Gatti's Restaurant in the High Street – which had luckily survived the Blitz – and were seated by the waiter. The menu was limited, of course, due to the rationing but they chose fish which was free of such restrictions. During the meal and a bottle of wine, Cora learnt more about her companion.

Hank told her about Detroit being the centre of the motor industry and how both he and his father had been employed as mechanical engineers until Hank joined the army after the Japanese bombed Pearl Harbour.

He looked somewhat rueful as he explained. 'The bombing came as a complete shock to our country. War was something that was happening elsewhere,' he said. 'But now we are as involved as everyone else. I know that many think but for that happening, we would have stayed out of the conflict . . . and who knows, maybe they are correct in their assumption.'

Cora sensed that her companion felt a certain shame about this and hurried to make him feel better about it.

'But you're here now. You aren't responsible, Hank.'

'Anyway, let's not talk about the war,' he said, 'what are your plans for when it's over?'

'I'm thinking of moving to London,' she said. 'I have no family, no ties. I just want a fresh start in a new place, away from all my bad memories.'

'No plans to get married and settle down then?'

'Not for a long time. I just want to live a little, do new things – enjoy life.'

'Then let's drink to that,' he said and raised his glass of wine to hers. 'I have an all-day pass on Sunday, are you free, Cora? I thought it would be great to see somewhere else other than Southampton. What do you say?'

Sunday was the only day that Cora didn't work and as she looked at her companion, she thought it would be a nice break. They arranged to meet at the train station at ten o'clock and take it from there.

Hank looked at his watch. 'Much as I'd like to stay with you, I'm afraid I have to get back to camp,' he said and called the waiter over and asked for the bill.

Outside, they parted until Sunday.

Cora walked home through the park, pleased she would be seeing the American again, wondering just how long she could keep from him the way she earned her money. If he ever discovered she was on the game that would be the last she'd see of him, of that she was sure.

In the Horse and Groom, the barmaid was calling time. She rang the bell hanging behind the bar. 'Time ladies and gentlemen, please!' She started to collect the empty glasses from the tables whilst urging the customers who were lingering to hurry.

'Come on you lot, drink up! If a copper walks in now, we'll lose our licence, so sup up and go home.' Eventually the bar emptied and she locked the doors.

Outside, the pimp Cairo Fred was urging two of his girls to work. 'Come along, you lazy bitches, enough hanging around. Go and find some more business!'

They muttered angrily as they walked away.

Fred leant against the wall and lit a cigarette. He loved the war, it brought so many clients and he was making money. But the girls needed a kick up the arse every now and then and he was the one to do it. The weekend had been very busy. So many men wanting a woman before they were shipped out. The last bit of tail before fighting the enemy was on most male minds and he was grateful for that. Everyone had a fiddle during wartime. The black market was thriving. Not that the spivs had much time for him. Fred knew that they despised him for living off immoral earnings, but he had a thick skin and they could keep their snide remarks as long as he was making money. They were no better; they just made their stash a different way, that's all. He saw Bert and Jimmy James – two brothers deeply involved with the black market – watching him with distasteful expressions, then they continued with their trading, swapping clothing coupons, ration books and petrol coupons. A wad of money exchanged hands.

Jimmy made his way to the back of the Lord Roberts pub where he had parked a small delivery van. Banging on the back door, he waited until it opened and took a case of Bourbon out of the van and carried it inside.

The landlord was delighted. 'The Yanks pay through the nose for this,' he said, eyes gleaming in anticipation of his rich reward. 'I'll take any you can get your hands on. Here.' He handed over an envelope full of money and walked the spiv to the door.

Jimmy was very pleased. He had made a deal with one of the American quartermasters at a GI camp whom he met in the Horse and Groom one night. The meeting had proved profitable to both. The Yank was saving to open his own business back in the States after the war and with his access to all the stores, he was sitting on a fortune.

Jimmy and Bert were hard men. They were leaders of

a small gang who were major racketeers and didn't take to anyone invading their patch. Their connections to those steeped in the black market spread like tentacles. Anyone who had anything under the counter to sell knew better than to trade with anyone else. A few had tried to get a better price, but they paid dearly for their betrayal. Noses were broken, homes trashed. They traded in fear and were very successful.

On Sunday morning, Cora met Hank and they decided to go to Bournemouth. It was a decent day weather wise. The sun shone and it wasn't cold. When they arrived, they walked down to the seafront and were sitting in a cafe looking out over the water, drinking coffee and eating egg on toast. It was such a treat as eggs were rationed. After, they walked around the shops, just window shopping but Cora found it frustrating being unable to purchase new clothes. But they did go into one shop where she bought a new hat, as no clothing coupons were required. She enjoyed trying several on with Hank helping her choose one, and to her delight he insisted he pay for it. She put it on her head with a broad grin and they walked out of the shop, Hank laughing at her obvious pleasure.

'It doesn't take much to make you happy, Cora!' he teased.

Laughing she said, 'In wartime it is the little things that matter.'

The day passed all too soon. They ate fish and chips out of the paper, sitting near the beach, went to a film and eventually caught a train back to Southampton.

Hank said he would walk her home but Cora didn't want him to see the one room she inhabited and where she did her business. She wanted that part of her life to be kept separate from this charming man, so made an excuse she had to go to visit a sick friend.

He slowly took her into his arms. 'Thanks for today, Cora. It was great. We'll have to do this again real soon.' He leant forward and kissed her gently.

'That would be lovely,' she replied, 'and thank you for my hat.'

'How can I get in touch with you?' he asked.

She hesitated. 'I'm in the Lord Roberts most evenings about six-thirty,' she told him. 'You can find me there.'

He looked a little surprised but didn't question her. 'Fine, I'll see you soon.'

As she walked away, she wished things were different, that she had a proper home where she could entertain this lovely man. She realised that if she was to continue to see Hank, things could become really difficult, keeping her work a secret, but she was determined to try.

It wasn't as if she enjoyed the way she made her money, having strangers use her for sex. Some treated her well as they fulfilled their desire, others didn't. To them, she was there to make sure they got their money's worth and they treated her without respect as a person and, sometimes, they were brutal. She'd been in fear of her life more than once. But among the prostitutes, word soon got around and these men met with a denial when they approached a brass, which in itself could be more than dangerous. Men, whose alcoholic-filled brutality came to the fore at such times, caused many a fight when they pestered the girls in a bar and the locals or other customers came to their rescue. But the military police, always on patrol around trouble spots, dealt with them very quickly.

She put her key in the door and made a cup of tea before going to bed.

Chapter Four

Belle had taken a night off and was spending the evening with Jackson Butler. He'd been very kind, bringing her some goods from the PX store and had arrived at the Horse and Groom, looking for her and bearing gifts of proper coffee, nylon stockings and tins of fruit. She was overwhelmed and had taken him home to offload the goods . . .

'Oh Jackson! This is so kind of you, you have no idea what a treat this is for me with the rationing. And nylon stockings! I could kiss you!' and she did, soundly.

He beamed with pleasure. 'Aw gee, Belle. It ain't nothing! Now how about we go and have a few beers?'

Since their first night together, Belle had been seeing Jackson regularly. Sometimes as a punter, although their relationship was different to when she took any other man to her bed for business. She'd grown fond of this young man who was finding the freedom of being in this country like discovering a gold mine. He couldn't quite get used to the freedom of movement it offered him and it delighted Belle to watch him grow.

They went into town and sat in a corner of the Spa Tavern, talking quietly, drinking their beer. Belle was aware of the hostile glances from some of the customers seeing her sitting with a black GI. She was used to this, it happened frequently when they were together and, most times, she chose to ignore it, but there was one couple sitting nearby and the woman was making her feelings very clear and in a loud enough voice to cause others to look round to see what she was complaining about.

'Well, I think it's disgusting!' said the woman. 'A white woman going out with a darkie! It isn't proper!'

Jackson, sensing Belle's anger rising, said quietly, 'Let's go.'

She flatly refused. 'No! You and I have as much right to sit here together as anyone else in this bar.' She glared at the woman. The chatter in the bar stopped.

Belle spoke up. 'What gives *you* the right to criticise? This soldier has come to fight in this war, to help to defend this country, your country! Soon he'll be sent over to France to face the enemy. He could be killed like so many others. If his blood *is* spilt, it will be red, like yours, not black, yellow or green. The colour of his skin won't matter then, madam!'

The woman was shocked at this heartfelt outburst. There was a deathly hush and then a voice was heard.

'Well said, young lady! We need all the help we can get to beat the Germans. Let me buy you both a drink!'

Belle having vented her spleen was astonished, as was

the woman who had started the whole thing. She got to her feet and dragged her husband out of the pub, muttering beneath her breath.

The gentleman who had come to her rescue came across the room, shook Jackson by the hand and asked, 'What are you both drinking?'

The bar chatter started up again and Belle smiled at the stranger.

'Two halves of bitter – and thank you.'

The stranger just winked at her and ordered the beer.

Jackson took her hand. 'You really are a feisty woman, Belle!'

She started laughing. 'No one tells me how to run my life, who I can go out with, who I can speak to. No one.'

'Calm down, honey, it's over with. I've received such treatment all my life, you get used to it.'

'Not in this country when you're with me, Jackson love.'

He looked thoughtful. 'When I do get shipped out, Belle, will you write to me? Keep in touch?'

She squeezed his hand. 'Of course I will.' As she looked into his large brown eyes, she knew that to her he was someone special. Someone she was growing fond of despite their differences. She'd not felt this way about any man ever since she and her husband had divorced. She knew she would miss him terribly when eventually he left these shores.

Plans for the invasion were now well under way with General Dwight Eisenhower in command. All coastal areas had been banned to visitors. Large scale military exercises

39

began. Amphibious operations were being practised as were airborne landings. Minesweepers were clearing enemy laid mines. The atmosphere within the town became tense with expectation. Leave was restricted but when the troops did manage a few hours out of camp, they made the most of it, which led to many a fracas in the dockland pubs as the men were letting their inner turmoil loose. Others sat in corners in quiet contemplation of what was ahead of them.

Hildy and Milt managed to see one another whenever he was free, which wasn't that often, and that pleased her mother, who made her feelings very clear.

'Good job when they all go! Then we can get back to normal,' she snapped one evening when Hildy was at home. 'I said as much at work this morning.'

Hildy's eyes flashed in anger. 'How can you say that? These men are facing untold odds. Many of them won't be coming back!'

This was her one fear. She and Milt had become close during the previous weeks and their relationship had blossomed and become physical. They would sometimes book into a hotel for the night, which had caused ructions in the Dickson household. Olive felt she was losing her grip on her daughter.

Milt had persuaded Hildy that she must be strong and lead a life of her own. He'd met Mrs Dickson on a few occasions when he'd been to the house to collect Hildy for a date and thought the old woman an evil old devil. He saw just how she used emotional blackmail to get to her daughter.

But Olive was unrepentant. 'Well, what do you expect?

War is war and lives are lost. In any case, when it's all over, these men will go home and forget the girls they met over here and if you think that isn't the case, think again.'

Hildy rose to her feet. 'But some of them get married, mother!' She grabbed her coat. 'I'm going out.'

Olive leant back in her chair, astounded at her daughter's outburst. Then the true significance of the remark penetrated her mind. Had Hildy decided to marry her GI? If so . . . what was to happen to her?

Cora and the other brasses were still kept busy despite the restrictions on the American troops. The French sailors came and went and now Canadian firefighters had moved into the town and there were the British troops too, who were also waiting to be shipped out and were longing for a woman.

She had still managed to keep her real occupation from Hank, whom she had been seeing regularly until the clamp down on leave. But she'd had a few scrapes in doing so. One night as she was sitting in the Horse and Groom waiting for clients, Hank had entered the bar. Cora had managed to slip out of another door before he saw her and she plied her trade elsewhere for a few days until she knew he was on exercises. But it had unsettled her.

This evening she was sitting in the Lord Roberts as usual before work when, to her surprise, Hank came into the bar and seeing her rushed over.

Kissing her briefly, he said, 'I hoped I would catch you. I've a few hours' leave and wondered if there was any way you could come out for a drink? God knows when I'll get another pass.'

41

She was so delighted to see him she immediately answered. 'Yes, I'm sure they won't mind me missing one night.'

He bought them both a drink and sat down. 'Your business must be mighty accommodating if you can just take time out like this,' he remarked casually.

She froze for just a moment. 'There's plenty who can cover for me,' she said.

'What is it you do?' he asked. 'You've never really told me.'

'We look after the troop's welfare,' she answered. 'Try and keep them from feeling homesick.' Well, that wasn't far from the truth, she thought.

Later, as they were sitting in a bar, one of her punters walked in with another GI and seeing her smiled.

'Hi Cora! How you doing?'

Then to her horror he grinned at her companion. 'Howdy Hank, great to get out of camp for a night, isn't it?'

Hank agreed and continued to talk to Cora as the soldier sat at a table.

'You know him?' she asked fearfully.

'Yep! We're in the same company,' he replied to her consternation.

Oh my God! she thought. If they get talking, he would discover her secret. And if he did, that would be the end of their friendship. She had never taken Hank to her bed. She had wanted their relationship to be different. Kissing and petting was as far as it had ever gone. Hank, thinking she was a good girl, hadn't pushed her for more and had respected her wishes. But now . . .

She was so lost in thought, she hadn't been listening until Hank said, 'Cora!'

'Sorry, sorry I was miles away for a minute. What did you say?'

'I said that I didn't know when I'd be free again. We're off to do some exercises for the next week.'

'Oh, right. Well, you know where to find me.' She caught hold of his hand. 'I'll miss you, Hank. You take care now.'

He put her hand to his lips. 'Make sure you do the same, Cora, honey. You've come to mean a lot to me.'

Although this thrilled her, it made the fear of discovery all the more of a problem. She really liked him, respected him, and if he found her out, she would be devastated.

The following morning, Hank's division was sent to Salisbury Plain on exercise for a week. On the third day, he was standing in a queue for food at the kitchen that had been set up, when the soldier who had seen him with Cora in the bar came and stood next to him. They were both covered in dirt as the rain had made the terrain a mud bath.

'Geez,' exclaimed the soldier, 'that was a hell of a morning. I'm soaked through to my underpants!'

'Me too,' agreed Hank. 'Man, I can't wait to get under a hot shower.'

They took their food over to a long table with bench seats and sat down to eat.

'I wonder how long it'll be before we get shipped out,' his companion said.

'Pretty soon, I guess. In one way I just want to get it over with, in another I dread the idea.'

'Know what you mean. Southampton isn't a bad place. The folks have treated us well.' He grinned broadly. 'I'll sure miss seeing Cora, I guess you will too?'

Hank's eyes narrowed. 'You seen much of her then?'

The soldier laughed. 'Every damned inch of her! Great body. For a whore, she's a great girl.' He rose from the bench. 'Gotta go. See you!'

Hank was in shock, unable to move. Cora, a whore? Not his Cora. The girl who had kept him at arm's length all the time he'd been seeing her. It couldn't be true . . . could it? He felt sick to his stomach.

Hank didn't have much time to dwell on his predicament over the next few days as the exercises continued. Fake battle lines were drawn and, as he walked behind a tank, slowly driving over the terrain to meet the supposed enemy, the realisation of what really lay ahead became apparent to all and sundry. It was a wake-up call. One that focused the mind and when the men piled into trucks to take them back to camp, they were a silent bunch as opposed to the air of jollity that had been uppermost on the outward journey.

They gathered ready to wash mud-packed uniforms and shower the dirt from their aching bodies after attending a debriefing with senior officers; they went over the results of the exercise then told the troop to get a good night's sleep because tomorrow they'd be off again.

There was a murmur of disappointment from the troops who had been hoping for a rest and a pass into town.

The officer glared at them. 'We're about to fight a war and you need to be ready or you won't be around to enjoy the pleasures of the flesh with anyone. Dismiss!'

Jackson Butler was on exercises in a different location. Crawling over rain-soaked ground, hiding from the other troops who were supposed to be the enemy. He jumped into a dugout only to find it was several inches under water which came up to his ankles and flooded his boots.

'Holy shit!' he exclaimed and yelled as another of his company threw himself into the hole, landing on top of him.

His comrade apologised as he untangled himself. 'Sorry, Jackson! Jesus Christ! This ain't no fun at all. I'm so fucking angry that if one of them Krauts came up here now I'd kill the bastard with my bare hands, I swear I would!'

Looking at the mud-spattered man beside him, Jackson started to laugh. 'You should just see yourself, man. You're covered from head to foot in mud. Hell, I doubt either of us will ever be clean again! Here . . .' he handed him a cigarette from a pack. 'I think we both deserve a smoke.'

At that moment, one of his officers appeared looking down on the two of them.

'What the hell are you playing at? This is not a fucking tea party, we're supposed to be fighting a war! Get up off your black arses and follow me.'

Jackson and his comrade dumped their cigarettes and, muttering beneath their breaths, clambered out of the dugout, ducking and diving at the sound of gun fire. Several hours later, they climbed wearily into trucks and were driven back to camp where, after a shower and hot meal, they tumbled into their bunks, ready for sleep.

One of the men was heard to say, 'If the damned Krauts don't kill us, I reckon we'll die of exhaustion!'

Jackson curled up under the covers and thought of Belle. He wished she were here with him, he longed to feel her warm flesh against his and her arms around him.

Belle was working, entertaining a Canadian firefighter, smiling, making him comfortable, seeing to his needs, her mind miles away – thinking of Jackson Butler.

Chapter Five

A week later, Cora was sitting quietly in the Lord Roberts sipping her half pint of bitter, when the door opened and Hank walked in. She, delighted to see him, waved and smiled, but he just nodded, walked to the bar and ordered a drink before wandering over to her and sitting down.

'Hank! How lovely to see you. How did the exercises go?'

'They were hell, really. We were soaked to the skin, cold and miserable, to be honest. We were all glad when they were over and we could sit in a hot bath and eat a decent meal.'

She was immediately sympathetic. 'How awful, but I guess it was essential in preparation for the real thing.'

'Yes, of course, we all realise that.' He took a good swig of his beer. 'So now, what I really want is to have sex with a woman until I'm exhausted – are you free?'

Cora was so shocked she was speechless for a moment. Hank had never spoken to her in such derogatory tone, but now she knew he'd discovered her secret. She sat up straight and glared at him.

'I never ever thought of you as being a callous person. You surprise me!'

He raised his eyebrows. '*I* surprise *you*! How do you think I felt when one of my buddies told me what you do for a living? Yet you have never ever let me get near you! How do you think I felt?'

'I didn't exactly lie,' she said quietly, 'I just didn't go into detail, but don't you understand? You were *different*. I didn't want you as a punter, with you I wanted to be me – as a person, just an ordinary girl, a girl you liked – as I liked you.'

There was a certain vulnerability in her voice which Hank recognised and which quelled his anger somewhat. 'Why do you do it, for Christ's sake?'

'Because I want a future! I have nothing. No one. I have to fend for myself and to do that I need money, money that will take me to London when I have enough. Enough to put all this behind me, to allow me to start a fresh life where no one knows me or anything about me. Can't you understand?' Cora was now the one who was angry.

Hank was at a loss for words. What she told him made sense, but he couldn't get rid of the images of this lovely girl in bed with other men. It was driving him crazy because to him, she was special.

He shook his head. 'I thought you were my girl. How wrong can a guy be?'

Cora fought the tears which threatened to come and rose from her seat.

'I'm really sorry, Hank, but that's who I am – and that's what I do.' She walked out of the bar, tears slowly trickling down her cheeks. She took a few steps along the street, then broke down and sobbed until there were no tears left to shed.

Inside the bar, Hank walked up to the counter. 'Have you got anything stronger than beer, landlord?'

Leaning closer so as not to be heard, the landlord said, 'I have some bourbon under the counter, Yank.'

'Fine, make it a large one, will you? And keep them coming!'

Belle locked her front door and started to make her way to the Horse and Groom when, in the dusk of the evening, she saw Cora leaning against the wall near the Lord Roberts. She was clearly in distress.

'Cora, whatever's the matter, love?'

'My lovely GI has found out that I'm on the game! Oh, Belle, I'm so miserable.'

Seeing the state of her friend, Belle took her by the arm and back to her room where she poured them both a stiff measure of gin and added some tonic.

'Here, love, drink this. I'll join you. Oh, Cora, life really is a bitch!'

'It was bound to happen. We met one of my punters one night and he was in the same company as Hank. It was only a matter of time.'

Belle nodded. 'He didn't like it, of course. That's understandable.'

'I never let him near me except for a few kisses and

cuddles and then just now, he asked me if I was free tonight as he wanted a woman. That really hurt.'

'Of course it did, but you can understand him. He must have had a hell of a shock when he found out. How did you leave him?'

'I told him that's what I did and walked out of the bar. So that's the end of a beautiful friendship.'

Belle, knowing of Cora's future plans, tried to cheer her.

'You listen to me! Pretty soon all these boys will be off to fight a war. They'll have other things on their mind and those lucky devils who survive will go home to their families. We won't even be remembered but you, you'll be off to London starting all over again. A new woman. You think about that instead, my love!'

'You're right, of course, it's just that I wanted a proper relationship, a real one, one that wasn't business. Hank treated me like a young innocent woman, not a brass, because deep down, I don't feel like one. Every time I take a man to my bed, I just think it's another step towards a better life.' She let out a deep sigh. 'I really can't work tonight, but I just don't want to be on my own.' She looked at Belle for support.

'Right. I'll take the night off too. You can bunk in with me. Oh, fuck it, let's just get plastered and I'll tell you how I came to be working the streets.'

It was quite a story.

Belle began. 'My parents were devoted churchgoers; I'm not surprised that comes as a shock to you,' she said, seeing the expression on her friend's face. 'I was dragged to church twice a day on Sundays, whether I liked it or not.

The only thing that made it bearable was the young vicar, who happened to be good-looking. I'd sit and stare at him throughout the service. Then one day as we were leaving, shaking hands with him outside, he suggested I might like to join the choir.'

'Well, you still have a great voice,' Cora chipped in having heard Belle sing many times in the Horse and Groom when the pianist played and everybody joined in.

'As you can imagine, I jumped at the chance and my parents were thrilled at the prospect. But what they didn't know was that very soon, the young vicar would make excuses for me to stay behind after the others left. At first he gave the reason that it was to help him put the music sheets away and tidy up, but deep down I knew differently.'

'What happened?'

'Nothing to begin with. He'd hold my hand just a little bit too long as he thanked me for helping, then he'd put his arm round my shoulder as he walked me to the door, then one evening he asked me back to the rectory to give me a copy of a new hymn we were to learn, made me a cup of tea and sat next to me on the sofa.'

'And?'

Belle shrugged. 'Well, one thing led to another and I left him no longer a virgin and – as I thought – madly in love.'

'Oh, Belle, that was so wrong of him! He used his position to seduce you.'

'But don't you see, I didn't care. We had an affair for several months until one evening his bishop called unexpectedly and saw us through the window.'

'Oh my God! What happened?'

'He was moved to another diocese and my parents were informed.'

'You weren't pregnant, were you?'

'Oh no, he wasn't entirely stupid, he took precautions, but my parents disowned me and kicked me out of the house.'

'How old were you?'

'Seventeen. I was working and rented a room near Canal Walk because it was the cheapest and the only one I could afford. One evening, I saw the girls working and got talking to one, found out I could earn more money as a brass and so I changed jobs.'

'But you once told me you were married.'

Belle gave a wry smile. 'Yes, another bad move. I met this man, managed to keep from him as to how I earned a living – I said I worked in a shop – and indeed, after a while, I left the streets and got such a job in a general store. We married and it was fine for a couple of years until he found out about my past and wanted me to go back on the streets because I could earn more money that way . . . that's when I kicked him out.'

'But you returned to doing tricks.'

'I did and made more money – but it was all mine. I've been doing it ever since. Like you, Cora, I'm saving, but for my retirement. I want a little bungalow with a small garden. I might even have a cat. Maybe open a B&B. I don't want to live with a man again. Sod that! And as for sex, well love, I've had enough of that to last two lifetimes.' She doubled up laughing until her stomach ached, then poured another drink.

But as she lay in bed that night, she silently admitted to herself that the things she'd told Cora about living alone were not strictly true. She was lonely. Yes, she had friends, but what she really wanted was to find a man who truly loved her, whom she could love back. A man to care for *her* – care *about* her. Someone she could lean on for a change. A man with whom she could sit quietly in the evenings, his arm around her shoulders, listening to the wireless.

She turned over with a deep sigh and shut her eyes, telling herself everyone had to have a dream or life would be unbearable. At least she'd have a bungalow to look forward to and that was more than most people aspired to.

Chapter Six

In the following weeks, life continued in Southampton. More troops were moved into camps around the town and every evening people listened avidly to the news, relieved to hear that Allied troops had taken Monte Cassino. It seemed that the Germans were now on the run. Newsreels in the cinemas were full of pictures of this success and Winston Churchill with his V-sign and famous cigar did much to cheer the population.

Life on Southampton's streets didn't change. The black market thrived, queues for food seemed to get longer, women spent time in the shops set up by the WVS, swapping and buying second-hand clothes – and the National loaf remained as unpalatable as ever.

The GIs who frequented the local pubs in The Ditches were generous enough with small food items, which they bought in their PX stores, and the children could be heard asking, 'Any gum chum?' whenever they saw an American uniform. Yet beneath this was the expectation and fear of the invasion.

* * *

Cora hadn't seen anything of Hank, which didn't surprise her but still made her sad. However, as the days passed and her nights were busy, she put the experience behind her until one evening, he walked into the Lord Roberts. Her breath caught in her throat as she watched him.

He walked straight up to the bar and ordered a drink, then picking up his glass he walked over to her and sat down.

Cora was sitting in silence and looked at him, wondering what he was going to say.

'Hello Cora. How are you?' he asked quietly.

'I'm fine, thanks. I'm very surprised to see you in here,' she said.

He stared at her. 'To be honest, I'm surprised too. But I can't get you out of my mind and it's driving me crazy!'

Her heart seemed to miss a beat. 'I didn't think you wanted to see me ever again after the last time,' she said.

'To be frank, I hate what you do. I hate every man you've taken to your bed, but I couldn't keep away any longer.'

'What's that supposed to mean?' she asked nervously.

'I guess I still want you to be my girl.'

She was stunned. 'Hank, how can that be when you know the business I'm in?'

'Well, I've given a lot of thought to what you said, how you felt about . . .' he was at a loss for a moment, 'your business. That it's a way to earn money to give you a future, so I'm hoping that these men don't mean anything to you.'

'But of course they don't! How could they?'

'In that case, will you be my girl again?'

She frowned. 'Can you live with what I do and still want me? Won't that come between us?'

He leant forward. 'Look, Cora. Pretty soon we'll be shipped across the Channel and I'm not sure just how long we'd have together, so let's just enjoy what time we have. No recriminations. What do you say?'

A smile crept slowly across her features. 'I'd like that, Hank. I've really missed you.'

'You have?' He looked pleased.

'Yes, why are you surprised?'

'I guess after our last meeting and, I admit I was unkind, I thought you wouldn't want anything more to do with me.'

She placed a finger over his lips. 'That was then, this is now. We won't ever mention it again. From here on in, I'm your girl. Right?'

He leant forward and kissed her. 'Right! Can I take you out for a drink to celebrate?'

'I can't think of anything I'd rather do.'

During the evening, Hank asked her about the night she lost her parents and her home and, as he listened, he could see how she'd suffered and began to understand how hard it had been for her to survive such a trauma.

'The Germans came over every night about the same time. We used to hear the sirens go and we knew we were in for another bad night. Mum used to make a flask of tea in case it went on for a long time. We didn't have a shelter so we used to crawl under the dining room table. We had blankets and pillows there to make us comfortable.' She took a sip of her drink. 'At first you'd hear the sound of the guns, then the planes and the whine of the bomb – then silence. That was the worst part because soon after the silence you'd hear an explosion. On this particular night it seemed worse than ever. There were more bombs exploding than before and they seemed to be getting nearer than ever. Every time we'd cling on to each other, wondering if it would be us next . . . and then it was.'

Hank caught her by the hand. 'Don't go on, honey, if it upsets you,' he said.

'No, I want you to know, then perhaps you'll understand.' She took a deep breath and continued.

'We heard the bomb. Then the silence and suddenly all hell broke loose it seemed. The ceiling caved in on top of us, there was dust everywhere, the table collapsed, then I don't remember anything until the air raid wardens and the firemen started to dig us out. All I remember was a strange voice saying, "Come along, miss, wake up, there's a good girl".'

'Oh, Cora, honey, I had no idea.' Hank's voice was full of sympathy.

Tears welled in her eyes as she said, 'They managed to pull me free and into an ambulance, but when I asked about my parents, the men went quiet – and then I knew.'

Hank called the barman over and asked for two brandies. When they arrived, he made her drink some. 'Here, this'll do you good.' He watched her closely as she did so. Then he asked for the bill.

'Come along, honey, drink up, I'm going to take you

home,' he said seeing the distress etched on her face. 'Gee, I'm sorry I asked. It was stupid of me.'

She gave a wan smile. 'No, I wanted you to know. Now you do.'

They walked silently through the unlit streets, using Cora's torch to light their way in the blackout, ignoring others who were out enjoying their evening, through The Ditches and to her room. When they were inside, she put on the kettle to make some tea. They were sitting side by side on the bed, waiting for the kettle to boil, Hank holding her in his arms as she cried silent tears. He stroked her hair and patted her back as you would a child, making soothing noises until she stopped grieving. Then he kissed her gently.

'I understand so much more now,' he told her. 'You have so much courage for someone so young; I only wish I could take the hurt away from you. I feel so useless.'

She looked up at him. 'Hank, will you make love to me?'

And he did, gently, with great tenderness and as he felt her relax, he hoped he went some way to help the mental anguish she'd been through that night. He prayed that being able to talk about it would be therapeutic for this lovely young woman who'd come to mean so much to him.

Olive couldn't wait for the invasion to begin. The event would bring an end to her worries. All those damned Yanks would be gone and her life would be back to normal. What she really meant was that she would once again have control over her daughter.

Ever since Hildy had taken up with 'that GI', as she thought of him, things had changed considerably. Hildy was out of the house more often and sometimes all night. When she'd accused her daughter of being a loose woman, no better than those on the streets, Hildy had not battered an eyelid, but had just looked at her mother.

'What I do is not any of your business, Mother. I'm a grown woman, not a child and you don't run my life for me.' Then she'd walked out of the room leaving Olive speechless.

Whenever Milt Miller came to the house, Olive was on edge. The young man was polite to her, but she knew that he could see through her duplicities and was aware of the emotional games she played, so she was very careful about what she said. Once when she'd questioned Hildy about an opinion she'd voiced which didn't agree with hers and had said as much, Milt had intervened.

'You forget, Mrs Dickson, that Hildy has a mind of her own.'

After that, she said little in front of him, keeping her spiteful and negative remarks for when she was alone with her daughter.

That evening, Milt and Hildy were taking a walk through the park together. The evening was pleasantly warm. They strolled slowly, holding hands and chatting about inconsequential things to keep both of them from thinking that soon they would have to part, knowing the future would be uncertain.

They sat on a bench and lit cigarettes. Milt placed his arm about her shoulders.

'Gee, Hildy, I can't tell you how happy I am that we got together. These past few weeks have been some of the happiest in my life, I want you to know that.'

There was an underlying sound of finality about his words that made her look at him.

'Have you heard something about the invasion?' she asked, tensing within his hold.

Feeling her stiffen, he kissed her cheek. 'No, honey, nothing definite but things are moving. More troops are being brought into the port daily. Something is going on, that's for sure and I've a feeling we'll be off before very long, so every moment we spend together is precious.'

'Oh, Milt. I'll miss you so much,' she said, her voice choking in her throat.

He cupped her face in his hand and looked at her. 'I know in the beginning we said we'd get together with no strings, but I don't want it to end when I leave.'

She was puzzled. 'What do you mean?'

'You know there isn't anyone in my life and, until now that's been just fine, but Hildy . . . will you write to me while I'm away and wait for me to come home? I want us to have a future together. How do you feel about that?'

'What do you mean?'

'I want you in my life after the war too, not just for now.'

She looked puzzled. 'How can that be?'

He burst out laughing. 'I thought that was fairly obvious. Will you marry me, Hildy?'

Her eyes shone as she held his gaze. 'There's nothing I'd like more, Sergeant. Of course I will!'

He smothered her with kisses. 'You've made me the happiest man alive. We'll have a good life together, I promise. I have the afternoon off tomorrow; we'll go and buy an engagement ring so, at least when I do ship out, I'll know it's official and . . .' he chuckled, 'it'll keep any other marauding men away from my girl.' He paused. 'Wait until you are wearing my ring before you tell your mother.'

She knew he was right. If she were to spill the beans to her mother when she got home, she'd hear nothing but aggravation and that certainly would spoil her happiness.

'You don't like my mother, do you?'

'No, honey, I don't. I won't lie to you. I think your mother is a selfish woman who bleeds you dry. She would spoil your life, if you let her.'

Letting out a deep sigh, Hildy agreed. 'Partly my own fault. I let her rule me during my teenage years and when I began to have a mind of my own and to grow up, she couldn't handle it and became worse.'

'Now don't you worry any more. I'm going to be around to sort out all your problems in the future.'

'You just make sure Milton Miller that you keep your bloody head down when you do cross the Channel, you understand?'

'Don't you worry, darling. I'm a good soldier; I know when to duck. Now come on, let's find a pub and drink to the future.'

Later he walked her home and kissed her goodnight at the door. 'I'll pick you up at the factory after your shift tomorrow and we'll go to Parkhouse and Wyatt to buy a ring, then out to lunch. I'm off duty until the morning, shall I book us a room for the night?'

She readily agreed wanting to spend as much time with him as she could before they were forced to part. 'I'll take a change of clothes with me to the factory.'

Once in her bedroom she pranced about like a teenager, muttering, 'Mrs Milt Miller. Hildy Miller.' Then she sat down, found a piece of paper and practised signing her name as Milt's wife. Eventually she climbed into bed and fell asleep.

The following morning, she packed an overnight bag and left the house for work before her mother was up, leaving a note to say she wouldn't be home that night. There was a bounce to her step as she made her way to her machine and she hummed away to herself as she happily contemplated the afternoon.

The foreman noticed her jollity and said, 'What's up with you today, Hildy? You look like the cat who's discovered a pint of cream.'

She grinned at him. 'Oh nothing really, just that life is good.'

He walked away, shaking his head, unconvinced by her answer, not noticing the small case she carried. Something had happened to her, he was sure, but what? At the end of the shift when he saw that she had changed into a dress and this time saw she was carrying a small case, his eyes narrowed. Was she leaving without telling him? Surely not, she was too professional in her job to do that, but where was she going? He turned away. Women! What man could ever understand them? Certainly not him. He'd been married for several years and they were still a mystery.

Had he continued to watch her, he'd have seen the GI waiting who walked over to his employee lifting her up in his arms and kissing her enthusiastically before they walked away holding hands.

Milt and Hildy walked to the jewellers, stopped outside and studied the rings on display in the window for a while, then walked inside the shop. Milt had a quiet word with the assistant, giving her an idea of the price he was prepared to pay and waited with Hildy whilst she chose a couple of trays filled with rings for them to look at.

Hildy's heart was pounding with excitement as she tried several rings and eventually chose a half hoop of emerald and diamonds. She put it on her finger, holding out her hand to see the effect.

'Oh, Milt, this one is lovely.'

'I like it too, but is it the one you really want, honey?'

She glanced back at the others before her and looking up, eyes sparkling with excitement, she said, 'Yes, this is the one without a doubt. I absolutely love it!'

He beamed at the assistant. 'I guess that's the one we'll take then.'

Hildy reluctantly removed it from her finger and passed it back over the counter and watched it being put into a ring box and a small bag. She waited patiently as Milt paid for it, put it in his pocket and then they left the shop together.

'Come on,' he said, 'I've booked a table for lunch at the Polygon Hotel to celebrate and then we'll go to our room.'

They walked across the park to the hotel and were led to their table.

'I hope you don't mind, darling, but I've pre-ordered our meal. I told the head waiter that this was a special occasion and he's promised to do us proud.'

Hildy was impressed as they were served prawn cocktail, followed by delicious steak, mushrooms, mixed vegetables and chips. As they tucked into their meal, a bellboy entered the dining room carrying an enormous bouquet of flowers and marched over to the table and presented it to Hildy.

'These are for you, madam,' he said.

She was overcome and felt herself blush as she took them from him, aware of the interest this had aroused from the other diners.

Milt chuckled at her discomfort. 'No need to be embarrassed, darling, how often does a person get engaged? It's a special day.'

'Oh Milt!' was all she could say.

He took the flowers from her and put them on an empty chair. With twinkling eyes, he said quietly, 'You can show your appreciation later.' Which made her blush even more.

After the meal, they were drinking coffee and talking. Milt was telling her that when he did eventually leave, it might be some time before she heard from him.

'Now you're not to worry. Troops move around a lot and it's not easy to get mail collected and posted. You're more likely to get several letters together so I'll number them on the back of the envelope so you'll know which comes first. You do the same.'

As she gazed at the strong features of the man beside her she realised that there would be a deep void in her life when he was eventually shipped out and she suddenly felt how it must be for those women whose husbands were already abroad; the families of the British Tommies already in the fray. At least she didn't have children to worry about, that must make the burden even worse. But she was determined not to show her fears. After all, that's what being an army wife was all about and Milt was a regular soldier.

Pushing back his seat, Milt said, 'Come along, let's go to our room.'

When they entered the bedroom, he took her into his arms and kissed her, then taking the package from his pocket he removed the ring from the box and placed it on her finger.

'There you are, darling. Now it's official!'

The stones sparkled in the sunlight pouring through the window. Flinging her arms around his neck she said, 'Oh, Milt, I do love you.'

He grinned broadly. 'Hell! I sure hope so.' He kissed her, lifted her off her feet and spun her round until they collapsed on the bed in a bundle.

She lay in his arms, content. They made love and slept, waking later to drink champagne that Milt had ordered and had been sitting in an ice bucket ready for them.

Later they dressed and went to the bar for a drink, then ate in the dining room before retiring for the night.

Waking early the next morning, Hildy didn't know when she'd been happier. She gazed at the ring on her finger, then at the sleeping figure beside her and prayed fervently that this wonderful man would come safely through the war and back to her because the alternative was too painful to contemplate.

She washed and dressed in her dungarees, then gently woke her fiancé. They drank a cup of coffee together before she had to go with Hank saying he'd be in touch.

Hildy knew that when she went home after work that day and faced her mother, there would be a scene, but she didn't care. She had a future before her with a man she loved and she wasn't going to let anyone spoil it. Her mother would just have to accept that her daughter was entitled to a life of her own.

Chapter Seven

The foreman at the factory was very relieved to see Hildy arrive as usual, dressed ready for work in her dungarees and carrying her case which she put away in her locker. If anything, she looked more chipper this morning than she did yesterday, which made him even more curious. It wasn't until he did his round of inspections later that he noticed the ring on her finger. He stopped beside her.

'Well, Hildy, you are a sly one. Congratulations! Who's the lucky man?'

She was delighted that at last she could share her good news and beamed at him.

'Sergeant Milt Miller, a GI I've been seeing. We got engaged last night.' She held out her hand for him to inspect her ring.

The foreman was impressed. 'That cost a few bob, love. Does that mean you'll be leaving us to live in the States then?'

'Eventually. We have to wait until the war is over, of

course, but Milt wanted to make it official before he was shipped out.'

'I'm happy for you, Hildy. I hope you won't have to wait too long to get hitched.' But as he walked away, he was concerned for the girl. War could be cruel, he just prayed that her man would come through unscathed. He'd seen too many families shattered when they opened the door to the telegraph boy, bearing the small envelope with bad news.

Later that day, Hildy walked slowly towards her home, knowing that when her mother heard about her engagement, all hell would break loose. Fortunately Olive was still at work so she had time to change, make a cup of tea and gather her thoughts, but her heart sank when she heard her mother's key in the front door.

As Olive walked into the kitchen, Hildy asked, 'Want a cup of tea, Mum? I've just boiled the kettle.'

Her mother gave her a scathing look. 'You decided to come home then!'

'I left you a note telling you I would be away last night,' Hildy said, pouring the tea into a cup and passing it across the table.

As she did so, Olive caught sight of the ring on her finger. Her eyes narrowed as she looked at her daughter. 'What's that all about?' she asked pointing to Hildy's hand.

'Me and Milt got engaged last night,' Hildy said and felt her stomach tighten as she did so. 'We're going to get married when the war is over.'

'How very selfish of you!' Her mother looked livid. 'You stand there and calmly tell me you're going to marry that Yank, without any thought to *my* welfare. You are just going to walk away and leave me to live alone. How could you do such a thing?'

Hildy sat down at the table, looking at Olive, she said, 'Yes, I suppose I am. I do have the right to some happiness, you know. You could be happy for me.'

'Happy? You know what happened to me – to us. Your father walked out on his marriage, how do you know this American won't do the same to you in another country? What will you do then I'd like to know?'

'Milt is *not* like my father. He loves me.'

Olive laughed scornfully. 'That's what he says now, you wait until you've been married a while, it'll all change, and in the meantime I have to manage, is that it?'

Hildy was at a loss as to how to get through to her mother.

'For heaven's sake, Mum, you aren't an old woman. You're only forty-six, in the prime of life. You have a job, you're earning money, you might even meet another man and get married again.'

Olive was incandescent with rage. 'Marry again, after all I've been through with your father? I'm just trying to stop you from making the same mistake.'

Hildy's anger erupted. 'No, you're not! You're trying to make sure you keep me here, with you, to spoil my chance of happiness just so you can have me at your beck and call, like I've been ever since Dad left.' She rose from her chair, grabbed her coat and, as she put it on, glared at her mother.

'I've had enough of your selfish ways and your emotional blackmail. I'm going to marry Milt and you won't stop me!' She walked out of the house, slamming the door behind her.

Olive sat at the table, outraged at her daughter's outburst and suddenly swiped the cups and saucers off the table, sending them crashing to the floor.

Trying to calm down, Hildy walked with her feelings in turmoil, oblivious to her surroundings, until she came to the pier. She entered and strolled along the walkway, looking out at the horizon wishing she could get away, to escape from the woman who for years had bled her emotionally dry. She sat down, lit a cigarette and admitted to herself that she hated the woman who'd given birth to her and was then filled with guilt. No one was supposed to hate their mother – it wasn't natural. Tears of frustration brimmed in her eyes. She had been so happy yesterday and now her mother had spoilt it for her yet again, as she had done consistently over the years whenever Hildy had a boyfriend. Her mother had so cleverly found something about them to criticise. A mention here, a word there, until the relationship would fail. But not this time.

This time, Hildy told herself, this time she'd met the man with whom she wanted to share the rest of her life and no miserable, self-centred woman was going to come between them. She'd move out if she had to. The more she thought of it, the better that idea became. She should have done it years ago. It would be good for Olive, make her stand on her own two feet for once. After all, she could afford the rent on their two-up two-down with the wages from her job. She could take a lodger, too, with the room that would become spare.

Thus inspired, Hildy went to an estate agent to enquire about a small furnished flat for herself and spent the afternoon looking at a couple that were available. The second one in the Polygon area was just what she needed, at a rent she could afford so she went to the bank to draw out some money for the deposit and was given the keys.

She walked home filled with determination. She let herself in and went straight upstairs to start packing her clothes. She could hear her mother banging about in the kitchen below, making her presence known, but Hildy ignored the noise and filled two suitcases. Then she carried them downstairs and put them by the door just as Olive stepped out of the kitchen. She looked at the suitcases and then at her daughter.

Taking a deep breath, Hildy said, 'I'm moving out, Mum. Under the circumstances I think it's the best thing.'

At that moment there was a knock on the door. It was a taxi Hildy had ordered earlier. She handed the cases to the driver, then a piece of paper and a key to her mother.

'Here is my address. I've got my ration book. I'm sorry it's come to this, but it's for the best,' and she walked out of the door towards the cab. It was only then that Olive found her voice.

'You selfish little bitch!' she screamed. 'Walking out on your own mother just for the sake of sex with some strange man. You'll live to regret it; see if you don't!'

Hildy closed the cab door, gave the driver the address and leant back in the seat trying to shut her ears to the abuse that was still being hurled at her.

'Bad day, love?' asked the taxi driver.

'Something like that,' she said and made him stop at a telephone box so she could call the base and leave a message for Milt with her new address.

That evening, Milt Miller arrived at her flat carrying a bunch of flowers. He gave her a hug and kissed her.

'Well, when I got your message I was surprised,' he said. Then looking round the rooms, he added, 'Nice place, just what you need. Is the rent expensive?'

When she told him, he said, 'That's great,' then taking a bundle of notes out of his pocket he gave them to her saying, 'this will help you along for a while.'

She looked at them with some surprise and started to decline his offer.

'Don't say any more, honey,' he said. 'We are engaged, this is the least I can do. I'll send you more whenever I can, after all, it's now my place to take care of you.'

Hildy was overwhelmed. Ever since her father had left, she had been the one to take care of her own and her mother's welfare. She who had to carry the burden that should have been her father's. Now here was a man who was going to look after *her*. She put her arms around Milt and kissed him.

'You have no idea just how much those words mean,' she told him.

'I told you, darling, that I had shoulders broad enough

to carry all your worries, but now I have to go. I borrowed a jeep so I could come and see you, but I've got to go back to camp. I'm not sure when I'm going to be free as we are out on exercises from tomorrow, I'll be in touch as soon as I get back.'

As he drove away, he knew that very soon they would be shipping out. He wasn't sure when, but the rumours around the camp had been rife. The top military brass had been meeting to choose the day for the landings, that was all he knew, but he couldn't and wouldn't say anything to Hildy. He realised just how difficult the decision to leave her mother must have been for her and no doubt Mrs Dickson wouldn't have made it any easier, but he was certain it was the right thing for Hildy.

During the next few days, Southampton became swamped with even more troops and vehicles. All along the streets surrounding the docks, tanks and their crew were lined up. As the local population went about their business, they saw the British Red Cross serving the troops hot drinks and sandwiches. Mobile canteens, run by the Church Army cared for the British troops. Every inch of the Empress Docks was filled with landing craft. The prime minister, complete with cigar, visited the troops to boost their morale and take a look at the final preparations for the forthcoming invasion.

Belle had seen little of Jackson Butler as most of the troops had been on exercises and she missed him. Of course leave had been cancelled for others who were also involved with final training, so business was slack.

The bar of the Horse and Groom was almost empty when Belle and Cora were sitting together that lunchtime chatting. Without the customers crowding the bar, the interior seemed even more dark and shabby, the stale smell of beer and tobacco seemed to cling to the walls, despite the fact that the bar doors were open trying to invite any casual drinkers. The pianist in the corner was sitting at the bar drinking a beer as it was hardly worth playing for a handful of people who were not exactly in the mood to celebrate anything.

Looking around the near empty bar, Belle asked, 'Is it me or is there a strange atmosphere in here today?'

'Funny,' Cora replied, 'I was just thinking the same. It reminds me of the Blitz, you know when you were having your supper waiting for the air raid siren to go, anticipating the worst.'

Belle finished her half of bitter. 'Come on, love, let's get out of here; its making me depressed. Let's go to the pictures, at least that'll cheer us up.' So that's what they did. But the British Pathé news, full of the troops fighting in various fields of battle, did little to lift their spirits.

The troops were at last given twenty-four hour leave. Although no information had been given out, the men knew that the invasion was imminent so they were determined to enjoy what they considered to be their last free time and they were hell-bent on enjoying themselves.

All the pubs around the docks were packed with all

nationalities. The military police were out in force as were the local constabulary, ready for unrest, but on the whole, it was trouble free. Yes, there was many a drunken soldier who was taken back to their different camps to sleep off the excess of alcohol, but the others just wanted to enjoy the time they had before being shipped out. To drink and get laid.

The local brasses were kept busy; they too realised that this may be the time to make a pile of money as the men queued for their services. The locals looked on with some amusement at the men standing in line outside various brothels. Others were disgusted saying the area around the town should be cleared by the police and all the prostitutes put behind bars. But the police were aware that would be unwise at this particular time and on the whole if the girls didn't cause any trouble, they were prepared to look the other way. That's how it was in wartime.

Cairo Fred drove his girls hard, thinking his cash flow would be sadly affected once the boys sailed across to France, taking their money with them. His girls complained bitterly, but he was not interested, only in the money they earned.

The law was different for those dealing in the black market. Men who dealt in American goods, filtered by the quartermasters who were on the fiddle, were syphoning off as much as they dare whilst they were able to do so. The racketeers loaded their vans. They took everything that was offered, but the local police had several of them under surveillance and pounced on them when their stocks were full. The courts were busy with a waiting list of cases to be dealt with.

As one of the judges remarked during a case, 'Greed is the downfall of many a criminal.'

At lunchtime, Cora waited in the Lord Roberts for Hank after hearing that leave had at last been given to the men, hoping that he would have a few hours free. She sat nervously waiting and looked up anxiously each time the door opened, until eventually he walked in and hurried over.

Taking hold of her hands he leant forward and kissed her.

'Gee, Cora, I was so worried I wouldn't get to see you before we shipped out.'

She felt the blood drain from her face. 'When are you going?'

'Nobody knows for sure, but very soon. That's all I know and this will probably be the last leave I get. I have to be back by midnight.'

Her heart sank, but not wanting his last night to be a sad one she forced a smile.

'If that's the case, what would you like to do?'

He gazed at her taking in every detail of her face so he could remember each part of it. 'Let's have a drink here, then go back to your place. I just want us to be alone.'

As they were sitting quietly together, he gave her an address to write to when he'd gone.

'Keep those letters coming, Cora, 'cause it's the only thing that keeps a man going when they are in a war zone.

I'll write back when I can – don't worry if you don't hear for a while – mail collection is uncertain.' He smiled and said, 'Let's get out of here.'

When they arrived at her room, they undressed and climbed into bed. Hank drew her into his arms and they just talked for a while and then they made love, taking their time, enjoying every touch, every kiss, unhurried in their need for each other, wanting this moment to last. To be remembered. To be cherished.

To Cora's delight, he'd brought some eggs and bacon with him which she cooked and they sat and ate together. When eventually it was time for him to leave, they stood in the doorway and clung to each other.

Cora watched him walk away, tears streaming down her face.

Jackson was curled up in bed with Belle on his final leave. She was trying to give him support mentally for what lay ahead, but strangely, he was the one who was the stronger of the two.

'Don't you worry none, Belle,' he told her. 'Whatever happens to me is in the good Lord's hands, but if my life is to be over soon, I have no regrets.' He gazed at her and kissed her cheek softly.

Belle could hardly contain her emotions and with tear-filled eyes she pleaded with him. 'Jackson, don't talk that way. I can't bear it.'

'Aw come on, honey, don't you fret none. Whatever happens, if I survive, you know I have to go home after to my family, but I'll never ever forget you, Belle. As long as I live, I'll never forget you. But you write like you promised me, won't you? That way we'll keep in touch.'

Taking a deep breath, Belle said, 'Yes, of course I will. But you listen to me, Jackson Butler, you make sure you write back and tell me you're alive and kicking!'

He burst out laughing. 'Belle, honey, you forget where I'm from! All my life I've been ducking and diving, no old German is gonna take me down – you hear?'

She couldn't help but smile at his confidence. 'I hear you loud and clear.'

Two days later, the troops were moving out of the town. The inhabitants of Southampton stood and watched for hours as company after company of troops of all nationalities marched through the streets of Southampton towards the ships waiting in the docks. The British troops marching tall and proud and in step, the Americans more casual, throwing their small packs of K-rations to the children waiting on the pavements. Cascades of English money was also thrown, the troops saying they had no further need of it. Despite the seriousness of the situation, there was an unexpected air of jollity about it all. Army trucks full of soldiers followed.

Cora and Belle were stationed in Latimer Street every day, both watching for their men. The Negro troops passed by and Belle caught sight of Jackson who waved and motioned with his hands for her to write. Belle nodded and blew him kisses, much to the delight of his comrades who teased him unmercifully.

There were several women pushing prams with black babies also waiting. Some crying, others cursing as they saw the father of their child who tried to keep out of sight.

One woman seeing her Negro boyfriend screamed out at him. 'You come back here, you bastard. This is your baby you've left me with!'

The man in question just kept marching, staring straight ahead.

Sergeant Milt Miller was marching beside his company of men when he saw Hildy searching the faces of the passing troops. She suddenly saw him and ran over, kissing him and walking next to him until they turned into the docks. She stood watching until the last line of men disappeared out of sight and she wept.

Cora, waiting further down the street, saw Hank in an army vehicle, who waved and called out to her.

'You take care of yourself!'

'You make sure you do the same,' she yelled back at him.

'Be sure to write,' he called. She nodded back, unable to speak as her emotions overcame her.

Inside the docks, the troops embarked in readiness, knowing they'd soon be crossing the English Channel to face the enemy. They coped with this knowledge in different ways. Some joked with their companions, others withdrew inside themselves. A few of them offered silent prayers. Others tried to cover hands that were shaking with fear trying to hide just how scared they were, trying to be men of strength.

To cover the mass assembly, smoke screens had been laid down and there were many complaints as the acrid smell seeped into the town; the population were unaware of the importance of the manoeuvre. But there was an air of tension in everybody, knowing that at any moment the invasion would begin for real. There was the faint possibility, if things went wrong, of seeing German troops walking through the town, but in their hearts they believed that the enemy would be defeated.

Chapter Eight

On 6th June 1944, the invasion of Normandy began. The sound of many planes flying overhead could be heard throughout the night and on into the dawn. The civilians poured out of houses and shops to watch, knowing that at last the day had come.

Sergeant Milt Miller was pushing his way through the men in his company, pressed together like sardines in the landing craft as they crossed the Channel, barking out orders, keeping his soldiers alert, not giving them too much time to think of anything but making their way as fast as they could out of the landing craft onto Omaha beach and keeping their heads down.

'Remember what you've been taught during the exercises. Those Krauts will be waiting and they won't be inviting you to stay and be friends. Show them the American GIs are up to the task and give them hell!'

'Yes, Sergeant!' they yelled in unison, now all pumped up, the adrenaline flowing through their veins.

Throughout the night, the RAF had pounded German batteries along the French coast and in the early morning, the US Eighth Air Force took over the attack. Mines were swept from the invasion route and engineers demolished beach obstacles as the troops landed behind them.

Milt's landing craft eventually stopped and the front opened. The men poured out, jumping into the cold water, holding their rifles aloft as all hell broke loose. The rattle of machine guns was deafening. Explosions from enemy positions filled the air as gun boats opened fire on them, trying to eliminate their gun placements and afford some backup for the invading troops. The water was waist high and the men struggled towards the beach, bodies dropping as they were brought down by German bullets. Cries from injured men could be heard. Blood stained the water. The lucky ones eventually found solid sand beneath their feet and raced to find shelter against the cliff face, soaking wet, scared, but triumphant.

In Southampton, Hildy leant against the wall of the factory, having watched the planes flying overhead, knowing that Milt would be on his way by now. They had spent his final night together in her flat, talking about the future and making plans for when he returned.

Listening to him, Hildy was impressed by his optimism; he didn't even consider that something might happen to destroy their future life together so she tried to be positive too and shut her mind to any negative thoughts.

'I'm not sure how long I'll stay in the army,' he told her. 'It just might be the time to quit and open up my own business, but we'll wait and see how the land lies when I return. But no matter what, we'll be together.' He looked at her and asked, 'Do you want to get married in Southampton with your family and friends around, or in the States?'

She couldn't help but give a sardonic smile. 'With my mother there – or not! I doubt she'd want to come and, if I'm honest, I'm not sure that would be a good idea anyway, she would do her very best to spoil the happiest day of my life knowing her.'

'You know, honey, I kind of feel sorry for her.'

'You do?'

'Well, it must be terrible for a woman like that, so wrapped up in herself. She'll never know true happiness and that's a great shame.'

Hildy nested in to him. 'You are an extraordinary man, Milt Miller.'

'Not really. I've learnt a lot about people through being in the army and in charge of men. People come in all different types. I've met wives and mothers like yours before. The most important thing is not to let them run your life or for sure, they'll destroy it.'

Milt had brought some food over from the PX store and they sat like a married couple sharing a meal and chatting before going to bed together. As she lay in his arms, Hildy prayed that the plans they'd made that night would come to fruition because she knew that this man was solid. One she loved, one she would be content to grow old with and she made a quiet pledge to her maker that if he would only bring Milt back alive, she'd be a good woman for the rest of her days.

The sound of a passing bus brought her back to the present and she returned to her work. Life had to go on and she'd sit down tonight and write her first letter to him.

During the following weeks, troops still marched through Southampton before being shipped across the Channel. Boats came back filled with wounded and German prisoners who were marched to barbed wire holdings inside the Western Docks to await removal to prison camps. They were watched by the locals who gazed at them with mixed emotions. This was the enemy? This bedraggled group of men who looked thoroughly dejected. They didn't look menacing at all.

By now, the troop movements became part of the norm and folks got on with their lives. They listened to Alvar Lidell reading the news every night to hear how the war was progressing and discussed it with each other as they queued for food.

The pubs were still busy with soldiers and sailors waiting to be shipped out – on top of the regulars who were stationed in Southampton dealing out supplies, making sure the troops were catered for before they left and keeping the military well stocked.

Belle and Cora were sitting in The Grapes, a pub in Oxford Street having a drink and a chat. They liked a change of scenery every now and again and The Grapes was a busy pub, situated nearer the docks. Belle was talking about Jackson Butler.

'You know the saddest thing is when Jackson does go

home after the war is over and he's demobilised, he'll go back to his family in Alabama and, once again, he'll be treated as a second-class citizen.'

'What do you mean?' asked Cora.

Belle explained about the segregation of the Negro in the southern states of America. 'If he'd had sex with a white woman there, he'd have been lynched.'

Cora was shocked. 'Oh my God!'

'But don't you see, Cora, here in this country he's had so much freedom. Here he could use the same bars as the whites and eat in the same restaurants. Here he was equal to them, he was respected as a soldier and as a man. What is going to happen to him when he goes home?'

'Do you think he'll get into trouble?'

'To be honest, I don't know, but it does worry me. You can understand why any Negro who was good enough to fight for his country should be respected and would be angry to be told to sit in the back of the bus and only use places designated to them. It's not right!'

'You really like him, don't you?'

Belle's voice softened. 'He was the first man in years to treat me like I was really special. Something to be cherished.' She looked at her friend and added, 'I can't tell you how good that made me feel.'

'You were special to him, Belle. You were not only his first woman but a white one who treated him like a man. You cared about him too and that must have meant a great deal to him.'

Smiling, Belle said, 'He did say he'd never forget me and as sure as hell I won't forget him. Oh for goodness' sake, stop all this. Let's have another drink. This bloody war isn't good for anyone, it messes with people's lives!'

The man in Belle's thoughts was holed up in a corner of a building with others from his company after they'd fought street by street, house by house, to clear the Germans from the area. During a lull in the fighting, his sergeant Milt Miller had told the men to take a break. The radio operator was reporting their position, waiting for further instructions.

After lighting a cigarette, Jackson took a swig from a water bottle, wishing it was like the beer he used to drink back in Southampton. He drew on his cigarette and let his mind wander back to those days and to Belle. What a great woman she was and what times they'd had together. He thought of how he'd felt her soft skin against his, how he'd held her ample bosom, stroked her thighs – and how she'd kissed him. He was sad at the thought that they'd never meet again. Yet he smiled as he remembered how delighted she was whenever he'd bought her food from the PX stores. Such a small thing to make a person happy. But she'd never asked for more. They'd been good together. He hadn't minded when his companions had teased him about his affair.

'You just want some white meat, man,' one had said. But it had been much more than that. She'd shown him respect as a man and affection that was sincere. Imagine! He a Negro. It would be something he'd carry with him for ever.

'Right! Saddle up, men, and follow me,' called Sergeant

Miller and they left the building, running, bent double, making their way deeper into enemy territory. Diving and ducking from one house to another, they searched each room for the enemy.

As they entered the next house, two Germans appeared at the top of the stairs and opened fire to bring one American down, but in seconds they were riddled with bullets and their bodies tumbled down the stairs. The GIs climbed over them and took the rest of the stairs warily, rifles at the ready, shooting those who got in their way. Jackson peeked in an open doorway and saw in the window of the room two Germans manning a machine gun. He took a grenade, pulled the pin and threw the grenade inside ducking back against the wall with his comrades for shelter. There was an explosion and the shooting stopped. Outside, Sherman tanks rumbled by and once the building was clear, the soldiers moved on to the next one.

It all happened so fast that there wasn't time to think of anything but getting the job done. Adrenaline kept them going. It was only in the quiet moments when they had a break that the men had time to realise the danger they had faced and how lucky they were to still be alive.

Chapter Nine

The British spirit always comes to the fore during adversity. Back in Southampton, women queued for food, chatting with each other, exchanging recipes, sharing information as to which shop had an unexpected delivery of something that was hard to come by. People grew vegetables and kept chickens, none of which many had done before, and the sex trade continued with the steady influx of troops. But prostitution was a dangerous game. The streets of Southampton at night were filled with those who were out to make a financial killing during the war and nothing was going to stop them from making money in many nefarious ways. Others took what they wanted without hesitation, as Belle discovered one night.

She was heading down Canal Walk on her way home, using her torch to shine her way, thankful that her night was over. All she wanted was a hot cup of tea and her own bed. Canal Walk was narrow and dark in the blackout. She passed one or two people who were leaving the Lord Roberts and eventually reached her door. She put her key in the lock, turned it and was suddenly pushed into the hallway, a hand over her mouth to stop her crying out.

A deep, rough voice said, 'Behave yourself and you won't get hurt, understand?'

Terrified, she nodded.

'Then take me to your room and don't turn on the light.' The man let go of her mouth, but kept a tight grip on her arm which he'd twisted behind her.

Trembling with fright, she did as she was told.

Once inside the room, the man spun her round to face him and shut the door. 'Take your clothes off!'

She hesitated and he slapped her round the face with such force she saw stars and she knew she was in trouble with no one to help her. She undressed.

For what seemed an eternity, the stranger abused her in a brutal fashion, making her cry out with pain.

'Shut your mouth!' he snarled as he drove himself inside her, grasping her ample bosom so tightly she grimaced, but she was too frightened to cry out.

Eventually, he'd satisfied himself and climbed off her. She lay still, wondering what he'd do next. He didn't say a word which was even more frightening, but she thought he was straightening his clothes. Then he opened the door and left, closing it quietly behind him.

Belle started to cry with relief, she'd been certain this man was going to kill her. She was bruised and bleeding and found it hard to move without pain, but she staggered to the door and locked it, putting the chair beneath the handle for added safety, then climbed back into bed, pulled the covers over her and sobbed.

The following morning, she was stiff and sore as she climbed out of bed and walked over to the basin to look in the mirror. She was shocked at her reflection. Her mouth was swollen and her eye was beginning to close, her cheek bruised. Her body was also beginning to show signs of bruising. Filling the basin with cold water, she bathed her face. She would have liked to sink into a bath, but didn't feel well enough to do so. Drinking a glass of water, she went back to bed.

It was here that Cora found her when she didn't show up at the Horse and Groom at lunchtime later that day. One of the other residents was leaving the house when Cora arrived and let her in. She knocked on Belle's door.

'Belle, it's Cora, are you in there?' She knocked again and waited as she could hear sounds of movement. When Belle eventually opened the door, Cora was shocked at what she saw.

'Oh my God! What happened to you?'

Tears trickled down Belle's face and she beckoned her friend inside.

It was some time before Cora heard the sad tale. First she helped her friend back to bed, made a cup of tea for them both, sat on the bed and listened whilst Belle told her of her ordeal.

At the end of the story, Cora asked, 'Have you any idea who it was?'

Shaking her head, she said, 'He wouldn't let me put the

light on, but he was tall and broad, he smelt of beer and tobacco. He wasn't in uniform because I couldn't feel any brass buttons, but I'd recognise his voice if I ever heard it again. He sounded north country to me.'

'Are you going to report this to the police? This was rape, Belle.'

Her friend gave a sardonic guffaw. 'What good would that do? Come on, love, it's a chance we all take on the job.'

'But you should see a doctor at least.'

Belle refused, 'No, I'll be fine. I won't be working for a while, but I would ask you to do me a favour.'

'Of course, anything.'

'Will you help me to take a bath? I need to soak in a hot tub to help my bruised body. And sod the five inches of water we're allowed; I need a full bath to sit in.'

'You stay put until I run the water,' said Cora, 'and I'll come and get you.'

When the bath was filled, Cora helped her friend into the water. She noticed the scratches and bruises on her body but made no mention of them as she washed Belle's back. She sat on the edge of the bath talking to her as Belle slid down and let the hot water ease her pain, wondering if they would ever discover the man who'd done this. Cora was thankful that her friend was alive to tell the sad tale, because any man who could do this was capable of anything.

She stayed with Belle, making her eat, letting her sleep and insisted on staying the night, sensing how nervous her friend was of being alone, wondering if she would be brave enough to continue with her work when she'd recovered.

*　*　*

Olive took off her green overall at the end of the day in the greengrocer's where she worked and hung it up behind the door. She called goodnight to her boss and made her way home. As she let herself into the house, she sighed deeply. It was so depressing to be alone. She missed Hildy more than she liked to admit and when she did so it was with anger that her daughter could have been so cold-blooded as to leave without a thought of how she would manage. Well, Hildy would be alone now her GI had gone to war and she wondered how that would affect her daughter; would the loneliness be enough to bring her back? But remembering the scene between them as Hildy left in the taxi, she knew in her heart that she would never return. She also knew that she'd said more than she should have at the time.

Making a cup of tea, she turned on the wireless for company. Perhaps she could take a lodger; after all, she did have a spare bedroom now. The money would be useful and it would be company. Not that she'd want anyone to encroach on her privacy. Oh no, they'd have to keep to their room, but it would mean there would be someone in the house. A presence. She could put a notice in the window of the local paper shop. She'd maybe do it tomorrow, her half-day when she went to do her shopping.

The following day, a new notice was put in the window at the newsagent's among the others.

Room to let to a quiet, respectable person. All enquiries in the evening at 4 Union Street. Ask for Mrs Dickson.

Hildy saw it as she entered the shop to buy a paper on her way to work. She always stopped to read the notices because often people advertised furniture and other things that were hard to come by in wartime and a bargain was often to be had.

She raised her eyebrows in surprise. It was the first sensible thing her mother had done in a long time. She entered the shop with a quiet smile to herself and bought her paper.

Two days later as Olive sat down to read the evening paper, there was a knock on her door. When she opened it she was surprised to see a well dressed man standing there.

'Mrs Dickson?'

'Yes, that's me.'

'I've come about the room to be let.'

This took her by surprise. Although she'd put the advert in the shop window, now actually faced with someone who was interested, she became uncertain. However, she was impressed by the man's appearance and he was in his early forties, not some youngster, which made her a bit more comfortable.

Seeing her hesitation, the stranger asked, 'Am I too late? Has the room gone?'

'No, no. You best come in and see it.' She took him upstairs and showed him the room which was spotlessly clean with a single bed. There was a small wardrobe, a hard-backed chair and chest of drawers in the window with a triple mirror on top.

He looked around and turning to her said, 'This seems to be fine.'

'How long were you thinking of staying?' she asked.

'At the moment, I'm not sure, but definitely for several weeks.'

'Right. The rent is seven and six a week and I don't do breakfast,' she said, 'and I want two weeks in advance.'

The stranger tried to hide a smile as he said, 'That's fine with me.' He put his hand in his pocket and counted out some money. 'I would like my own key though.'

Seeing the cash in his hand, Olive said, 'That's fine, but you have only the right to the room and bathroom, not the rest of the house and I won't have you bringing women back here, Mr . . . ?'

'Joe Keating, and I can assure you, I will not be entertaining anyone here, Mrs Dickson, but I'd like to move in later tonight.' He waited for her answer.

'That'll be fine,' she said and took the money. 'If you come downstairs, I'll get your key.' She showed him where the bathroom was first, then made her way to her sitting room, took out Hildy's key and gave it to him.

'I hope you're not a noisy person, Mr Keating?'

'I'll be as quiet as a mouse,' he said with an amused smile. 'I'll be back later with my things and thank you.'

Olive went back to her sitting room and sat down. Having made her decision to take a stranger into her home, she was now filled with trepidation. Had she done the right thing? She looked at the money her new lodger had given her and was pleased. That at least would pay her rent and she wouldn't have to worry about getting a breakfast. She certainly didn't want the worry of that with the rationing, it was difficult enough catering for herself without having to worry about another. Then she sat back and smiled with some satisfaction. If Hildy asked to come back now, she could say she didn't have any room for her.

At the end of the week, Belle felt well enough to go out of the house. She met Cora and some of the other brasses in the Horse and Groom where she warned them about the stranger who'd attacked her. They were all horrified at what had befallen their friend, although each of them had met with violent punters at some time in their lives, so they could understand how dangerous her situation had been.

'Bloody hell, Belle!' said one. 'You was lucky to come out alive by the sound of it!'

'I thought I was a goner,' she admitted, and looking around her, she said, 'I'm not at all sure I can face taking anyone back to my house again. That bugger scared the shit out of me! I've had some dodgy punters in the past but this one was terrifying. I thought he was going to do me and that's a fact.'

'What will you do?' asked Cora.

Shrugging, Belle said, 'I'll have to get a job. I'll buy tonight's *Evening Echo* and see what's on offer. You lot be careful; this man is dangerous.' Belle went on to describe him as best she could.

* * *

Later that night, she pored over the 'Situations Vacant' in the local paper. With so many men off to war, there was no shortage of jobs on offer. She didn't fancy working in a shop, she considered being a bus conductor, but the best wages on offer were in the factory that used to be Sunlight Laundry which was now making parts for Spitfires. She still had dreams of owning a bungalow so decided to go along in the morning and apply for the vacancy.

Before getting into bed, Belle checked that she'd locked her door then placed a chair under the handle. Her devastating experience had left her feeling edgy. When she walked home, she kept glancing behind her to make sure she wasn't followed and occasionally she had nightmares where she relived every terrifying moment. But she was a strong woman and she coped with it all, determined to get past this and start her new life.

The following morning, her interview went well, and to her delight, Belle was taken on. The foreman told her they were short of staff at the moment and when she said she could start at once if he liked, he was more than pleased.

'I'll take you to meet Hildy Dickson; she'll show you the ropes and train you. You seem pretty bright to me so I expect you'll pick it up fairly quickly. She'll kit you out in a pair of dungarees. Come with me.'

As they left his office and walked through the factory, the buzz from the machines filled the air. Belle supposed you'd get used to the noise eventually.

They stopped beside a machine and the foreman tapped

the girl working it on the shoulder and gestured for her to switch off.

'Hildy, this is Belle Newman. I've just taken her on. Show her the ropes, will you, love?'

Hildy smiled at Belle. 'Of course, come with me,' and she took her to a store and found a pair of dungarees that fitted, then back to a machine that was free and unmanned.

For the rest of the morning, Belle was instructed as to how she was to work. It seemed entirely alien to her, but nevertheless she enjoyed the experience and at lunchtime, Hildy took her into the canteen for a meal.

They queued for food, which was free as it was financed by the government, so the girls helped themselves and settled down on a bench before a long table with other workers. In the background on the radio, *Workers' Playtime* could be heard and the girls were all chatting.

Hildy sipped her tea and turning to Belle said, 'You pick things up really quickly. Before long you'll be able to manage a machine on your own.'

Belle grimaced. 'Don't know about that,' she said.

'Trust me, you will. I've trained enough girls to know.' Hildy had noticed that beneath Belle's make-up, there were traces of bruising on her face which intrigued her and she wondered what the story was behind this young woman – but it wasn't her place to pry. Everybody had a story, but not everyone wanted to share it. They returned to the factory floor half an hour later.

That night Belle sat down and wrote a long letter to Jackson Butler, telling him she had a new job, but not the reason for the change. As she wrote she prayed that he was safe and still in one piece. She searched the mail for a letter from him, but as yet she'd heard nothing and clung to the memory of him saying it would take time for the mail to come through.

As she climbed into bed, it gave her a certain pleasure to know that no longer did she need to use her bed to make money by selling her body.

Over in France, the battle for supremacy and ground continued. The Allies had linked up the beachheads to form a continuous front. The Americans fought on, taking ground, moving on. But it took two long and weary weeks for them to break through until eventually Cherbourg was theirs. The troops took a well-earned rest as the kitchens were set up and the food cooked.

Sergeant Milt Miller was proud of his men and told them so as they sat eating the hot, steaming food. He walked among them seeing they were alright, telling them what a good job they'd done, before partaking of any food himself.

He strolled over to a bunch of men sitting on the ground in a circle. They moved up to make a space for him.

'Thanks,' he said as he sat down. 'What's your name, soldier?' he asked the man next to him.

'Hank Mason, Sergeant. I remember seeing you around in Southampton.'

'That seems an age ago, doesn't it?' Milt remarked.

'Sure does. Like to be back there now,' said Hank.

'Did you leave a girl behind?'

Hank hesitated. 'Well I did meet someone, but we said it was just friendship, things being so unsettled. You know how it is in wartime.'

With a slow smile, Milt agreed. 'True, however I did meet a lady and we became engaged before I left. She's coming to the States when this is all over and we'll be married.'

'That's great. Congratulations!'

'Now we're here for a while, I'm hoping we'll get some mail. That'll cheer the men after such a hard time.'

'Yes, Cora promised to write. I told her how important it was when you're away.'

Milt rose to his feet. 'Let's hope the pony express gets through then.'

They were not disappointed and towards the evening the men gathered around as the mail arrived. They stood listening for their names to be called and the lucky ones took their mail off to a quiet corner to read the contents.

'Jackson Butler!' called the soldier delivering the letters.

Jackson pushed forward, retrieved two letters and took them away. They were from Belle. He sat on the ground and opened the first one.

Dearest Jackson,
I do so hope you are alive and well and that you get this letter safely. It was really hard to see you driven off that day to the docks before you sailed for France. I miss you, lovely boy, and wish with all my heart you were here now, so I could hold you close to me.

It went on to tell him bits of gossip about the Horse and Groom and her friends.

Now you make sure you keep your head down. I'm looking forward to hearing that you're safe and sound.
Lots of love,
Belle
xxx

Jackson read it again, lit a cigarette and then opened the other letter.

Dearest Jackson,
I have news you'll never believe. I've given up my old profession and am working in a factory. How about that? I am now an honest woman! I'm learning how to work a machine which makes parts for Spitfires. It's such a change and I'm loving it and soon I'm told I'll be good enough to work the machine on my own. I feel like a kid taking school exams.
Been watching the news and hoping you are fine. Take care of yourself.
Much love,
Belle
xxx

He was delighted to hear from Belle and surprised, but pleased she was off the streets. In his mind she was far too good a woman to be selling herself, but at the same time realising had she not have been doing so, they would never have got together. He took out a pad from his kit bag and started to write back to her.

Milt had a letter from Hildy and a couple from home. Much as he wanted to read them, he had to get his men settled for the night so after he was finished he'd have time.

The cook made some coffee and handed it to Milt. 'Here you are, Sergeant. I guess you could use one of these.'

Milt thanked him and took it to his tent. He read the family ones first. All was well with them and they brought him up to date with family news. He put these in his pocket and opened one from Hildy.

Darling Milt,
I can't tell you how much I miss you and how I long for the day when you return and we can be together. I keep as busy as I can to fill the empty evenings. My friends and I go to the pictures and watch the newsreels. My heart is in my mouth as I watch the fighting and wonder if you are safe.

We're busy in the factory and at the moment I'm teaching a new girl, Belle Newman, how to work a machine. We are short-staffed and have advertised for more woman power!

Won't it be wonderful when the war is over and we can start our lives together? You keep safe, you hear! I'll write again soon.

All my love for ever,
Hildy
xxxx

He undressed, climbed into bed and read the letter one more time before falling asleep.

Not everyone who'd received mail was happy. Some men had received Dear John letters breaking off relationships and engagements. Others had received news of a death in their families and were unable to do anything about it other than to write and express their sympathies, others wrote in anger. But this was wartime and such things were inevitable.

Chapter Ten

Olive was pleased with her lodger. He was quiet and tidy in the bathroom, but kept his bedroom door locked, as she found out one day when she tried the door.

If they ever met in the hallway, he was polite but never paused to chat. She was now becoming curious about the man. Was did he do? If she tried to question him, he was evasive. Like the other day when she met him as he walked through the front door on her afternoon off.

'Good afternoon, Mrs Dickson,' he said, tipping his hat.

'Good afternoon, Mr Keating. Your half-day too?'

'Not really, so if you'll excuse me, I have some paperwork to see to,' and he left her standing as he walked up the stairs.

Her eyes narrowed. She didn't like being dismissed so readily. She was so used to being in control that his attitude irked her somewhat. But there was nothing she could do about it and the money he paid for his rent was more than useful.

In his bedroom, Joe Keating smiled to himself. *Nosey old woman*, he thought. It gave him a certain pleasure in being evasive. It was none of her business what he did. He removed his jacket, and taking a sheaf of papers from a briefcase, he sat on the bed, reading through them and taking notes.

Cora was still working the streets, much to Belle's consternation. After her experience, she worried about her friend and tried to persuade her to join her working at the factory.

'Look, love,' said Belle as they sat in the Horse and Groom early one evening, 'the money isn't at all bad and you can work overtime if you want. It's not difficult. I'm working my own machine now. We could get a small flat between us and share.'

Cora looked thoughtful. 'Do you think I'd be able to work a machine again? My stint in the factory was brief and a long time ago. Remember, Belle, I've been a brass since just after my parents died. I don't really know anything else now.'

'Oh, Cora, you don't know how sad that makes me feel to hear you say that. You are young and beautiful. You have your whole future in front of you. You shouldn't be on the streets anyway; you're not meant for that kind of life. If you stick at it, you'll age before your years. Trust me, I know!'

'I'll think about it, promise. Oh, look, that man over there just smiled at me. I think he was in The Grapes the other evening.' She looked away quickly.

'Perhaps he fancies you,' Belle laughed. 'He's well dressed, clean. Maybe he'll ask you for a date.' She roared with laughter at the shocked expression on Cora's face. 'You could do a lot worse, love.'

'Oh, for goodness' sake, will you behave! Anyway, he's far too old for me.'

'Well, I wouldn't turn him down, but it isn't me he's interested in,' said Belle. 'More's the pity.'

Cora finished her half of beer and, getting up from her seat, she said, 'Well, I'd best start work.'

'Think about what I said, coming to work with me, right?'

'I will, Belle, I will.' She walked out of the door.

Belle sat and finished her drink, thinking of the many years she'd sat in this bar and others, looking for punters. When one man came over to her and propositioned her, she just smiled at him.

'Sorry, love, I've retired.' Then she left the bar and walked home, made a cup of tea and sat down to read the letters from Jackson Butler that had eventually arrived. She was so relieved that he was alive and well. He didn't say much about the fighting except that it had been bad.

But then, Belle, I think about you. The times we had, how you would cuddle into me after we made love. I wish we were together again now.

She brushed the tears away as she read them. If anything happened to him, she would never know. After all, it would be his family who would be told the bad news, certainly not her. They wouldn't know of her relationship with their son, and if they ever did, the knowledge that he'd been with a white woman . . . she couldn't imagine the effect that would have. With a sigh, she undressed and climbed into bed.

Cora entered the bar of The Grapes just before closing time. She was weary and ordered a gin and tonic. A British soldier came over to her. He'd been drinking heavily and his speech was slurred.

'Hello gorgeous! I've got a couple of hours before I'm due back at camp and I'm going to spend them with you.'

'No, I'm afraid you're not,' she said quietly.

'What's the matter? My money not good enough?'

She looked up at him. 'That's not the point; I've finished working for the night.'

He became abusive but thankfully the landlord came over and grabbed him by the arm.

'That's enough, son. Leave the lady alone or I'll chuck you out!'

Another soldier came over and apologised. 'Sorry, I'll take him back to camp when I've finished my drink.' He led his colleague away and a little later the two of them left the bar.

Cora was relieved. The last thing she needed was a belligerent punter. She'd been thinking about Belle's idea and the drunken soldier had helped her come to a decision. Belle was right. It was time to move on. She finished the last of her drink and left the pub.

There was no moon that night and Canal Walk was darker than ever. She switched on her torch and started to make her way home. She'd passed the Lord Roberts when she was suddenly grabbed roughly by the arm.

'Right you, little bitch! Who do you think you are, turning me and my money down?'

The smell of alcohol from the man's breath filled her nostrils and when she shone her torch into his face she recognised the drunken soldier who'd approached her earlier.

'Leave me alone!' she cried and tried to shake off his hold. To no avail. Now she was really scared, but before she could scream or call out, the man was sent flying and hit the wall behind him, sinking to the ground, unconscious.

A soft voice said, 'Let me walk you home, miss.'

In the torchlight, she saw it was a man she'd seen in the Horse and Groom.

'You'll be perfectly safe with me,' he said quietly, taking her arm. 'Now, which way do we go? The soldier will be out for the count for some time, so don't you worry about him.'

Cora didn't hesitate and let the stranger walk her home. He waited until she'd opened her front door and turned to thank him.

'My pleasure, but you really shouldn't be on the streets, you are far too good for that.' Then he walked away, disappearing into the darkness.

Cora was trembling, remembering how her friend Belle had fared and felt lucky that she hadn't ended up the same way. Had it not been for that stranger . . . well, it didn't bear thinking about.

* * *

The following morning, she knocked on Belle's door in time to catch her before she left for the factory. Her friend was surprised to see her.

'What the hell are you doing here at this hour? Are you alright?'

Cora quickly told her what had happened the previous night. 'So I wondered if I could come to the factory with you and apply for a job?'

Belle shut the door and grinned broadly. 'Well, you're full of surprises! Yes, come with me, I'll introduce you to the foreman and put in a good word for you.' She tucked her arm through Cora's and they set off.

The foreman was delighted to have another worker and when Belle left them to go to her machine, the foreman took details from Cora and asked, 'You able to start now, love?'

'Yes, if you like.'

'Then come with me.' He led her to the factory floor, introduced her to Hildy and left the two of them to get on with an introduction to the machine which Cora would learn to use.

'I have used a similar machine before,' Cora said, 'but it was a long time ago.'

'Well, let's see you get on,' Hildy replied.

At lunchtime in the canteen, Belle joined the two of them over lunch. She smiled at Cora. 'I can't tell you how happy I am that you decided to work here. It's alright, isn't it?' she turned to Hildy for confirmation.

'It's not at all bad as jobs go these days. You can earn

108

more money by working overtime – once you are able to work on your own, of course. You'll be fine, you'll see.'

'Hildy is a good teacher,' Belle said, 'mind you, don't let her catch you slacking because she can be a bit hard.'

'It's part of my job,' Hildy explained. 'Some girls try it on . . . but only once. If they don't pull their weight they're out of a job. But I know I won't have any trouble with you two.'

And so Southampton lost two of their ladies of the night.

Chapter Eleven

Hildy let herself into her flat at the end of her working day. She undressed, ran a bath and soaked her aching body in the hot water. She'd worked overtime and was weary, but she was saving her money for the time that she went to America and married Milt.

She lay back in the bath, slopping water over her shoulders with the wet sponge. God, she wished he was here now, she missed him so much, but at least she was now receiving mail from him. He sounded cheerful. The men in his company were doing a good job and he was proud of them, but of course, like her, he couldn't wait for the war to be over so they could start a life together.

For her part, she was relieved that her mother had taken in a lodger and was proving that, when necessary, she was well able to look after herself. Hildy hadn't called on her. What was the point? She'd only be met with verbal grief. The day she'd walked out of the family house she felt as if a weight had been removed from her shoulders and when the day came that she sailed away from Southampton to a new life, she would have no feelings of guilt. She'd served her time as a daughter and been unloved by a woman who could only think of herself.

Joe Keating was walking along the street when he saw the young woman he'd saved from the attentions of the drunken soldier the other night. She had a cigarette in her mouth and appeared to be searching for a light. He stopped beside her and handed her his lighter.

'Here, try this.'

Cora looked up and smiled when she recognised him. 'Thank you. You've come to my rescue yet again!'

'I'd hardly call this a rescue. That sounds far too dramatic . . . Miss?'

'Cora Barnes, and you are?'

'Joe Keating, at your service. Where are you off to?'

'I've just finished work and am going in search of a good cup of tea.'

Looking at his watch, he said, 'Twelve o'clock. You're starting early, aren't you?'

For a moment she puzzled over his remark, then she started to laugh. 'I have a new job, Mr Keating. I am working in a factory these days.'

'You are?' He looked surprised, yet pleased. 'I'm happy to hear that; I told you that you were too good to work on the streets.'

'That's right, you did and to be honest it was the night you came to my rescue that made me change my occupation. I was really scared and decided to quit whilst I was ahead, so to speak.'

He grinned broadly. 'I think this calls for a celebration. Would you allow me to buy you that cup of tea?'

His invitation was so unexpected that for a moment Cora hesitated.

'You'll be perfectly safe with me, Miss Barnes,' he said, trying to hide a smile.

She burst out laughing. 'Of that I'm in no doubt! Thank you, I'd be delighted.'

They found a nearby cafe and sat down at a table near the window.

'Would you like a sandwich or something?' asked Joe.

'Oh, no thanks, a cup of tea will be fine.' She looked at her companion and, filled with curiosity, asked, 'Do you work around here, Mr Keating?'

'Yes, at the moment I work for the National Provincial Bank in an advisory capacity. The bank's introducing a new system and I'm here to oversee it.'

'You are?'

He looked amused at her surprise. 'What did you think I did for a living?'

Cora chuckled and, with twinkling eyes, said, 'Oh, I don't know. Nothing as mundane as that.' She gave the matter a moment's thought. 'I was convinced it was something far more exciting. To me, you are a man of mystery.'

He started to laugh. 'Really? No, I'm just an ordinary man trying to make a living.'

'I don't think you are ordinary at all. I would say there is far more to you than that: I'm convinced you are a man with a secret past . . . or present even.'

'You have too lively an imagination, young lady.'

At that moment, the waitress served the tea and further conversation on the matter was closed. They spoke about the war and D-Day, the number of troops who'd passed through the town, the fighting going on across the Channel and how they hoped it would all be over soon.

'What will you do when that day comes?' asked Joe.

'After celebrating, I'm going to move up to London and start a new life,' said Cora. 'I've been saving every penny I've earned with that in mind.'

'Will you be returning to your old occupation?' he asked.

'Certainly not! I want to put that all behind me. I'll get a job in a shop somewhere, a nice little flat and begin to live! I'll bury my past and start again.'

'That sounds like a great idea, I wish you luck.' He looked at his watch. 'Much as I'd love to sit and chat, I've an appointment.' He called the waitress over and paid the bill.

They rose from their chairs and left the cafe.

'Thanks for the tea, Mr Keating – it was kind of you.'

He smiled softly. 'The pleasure was all mine. You take care of yourself now.'

Joe smiled to himself as he walked away. What a delightful girl Cora Barnes was. He hoped she would fulfil her wishes.

Cora was telling Belle about her encounter with Joe Keating. 'He took me for a cup of tea, Belle! He says he works for the National Provincial Bank.'

Her friend looked sceptical. 'No, there's more to him

113

than that. You've seen the way he dresses. Those suits cost a packet and are made to measure would be my guess. You be careful, Cora, love. Don't get involved.'

'That's hardly likely, Belle. We only met by chance on both occasions.'

'I know, but I'm a great believer in fate. I think people come into our lives for a reason.'

'Oh, for heaven's sake! You sound like an old gypsy telling fortunes.'

'Maybe, but I'm seldom wrong. You just remember my words.'

On the battlefields in France, Sergeant Miller was certainly glad that Jackson Butler was in his life. They were in a small town, advancing with their company. Sherman tanks led the assault, with the soldiers moving in behind. The fighting was fierce as the town was well defended, the troops dived for cover wherever they could before moving on – the tanks climbing over rubble, advancing deeper into enemy territory. The sound of explosions and the smell of cordite filled the air. Cries of pain could be heard as the enemy made its mark. The ground was spattered with blood as both sides suffered casualties. Grenades were thrown and body parts flew into the air.

Soldiers moved on further with bullets flying around them. Just as Sergeant Miller urged his men to move out, Jackson spotted a sniper in a window about to take a shot at his sergeant, but he brought Milt down with a rugby tackle, and then lifting his rifle, shot the sniper dead.

As Milt brushed the dust from his face, he realised

what had happened. He looked at Jackson with gratitude, 'Thanks, I owe you.'

Jackson brushed his thanks aside. 'I got lucky, Sergeant.'

Milt grinned. 'No, soldier, I was the one who got lucky!' Getting to his feet, Miller called to his men. 'Move out!'

They spent the next few hours fighting every inch of the way into the town. As the casualties occurred, the call of 'Medic!' could be heard many times during the advance until the town was safely in the hands of the American troops.

It was only then that the locals, who had been in hiding, cheered the victors as they established their stronghold.

Reconnaissance parties were sent out, to scour the buildings and shots were heard as hidden German troops were found. Then those who surrendered were led away, hands in the air.

Eventually camp was made and the surviving soldiers took a well-earned break. Milt sought out Jackson Butler and handed him a silver flask. 'Here, take a swig of this, Butler, because today you really earned it. My girl will be more than grateful you're a good shot!'

Jackson took the flask, and with a broad grin, he said, 'To the lucky lady!' and drank.

The burning liquid felt good as it passed down his throat. He handed the flask back. 'Thanks, Sergeant.'

Sitting on the ground, leaning against what was left of a wall, Jackson took out a pack of cigarettes and lit one. Apart from feeling dirty after all the fighting and the debris, he was happy to still be alive. Today had been really bad and he knew that they had lost some good men. He said a silent prayer, thanking the Lord for his salvation and praying he would come out of the war in one piece.

For his part, Sergeant Milt Miller knew just how lucky he was to still be alive. Had it not been for Jackson Butler whose sharp eyes had spotted the sniper, he would be a dead man. He certainly wouldn't be putting that in his next letter to Hildy!

Hank Mason had made it through the day, too. But as he sat drinking a cup of coffee, his hands were trembling. He had been so lucky. Two men beside him had been killed. He remembered the look of surprise on the face of one of them as a bullet entered his heart and he fell. He wondered how much longer the fighting would last and would he still be standing?

He was not alone in such thoughts. Every man who had survived this day wondered the very same thing, knowing that ahead of them lay many a day like today.

Chapter Twelve

A new threat emerged. The Germans were sending over bombs called V-1s, buzz bombs or doodlebugs as the locals called them. The public had been warned to take cover if they heard the curious engine noise stop or if they saw the flame from the bomb disappear. It took seconds before the explosion. The south of England had been shaken for thirty long hours. It was like the Blitz all over again. Southampton was fortunate; there were only three attacks, two in Bitterne, but luckily without fatalities.

Belle and Cora decided to share accommodation now they were both working. They applied to be on different shifts so as not to be with each other twenty-four hours a day, which they considered would be too much, even though they were such close friends. It worked well as they shared the household chores and the cooking.

They remained in the same vicinity where the flats were cheaper and they were near their place of work. However, they still managed to spend an evening out together, going to the cinema, enjoying the fleshpots and they still kept in touch with their old associates.

It was on one such occasion, sitting in the Horse and Groom, talking to their old mates that Belle suddenly turned pale and spilt her glass of beer.

Cora was the first to realise that something was wrong. 'What is it, Belle?' she asked.

'Those two men, standing at the bar. The big one . . . I heard his voice, that's the one who raped me!'

Cora looked across the bar at the men. They looked like dockers, in their shabby trousers and jackets. One was wearing a flat cap.

'Which one?' whispered Cora.

Looking down into her lap so as not to be noticed, Belle said, 'The one without the cap. I'd know that voice anywhere.'

The other girls looked over at the men.

'Don't any of you have anything to do with him and don't leave here alone like I did,' Belle warned.

'What do you want to do, Belle?' asked Cora. 'Do you want to leave?'

Belle was now really agitated. 'Yes, let's go.' She rose from the chair.

The man at the bar looked over. He saw Belle and watched her carefully as she walked to the door. She looked back over her shoulder at him and saw the grin on his face. She walked outside and was violently sick.

Cora was standing over her trying to comfort her when a quiet voice asked, 'What's the problem? Is your friend ill? Can I help?'

It was Joe Keating.

Very quietly Cora explained. 'There's a man at the bar who attacked my friend Belle a few months back and she recognised him. She's in shock.'

'What does he look like?' asked Keating.

Cora described him.

'Right, well you take your friend home, I'll go into the bar and make sure he doesn't follow you, if he does, I'll come and walk with you.'

Cora thanked him and quickly led Belle away.

Joe Keating walked into the bar and saw the two men. He walked up to the counter and, standing beside them, ordered a drink. The men continued to chat, so Joe sat at a nearby table watching, until much later when the men left together.

The following night there was a report in the *Southern Evening Echo* about a dockworker found badly beaten near Canal Walk who had been hospitalised with serious injuries.

It was the main topic of gossip in the Horse and Groom when it was discovered it had been a customer who'd been drinking in the bar the night before. It wasn't long before the brasses realised it was the man who'd attacked Belle and they made sure she was told about it.

'Oh my God!' Cora exclaimed, then turning to her friend asked, 'Do you think that Mr Keating had anything to do with it?'

'Don't be silly,' said Belle, 'why would he get so involved?'

But just at that moment, one of the brasses came over and told them the man had upset a couple of men in the bar and after he left, they followed. 'Draw your own conclusions,' she said.

Belle glanced over at Cora. 'There you are then!'

'So I was wrong, thank goodness for that.'

Chapter Thirteen

Meanwhile, in France, territory was being won and lost. Troops gained a foothold only to be driven back. The fighting was fierce, but eventually things began to change. Heavy bombings had disrupted the German communications and destroyed their fire power. Now, in some areas, they were prepared to surrender at the sight of the invading troops. Lines of German prisoners filled the roadsides as American and British tanks passed through in various areas of France.

Nevertheless, some strongholds were still well defended. It was here that Milt and his company were still fighting. Food was short, sleep was brief. The troops were tired and dirty, all of them longing for a respite, a hot meal and a wash.

The company was holed up on farmland, with a German company approaching through the fields of corn. Some of the men were in a cow shed, some in an old barn, Jackson and a few others crouched down in what had been a pigsty.

'Jesus, this place stinks!' exclaimed Jackson in disgust. 'I ain't never gonna get the smell out of my uniform.'

One of his mates burst out laughing. 'You ain't got no hope of getting laid again if you don't. Even Belle wouldn't have you smelling like that.'

An eruption of gunfire stilled any further conversation.

Machine-gun fire rattled as the Americans fired on the approaching enemy and, when they were closer, a flame thrower turned the growing corn into a furnace. Screams of pain could be heard. Men, in flames ran in panic.

'Move out!' yelled Milt. His men moved forward, firing as they went, stopping to throw grenades, moving forward again whilst their own planes flew over, dropping bombs on the German lines, until eventually the field was theirs.

Jackson got to his feet and cheered, holding his rifle in the air in triumph. A shot rang out and he fell to the ground. Another sounded and the German who'd fired at Jackson also fell to the ground.

Milt came running, calling, 'Medic!' loudly. He reached Jackson. 'You bloody fool! What the hell were you thinking?' He stooped down beside Jackson, and covered the wound on his shoulder with a pack to stem the bleeding.

'Sorry, Sergeant. I wasn't thinking.' He winced with pain. A medic knelt beside him and tended to him, giving him an injection before dressing the wound.

'Am I gonna die?' asked Jackson fearfully.

'No, soldier; you'll be fine, but we must get you to a field hospital. They'll take care of you. Although you'll be going home would be my guess.'

Jackson let out a sigh of relief. The thought of dying on

the battlefield and never seeing his family again had always been at the back of his mind, but he'd accepted it as a price you had to pay for war. Now it seemed possible that he had been spared. He gave a silent prayer, knowing how stupid he'd been and how fortunate.

A couple of weeks later, Belle opened a letter from Jackson. As she read it, she let out a cry of alarm.

'What's the matter?' asked Cora.

'Jackson's been injured!' She read on. 'He's fine, thank God. He's being shipped back here to the hospital at Netley apparently. He'll let me know when. He says he caught a bullet in his shoulder and has had an operation, but in time he'll be fine. He's been in a field hospital.'

'Oh, Belle, you'll be able to visit him so you will see him again, after all.' Then she saw her friend was in tears. Rushing to her side, she held her close. 'He's alive, Belle! Don't cry.'

'I know and thank God for that, it's just that I thought I'd never see him again and now I will – I'm so happy!'

Cora started to laugh. 'It's no wonder that men can never understand a woman. I'll make us a cup of tea – that puts everything right.'

Three weeks later, Belle took a bus to the hospital in Netley, which had been taken over by the American army. She stopped at the reception desk and asked to see Private Jackson Butler and was directed to one of the wards.

Her heart was beating rapidly; she took a deep breath and walked on. Every bed was full. Nurses were busy tending to the patients, but one of them stopped to tell Belle which bed she was looking for. It was at the far end by a window.

Jackson was propped up on his pillows, one shoulder bandaged and in a sling, eyes closed. Belle stood and looked at him, trying to fight back the tears.

'Hello Jackson, love,' she said softly.

He opened his eyes and when he saw who was standing beside him, he grinned broadly. 'Belle!'

She leant over and kissed him. 'Didn't I tell you to duck and didn't you promise me that you would?'

He hugged her with one arm until she could hardly breathe. 'Oh, Belle, I can't tell you how good it is to see you. How are you?'

She sat in the chair beside the bed. 'More to the point, how are *you*?'

He grimaced. 'Fine, I'm fine. I caught a bullet in my shoulder, but after an operation, it'll mend in time. They're gonna send me home, Belle.'

'At least you won't have to go back to the fighting.'

He took her hand. 'It was pretty hairy out there, Belle; we lost a lot of good men. But we had a great sergeant who kept us as safe as it was possible. Milt Miller's a good soldier.'

'Milt Miller? Our supervisor at the factory is engaged to a Milt Miller, a sergeant. It must be the same man.'

'Well, you tell her from me, he's fine.' His expression softened as he gazed at her. 'I sure missed you, Belle. I thought about you a lot. I wish I could come back and convalesce with you.'

'No more than I do, darling. I would take such care of you, you wouldn't believe.'

A nurse came over and asked Belle if she'd like a cup of tea.

Belle thanked her and said she'd love one. Then asked, 'How long will Private Butler be staying here?'

'At least a couple more weeks.' She looked at her patient. 'Well, Private, you look pretty chipper.' Then to Belle she said, 'Having a visitor does the men so much good, but unfortunately most of the men here have to wait to get back home first.' Looking at Jackson, she added, 'You're a lucky man!'

He chuckled and said, 'Nurse, you have no idea just how lucky.'

When they were alone, Jackson said quietly. 'Gee, Belle, I want so much to hold you and feel you close to me.'

She caressed his face. 'I know, I feel the same. We had such good times together, didn't we?'

'We sure did, honey, and when I go home, that's what I'll remember most of all. You made me feel like a man, just like any other.'

'You were more of a man than many I've known, Jackson; you just remember that.'

But in her heart she knew that when he returned to Alabama, the same old restrictions would be facing him and she worried as to how it would affect him. But she kept these thoughts to herself.

She stayed until visiting time was over, promising to come again the following day and every day until he was shipped home.

'Can you manage to do that with your job?'

'Yes. I'm on an early shift so my afternoons are free.'

'Belle, honey, I'm so glad you ain't on the streets no more.'

'Me too,' she agreed. 'Working in a factory is great and I'm enjoying it.'

'Why did you decide to change your job?'

There was no way Belle was going to tell him the truth. 'I heard of a job going in the factory. The money was good and I could please myself as to what hours I worked. It was time for a change. Cora, one of the other girls, now works with me. We share a flat, so it's a whole new life.'

A nurse came to tell her visiting hours were over. She kissed Jackson goodbye until the following day when she would return.

'No flirting with the nurses now,' she laughed as she rose to leave.

'There's only one woman for me, you know that, Belle, honey.' And he watched her leave, waving to her as she looked back from the doorway.

The following morning, Belle was able to give Hildy the news that her fiancé was fine. She told Hildy what Jackson had said about Milt being a good soldier and saw how pleased her supervisor was.

'I just pray he comes through it all, so we can be together again. I'm glad your friend is okay. When I write to Milt, I'll tell him about Jackson. He'll be pleased to have news of one of his men.'

* * *

During the next two weeks, Belle spent her afternoons at the hospital. After a few days, Jackson was able to walk with her in the grounds. They would find a secluded spot away from prying eyes where they could snuggle up together and exchange kisses and one afternoon, Jackson was allowed out of the hospital grounds for the afternoon. They took a taxi to Belle's flat where they were able to climb into bed and make love once again.

As they lay together, content to be with each other, Belle said, 'I'm really going to miss you when you leave . . . again!'

'Me too, honey, but you know there ain't no way we can be together. Folks have learnt a certain amount of tolerance during wartime, but after . . . we'd have no chance and I wouldn't dream of putting you in a situation like that.' He kissed the tip of her nose. 'You will meet some nice guy and settle down. A man who will take care of you, who will be acceptable to your friends and others. You know I'm being honest, honey. That's life. That's reality.'

She knew he was right, but it didn't help the way she was feeling.

That evening, she received a telegram from Jackson saying he'd just been told he was being moved out the following morning and he would write. Although she knew it was coming at some point, she was devastated.

Chapter Fourteen

It took Belle some time to get over the departure of Jackson Butler. Cora was in despair trying to cheer her friend, but Belle would go to work, cook a meal, wash up and go to bed. Eventually she began to emerge from her depression and was more her old self.

It was her birthday on the Saturday and Cora suggested that they get some friends together at the Lord Roberts and have a party and, to that end, the word spread. Everyone took something to eat and the landlord gave the first drink for free. It turned out to be quite a night.

Belle was a popular woman and all evening long folk gathered, bringing gifts and cards. The pianist was playing and before long the sound of singing echoed round Canal Walk. 'Roll Me Over in the Clover' was followed by 'Roll Out the Barrel' and so on.

Towards the end of the evening, Belle, now well lubricated with alcohol, stood in the middle of the bar and started to sing 'We'll Meet Again' and her husky voice filled with emotion. The bar was silent until she'd finished, then the applause rang out, but Cora saw the tears in her eyes and knew that she'd been thinking of Jackson.

Belle walked back to her seat, but didn't sit down. She looked at Cora and with a tremble in her voice said, 'Let's go home.'

Hildy had written to Milt telling him about Jackson and that he'd been shipped home. She was very surprised when she received an answer. Milt told her that Jackson had saved his life and the following day during lunch break, she shared the news with Belle.

'It seems that your man saw a sniper about to shoot Milt and pushed him down on the ground, then shot the sniper.'

Belle was puffed up with pride. 'That's marvellous,' she said. 'My Jackson is a special kind of man.'

'Well, next time you write, you thank him for me.'

'I certainly will,' said Belle, wondering if she'd hear once Jackson was home.

Three weeks later, Belle was sitting in her dressing gown having a cup of tea, when she heard the postman put something through the letter box. There on the mat was a letter with an American stamp on it. Picking it up, she hurried back to the kitchen, sat down and opened the envelope.

My dearest Belle,
Well, here I am back in Alabama with my family.
The shoulder is healing well and pretty soon I'll

be just fine. I'm no longer a soldier, but have been honourably discharged due to my injury. I've got a Purple Heart for my trouble. I guess that's a whole lot better than a casket with a flag.

It's great to see my family again, but after being away and in another world, I can't see me sticking around here for much longer. Nothing has changed, Belle. The fact that I fought for my country don't make no difference no more. The black man is still a no count nigger as far as white folk living here think and I'm damned if I'm going to be told to sit in the back of a bus!

I'm taking the money I saved in the army and am going to New York to find work. New York is more open minded to men like me. OK, I can't find a job that gives me no real standing in society, but I can wait tables, earn money and at least be treated better that here in the south.

I ain't never ever going to forget you, Belle, honey. You treated me with respect for the first time in my life and that was real special. You are real special, I want you to know that. I'm leaving in a couple of days' time and when I'm settled I'll write again.

I miss you like hell.

You look after yourself now.

All my love,

Jackson

She read the letter several times. It was as she thought. He was now too much of a man to be treated with contempt and she felt he'd made a good choice to move to New York. She remembered how the GIs from the northern states of America had not been the ones to take offence at seeing a black man in their midst; they were treated like any other soldier. It had been those from the southern states who'd been so outraged due to their upbringing. She'd have to wait to hear from him again with an address to which she could reply, but she was delighted that he had written.

Joe Keating knocked on Olive's kitchen door and gave her his notice. She was surprised and disappointed. After all her lodger had come and gone quietly, paid his rent on time and had been no trouble.

'I'll be leaving tomorrow,' he told her.

'But you've paid until the end of the week,' she argued.

'Yes, I'm aware of that.'

'I hope you're not expecting a rebate?'

Joe could see the woman was ready for battle and thought what an unpleasant creature she was.

'No, Mrs Dickson, I'm not. After all, it's my choice as to when I leave, not yours.' He turned and walked upstairs.

She didn't say a word. There was a coldness in his tone that took her by surprise. Until then he'd been polite and affable, but today was very different. It made her a tad uncomfortable, which for her was a new experience.

That evening, Joe went out for a meal, then went to the cinema. At the end of the programme, as he walked down the stairs from the circle to the foyer, he saw Cora Barnes with her friend.

'Good evening, ladies.'

They both turned and looked surprised. 'Hello Mr Keating,' said Cora, 'and how are you?'

'Fine, thank you.' He nodded to Belle. Then putting his hand in his pocket he took out a small card. Handing it to Cora he said, 'When eventually you do come to London, give me a call. I might be able to find you a job.' With a smile, he walked away.

They both looked at the card. It said 'Joe Keating. Business Consultant' and an address of a London bank, with a phone number.

Belle glared at her friend. 'You be very careful of that man!'

Cora laughed loudly. 'Oh, Belle, he's a nice bloke and that was really kind of him.'

Belle looked at her in astonishment. 'There's kind, but make sure there aren't any strings attached. These days no one does anything for nothing. You know that!'

'I probably won't ever need his help, but I'll keep it because you never know.'

Belle didn't reply.

It was now late August and the news of the war was good. Paris had been liberated by the French and the tricolour flag replaced the Nazi swastika on the Eiffel Tower. It wasn't all joyful in the beginning: collaborators were dragged through the streets and beaten and police had to protect captured German officers from being lynched. But eventually the celebrations began.

This was heartening news for troops still fighting in other parts of the country. It spurred them on with the thought that the fighting would soon be at an end and they could return to the safety of their homes.

Hank Mason wrote to Cora telling her all this. Her letters had been a constant comfort during the tough days and he was grateful to her. He was especially pleased to read that she was no longer working the streets of Southampton's docklands. He wrote:

So pleased you are now working in a safer environment, Cora. So you are really my girl now!

This made her smile. She had enjoyed their relationship, but that was all it was and his friendly letters to her made that clear.

She really liked Hank, but she wasn't in love with him. She could hardly wait for the war to end so she could move to the big city and start anew. The thought of it did scare her a little. Southampton was familiar and London wasn't, but she was still determined to go. If she did find it hard to find work, she still had Joe Keating's card, but she'd only contact him in an emergency.

In bed at night, she'd try to picture her future and make plans. Eventually she wanted a nice flat with two bedrooms, in case she had guests. But realised this wasn't going to happen at once. It took time to find a nice place and she'd probably like to be outside the confines of the city. She didn't know the area and would have to explore before deciding where she'd like to live. It excited her and scared her at the same time. But she was determined to be a new woman in every way. No one would know of her background so she could reinvent herself. She liked that idea.

Chapter Fifteen

The autumn passed and winter began. It was severe and bitterly cold and there was a shortage of coal. People were burning old furniture to try and keep warm. Food queues grew longer and the rationing was still meagre. Headlines in the paper reported that Glenn Miller, the popular band leader, was missing over the Channel, which saddened thousands who'd danced to his music.

At Christmas, however, the Canadians sent over a supply of beautiful red apples for the children and bananas. For some, it was the first time they'd seen this fruit, so imagine the scene when they were shown how to take off the peel before eating this strange phenomenon. The American troops still stationed in the town gave parties for the children and American candy was handed out, which delighted the children more than anything else.

Cora and Belle managed to buy a small sack of coal from one of their friends, but they didn't ask where it came from; they were just delighted to be warm. They purchased a chicken, made paper chains out of crêpe paper and hung them around the small sitting room to try to make it look festive and Belle found some paper Chinese lanterns from a box of old decorations. On Christmas Eve, they went to a carol service at St. Michael's Church.

As they settled in their pew, Belle looked around at the packed congregation, all huddled up in thick coats and scarves, but nevertheless there was a festive feel to the church, decorated with holly and berries, with the scene of the Nativity before the alter.

She knelt down and said her prayers – they were like so many others there, praying for an end to the war and the safe return of their loved ones.

Prayers were read and carols sung, the vicar filling the air with incense as he walked down the aisle, swinging the thurible on its long golden chain.

Belle loved the atmosphere created during a service; she admired the theatre of it all. It was a performance like no other and it cleansed her soul.

As she sat listening to the sermon, her mind wandered. She thought back to how she'd started her life on the streets of Southampton's docklands, of the many men who'd paid for her services, knowing that many of them would not be returning home and she hoped she'd been able to give them some comfort in a strange land. Some she remembered clearly, others were a blur. Some she didn't want to recall at all, but they were in the minority. It had been a tough way to earn a living, but she didn't regret it. Now she was living a different kind of life, although she did wonder what she'd do after the war was over and the factory closed.

136

Cora would be off to London and she'd be alone again. She didn't relish that fact at all.

Cora felt tears trickle down her face as she sat staring at the altar. This was the fourth Christmas she'd spent without her parents. As a family, they'd always attend this carol service and suddenly it brought back the desolation of her loss.

On Christmas Eve, she and her mother would have prepared the vegetables for the Christmas dinner, made mince pies and wrapped gifts, placing them around the Christmas tree. Then they would have all had a small glass of sherry before making their way to the church.

Her mother Jessy was a gentle woman, a good mother and wife, and Cora knew that had she known how her daughter had earned her money, selling her body, she would have been appalled and ashamed. A sob caught in Cora's throat and she closed her eyes, trying to get the thought from her mind. But at least now, she told herself, she was earning money in a way that would have met with her mother's approval, so thanked the Lord for that.

She couldn't wait to be able to move to London without anyone knowing of her shameful past. She would miss her friend Belle who had stood by her, but she had to make this move alone.

The girls trudged home in the cold, banking up the fire as soon as they stepped inside the flat. They had managed to buy some logs which helped to eke out their coal supply. Belle poured them a gin and tonic each and they sat warming themselves before the fire.

'Well, I wonder where we'll be this time next year?'

Belle muttered. 'I hope to God the war will be over long before that.'

'Oh, Belle, it can't possibly last that long surely?'

'Let's hope not.' She cut a couple of slices of bread and, putting them on a toasting fork, held them against the flames. 'I long for roast beef and Yorkshire pudding,' she said wistfully.

'I want a bar of Cadbury chocolate and ice cream,' Cora said.

'I want to soak in a hot bath, with water up to the waste pipe.' Belle said with a grin.

'I want to go shopping for clothes that are not utility and without the need for coupons.' Cora started to laugh. 'One day, Belle. One day.'

Finally on 8th May 1945, the girls got their wish. The Germans had surrendered and Winston Churchill made his broadcast to the nation with the good news.

Thousands gathered at the Civic Centre in Southampton to celebrate VE Day. They cheered, danced and sang, some draped in British flags. 'There'll Always Be An England' rang out. Troops from foreign lands joined in, knowing that for them it was all over too.

Belle was in the arms of an American GI, dancing to the music which was being played over loudspeakers, and Cora was doing the same with a Polish airman. People were kissing each other, carried away with joy that the war was over. The pubs were full, music played, people were ecstatic. But for those who'd lost kinfolk it was a muted celebration.

'The boys will all be coming home!' cried Belle, flinging her arm around Cora's shoulder. 'Your man Hank, Hildy's fiancé Milt, thank God for that!'

All the staff working in the munitions factory had been called to the canteen to hear the good news and listen to Winston Churchill speak. There was silence as they sat, hardly breathing with excitement. At the end of the speech, cheering began. Hildy Dickson found she was crying. Her Milt had come through safely. They could be married! He had never doubted the fact, but she had been terrified that she could have lost him. The knowledge that now he really was safe was all too much for her and she sobbed uncontrollably.

The girl sitting next to her put an arm round her shoulders. 'Don't cry, Hildy, love, it's all over. Your man will be coming home.'

Mopping her tears and blowing her nose, Hildy said, 'I know, but it's just such a relief.'

They were given an extra half an hour lunch break before returning to their machines, then they all began wondering just how much longer they would be employed, but delighted that Spitfires would no longer be needed to fight the enemy.

In London, crowds gathered in front of Buckingham Palace and cheered wildly as the royal family came out onto the balcony. Earlier they'd listened to the King's speech. It was a great celebration nationwide.

Olive Dickson heard the news in the shop where she worked. People from the street gathered to listen to Churchill as the owner turned up the volume on the wireless. It was the only topic of conversation for the rest of the day.

As she put the key into her front door and entered her empty house, she felt very much alone. Yes, she was pleased the war was over, of course she was, but that meant that Hildy would be free to marry her GI and leave Southampton for good.

She made a cup of tea and sat down. She really was alone now. She had no close friends. Her neighbours just nodded when they saw her and walked on. It was her own fault, of course. She hadn't gone out of her way to make friends because she hadn't needed them. She had Hildy at her beck and call – but not any longer. Even if they were on speaking terms, in time her daughter would leave to cross the Atlantic to another country and she'd probably never see her again. Her lodger had gone too. Not that she saw much of him, but it was a comfort to know he was in the house. Well, she'd just have to advertise again. But now, would there be anyone needing accommodation? She let out a deep sigh.

During the days that followed, street parties were organised. Tables were set out in the streets, women raided their pantries and food was produced. Paper hats were found and bunting hung from windows and roofs. Pianos were wheeled out onto the street. Old grievances were buried. The whole atmosphere in the country changed. Folk wandered around with broad grins, hardly able to believe the good news. It was a joyous time for most.

For those who'd lost members of their family, it was a mixed blessing. No more men and women needed to die and everyone was relieved about that, but so many had paid the ultimate sacrifice and there were many houses filled with sadness and broken hearts.

As the celebrations continued, Hildy sat reading a letter from Milt.

> *My darling,*
> *I can't tell you how I feel right now, knowing that the fighting is over and we can all go home. As yet I don't know if we'll be shipped back to Southampton to be repatriated. I certainly hope so because I can't wait to see you again. Then we'll have to make plans for you to come to America where we can get married. Just be patient, my love, and know that it is now possible. I'll write when I know what's happening.*
> *All my love always,*
> *Milt*

A few weeks later, Cora was wondering if it was time for her to move out of Southampton and put her plan for a new life into place. She decided to take a day off and go to London to look for work. It was the only way. She didn't want to give up her job until she'd found another, that would be foolish. She told Belle of her plans.

'I'll get an early train, buy a paper and visit a couple of employment exchanges to see if they have anything to offer.'

Belle's heart sank. She knew this day would come and she wanted her friend to get a new start, but Belle knew she would leave a deep void in her own life. They'd been through so much together.

'That's a good idea,' she agreed. 'Put your toe in the water so to speak. Well, good luck, love. Hope it goes well.'

The following morning, Cora found a seat in a carriage and watched the countryside pass by as she sat beside the window, her heart beating faster with excitement and a certain trepidation.

When she arrived at Waterloo and walked out of the station, she could still see the signs of war as she looked at the stacks of sand-filled sacks piled high in front of official looking buildings. She bought a couple of papers and went inside a cafe to read them, ordering a pot of tea. She turned to the situations vacant and began her search.

By the end of the day, Cora was exhausted and disappointed. So far she'd not been able to find suitable employment as her lack of training had held her back in many instances. Women who had taken over men's positions in various establishments were now expected to step down when the men returned from the war and it made the situation even worse for her.

There were menial jobs on offer, but none that appealed to her. She didn't fancy washing out public toilets, or sweeping streets. If she was going to start a fresh life, she at least wanted to start with a job that paid well and gave her some satisfaction. She'd been to employment agencies and left her name and address should they have anything to offer in the future, but she caught a late train home feeling weary and dejected.

Belle, in her nightdress and dressing gown, heard the front door open. She waited to see how her friend had made out with mixed feelings, but as soon as she saw the look on Cora's face, she knew that the day had not been a success and quietly breathed a sigh of relief.

Cora sat down and immediately removed her shoes and massaged her aching feet.

'Bloody waste of time that was!' she exclaimed.

'What happened?' asked Belle as she put on the kettle to make her friend a cup of tea.

Cora told her of her attempts to find a job. It was a long and sorry tale.

'So what will you do?' asked Belle.

'I'll leave it for a few weeks and try again.' At the back of her mind, she thought that if the same thing happened she'd contact Joe Keating. After all, he'd offered to find her work and if she couldn't do it by herself, she'd have no option. Not if she was determined to move to the metropolis.

A month later saw her once again on a train heading for Waterloo Station.

By late afternoon, Cora was totally frustrated. She had decided that she'd really like to work in one of the department stores, but when she'd enquired, she was told there were no positions vacant. In desperation, she'd tried cafes and restaurants for a job as a waitress, but those she'd tried wanted people with experience. She sat on a bench in a park, lit a cigarette and took out Joe Keating's card and read it. Across the road was a phone booth and after giving the matter some considerable thought, she walked across the road, put her money in the box, dialled a number then pressed button 'A' when she heard a voice answer.

'Joe Keating, Business Consultant.' It was a woman speaking.

'Could I speak to Mr Keating, please?'

'May I ask who is calling?'

'Miss Cora Barnes from Southampton.'

'Please hold the line.'

Cora waited, her heart pounding. What if he didn't remember her?

'Well, Miss Cora Barnes, this is a pleasant surprise. What can I do for you?'

The relief she felt was enormous when she heard his voice. 'I'm here in London looking for a job and I'm not having any luck and you did tell me to call you if I needed any help. So here I am!'

She heard a soft chuckle on the line. 'Indeed you are. Where are you?'

'I'm not at all sure,' she said. 'I'm in a call box.'

'Look at the notice on the wall of the box and there will be an address.'

She did as she was told and eventually found it and relayed the information.

'Fine, wait outside and I'll pick you up in ten minutes.' He replaced the receiver.

Cora stepped outside and let out a deep breath. *Belle will be furious with me*, she thought, but I'm desperate. It can't do any harm just to talk to the man.

A few minutes later, a cab pulled up and Joe opened his door and beckoned to her. Feeling more than a little nervous, she walked over and climbed inside.

'How nice to see you – you look well,' he said smiling at her. 'We'll go for a quiet drink and chat and you can tell me what's happened during your search.'

'That's kind of you,' she said and sat looking out at the passing scenery, not knowing what else to say.

The cab pulled up outside a small hotel and they got out. Joe paid the cab driver and taking her arm, led her inside to a small, well furnished cocktail lounge where a waiter came over to take their order.

'What would you like?' he asked. At her hesitation, he said, 'Are you thirsty after your long day?'

She nodded.

'Two Tom Collins,' he told the waiter and looking at Cora he said, 'You'll find it very refreshing, I promise. Now, tell me about your day.'

Cora explained that this was her second time in London searching for employment. She told him where she'd been and the lack of success she'd had.

'It seems an impossibility to find work; after all, I've no training in anything.'

'What kind of job are you looking for?'

'I'd really like to work in a nice shop, you know, selling women's clothes. I so want to be surrounded by beautiful things for a change. Does that sound ridiculous?'

'Absolutely not! I fully understand that. You want to leave the seedy streets behind with your past, right?'

'You do understand!' She relaxed in her chair. 'That's exactly how I feel, but the big department stores don't have any vacancies.'

He handed her a tall glass the waiter had just delivered. 'Here, try this.'

Cora took a sip and liked it. 'Oh that just hits the spot, doesn't it? Thank you.' She took another and put the glass down on the table.

Joe looked thoughtful. 'I don't think a big store is a good idea, Cora. A small shop is where you should start and where you'll learn the business of selling. You have a natural charm, so you'll do well with the customers, but you need to learn the trade.'

She looked crestfallen. 'Where do I find a place like that?'

'You don't, I will. You just have to be patient and give me time.'

'Really? You can do this?' Her look of surprise amused him.

'Yes, I can. Didn't I tell you some time ago to get in touch with me and I'd find you a job?'

She looked a little embarrassed. 'You did.'

He chuckled softly. 'I am a man of my word; I want you to know that.' He paused. 'Have you thought about living accommodation?'

'Not yet. I needed work before I could look for a place to stay and . . . it would have to be small and inexpensive.' She frowned. 'Can you suggest somewhere? As I don't know the city at all.'

'Now, Cora, don't worry, we'll sort something out when I find you a job. Have you eaten?' he asked.

'I stopped for a sandwich this morning, that's all.'

'Right, then. Drink up and we'll go into the dining room to have a meal before you set off back to Southampton.'

She was about to protest, but Joe wouldn't listen. 'I know how tiring a day in London can be. Come along, you'll feel better with some food inside you.'

The dining room was elegant. The chandeliers glistened in the light. The tables looked pristine with their white cloths and silver cutlery. It had an air of sophistication and money and Cora felt she should be dressed in jewels and fur to match the elegant surroundings. But Joe soon put her at her ease.

They talked about the war ending, of the men who would be returning home, of those families who would be mourning the loss of some and of the future.

'There is so much rebuilding to be done, here and in other towns that were severely bombed,' Joe said. 'There are still shortages, but eventually we'll get back to normal again, it'll just take time.'

It was a pleasant hour and a half and after they'd eaten, Joe called a cab and drove her to the station. He took note of her address and told her he'd be in touch.

'Thank you so much,' said Cora as she climbed out of the cab.

'Don't mention it, my dear young lady. It's my pleasure.'

'To my rescue yet again!' Cora exclaimed with a grin. She could hear his laughter as she walked towards the entrance.

147

As she sat on the train on the way home, she wasn't feeling downhearted any more. Mr Keating said he would find her work and somehow she believed him. Belle said people came into your lives for a reason; maybe this was why he was in hers. She fervently hoped so.

Chapter Sixteen

Hildy could hardly contain her excitement. Milt had written to say he would be shipped to Southampton to a camp in Tidworth before being sent home and he'd try to get permission to see her.

> There's no way they're going to stop me from seeing you, darling, even if I have to go AWOL to do it! However, the fact that we are engaged makes it more hopeful because we'll have to make plans for the future. I can't wait to see you, Hildy. God! It seems a lifetime ago that we were together and believe me, it's seemed a very long war.
>
> I want to catch the mail so must close. I'm counting the days.
>
> All my love for ever,
> Milt

She was not only delighted with the news of his

homecoming, but relieved too. The factory would be closing down soon and all the staff were worried about finding jobs elsewhere, but for her, she hoped it wouldn't be long before she'd be leaving to be with Milt in America. It was a somewhat daunting change, but she had no reason to stay. She felt no responsibility towards her mother, which in one way was so sad. But if she was being honest, leaving her behind would be like a weight lifted from her shoulders. Still being in the same town, it was as if there was an invisible bond holding them together, even if it was tenuous.

Two weeks later, the ship carrying American troops back to England for repatriation docked in Southampton and three days after, Hildy was in her flat waiting for Milt to arrive. She was a nervous wreck. By mid-morning she'd changed her clothes several times until she eventually decided what to wear. Her hands were trembling with excitement and anticipation. Would he have changed? Would she still feel the same when she saw him? Would *he* still feel the same? She sat down in a chair at the thought. How dreadful that would be if he didn't. The doorbell rang and for a moment she couldn't move, then she got to her feet and rushed to the door.

Milt stood there, a broad grin on his face. 'Hello Hildy.'

She flung her arms around him and burst into tears.

Milt picked her up and carried her into the living room saying, 'Well, honey, I've never reduced a woman to tears before and I only said "hello".'

She held his face and kissed him longingly. 'Oh, Milt, I'm so happy to see you.'

150

Laughing he said, 'Thank goodness for that, for a moment you had me worried.' He gazed at her and said, 'God, you've no idea how much I've longed to see you, to hold you. You look great.'

She led him to the settee and as they sat holding hands, she thought he looked older and careworn. The months of warfare had taken its toll which was to be expected and Milt looked as if he'd been through hell. There were dark circles under his eyes, he'd lost weight, but it didn't matter because he was here in one piece. She'd take care of him, make him whole again.

'I'll put the kettle on,' she said, 'and make a cup of tea.'

He chuckled and took a small packet from his bag and handed it to her. 'Coffee,' he said. 'Sorry, honey, but I'm an American who has yet to really enjoy the English habit of drinking tea.'

He watched her through the open kitchen door as she busied herself and felt himself begin to unwind. This was the sort of peaceful domestic scene he'd envisaged through the war. It was the one thing that kept him sane in moments of carnage. Guns firing, bombs exploding, dead bodies, the smell of cordite and the sight of blood. He knew that these things would remain with him for a time, but with Hildy he could begin a new life, something with purpose, unlike war, which seemed to have little.

Walking into the kitchen, he enveloped her into his arms. 'Leave the coffee, let's go to bed.'

It was now over three weeks since Cora had met with Joe Keating in London, but so far she'd not heard from him.

She'd began to believe that her hopes were lost when one morning Belle collected the mail from the mat and handed her an envelope.

'This is for you – it looks very official; the address is printed.'

Cora opened it and saw the heading. *Joe Keating, Business Consultant.* Holding her breath, she began to read.

> *Dear Miss Barnes,*
> *I apologise for taking so long, but at last I do have some good news for you. There is a vacancy for an assistant in a small dress shop off Tottenham Court Road called Lyntons, Number 122, Percy Street and I have made an appointment for you for an interview with the manageress on Thursday at 2.30. I think it's just what you're looking for.*
> *Good luck!*
> *Joe Keating*

Seeing the look of glee on Cora's face, Belle asked, 'Good news?'

'Yes, I've an interview for a job in London on Thursday next!'

'Oh my goodness, that's great. Was it from an agency?'

Cora hesitated then said, 'No. It's from Joe Keating.'

Belle looked astonished. 'Joe Keating? You got in touch with that man?'

Hearing the note of censure in Belle's voice, Cora stood her ground. 'Yes, Belle, I did. I spent fruitless hours searching for work and I was desperate, so I rang him.'

'And?'

'We met, had a drink and a chat and he said he'd find me work – and he has.'

'What's the catch?' Belle asked.

'There is no catch. He promised to help me if I was stuck and he has, thank God! Mind you, I've got to get through the interview first.'

Belle sat back in her chair and glared at her friend. 'I wouldn't worry about that, Cora. I would think it's a certainty. Joe Keating wouldn't have told you about it otherwise.'

'Why do you say that?'

'Call it a gut feeling. That man has his finger in a lot of pies, I would say. Anyway, good luck. Just be careful there isn't a price to pay for his good deed that's all!'

'What do you mean?'

'Listen, love, call me a sceptic, but I've been around too long and I've learnt a thing or two. People seldom do things without some agenda, especially where men are concerned. Just watch your step is all I'm saying.' She rose from her chair and went upstairs.

Cora was now perplexed. Belle was a wise woman but in this case she was wrong . . . or Cora hoped she was wrong. In any case, she wasn't a fool. As far as she was concerned, there would be no strings, she'd make sure of that.

The following Thursday, she dressed smartly in her best costume and hat, caught a train and a taxi to the address she'd been given and after she'd paid the driver, she looked in the window of the shop. It was tastefully dressed with three mannequins wearing stylish dresses, hats, and handbags draped on their arms. One or two other hats were placed on draped material. It all looked very classy. Taking a deep breath, she entered.

A bell pinged as she opened the door and an elegant woman behind the counter looked up and smiled. 'Can I help you?' she asked.

'I'm Cora Barnes; I've come for an interview with the manageress.'

The smile disappeared. 'Oh yes, well I am the manageress, come through to the back, will you.' She nodded to another assistant to take over and then took Cora through a curtained off room which served as an office.

'Please sit down, Miss Barnes. Now I believe you have no experience in this type of work, is that correct?' There was a coldness in her tone which made Cora edgy.

'Yes. I've been working in a munitions factory, doing my bit for the war effort, you know. But now I want to start a new career. I love clothes and would very much like to be in this kind of business.'

'I can see by your apparel that you have taste, thank goodness, and it's imperative in this business, of course.' She took down details of age and address, then discussed a salary. 'We do pay commission too,' she told Cora, 'so if your sales are above a certain amount you will be rewarded for your work. I like my assistants to wear black skirts and white blouses – will that be a problem?'

'Not at all,' said Cora, wondering how on earth she'd

find enough clothing coupons to purchase such items.

Cora eventually rose to leave with a job starting in three weeks' time.

'That will give you time to find living accommodation,' she was told once the manageress discovered she'd nowhere to stay in the city.

Cora left the shop with her head in a whirl. Outside, she stood against the wall to catch her breath. She couldn't make sense of the change of attitude of the woman who'd interviewed her – perhaps she was just a hard taskmaster – but she'd achieved her aim. Now she'd have to find somewhere to live and she had no idea where or how much it would cost.

'Are congratulations in order?'

She looked round in surprise to see Joe Keating standing, smiling at her.

'Mr Keating! Where did you spring from?'

'Joe, please. I knew when your appointment was so thought we could celebrate over lunch. Besides, you have to find somewhere to stay, don't you?'

Suddenly Cora heard Belle's warning ringing in her ears and she hesitated, but she also realised she still needed his help so she agreed.

They went to a nearby restaurant and sat down at a table. After ordering, Cora looked at her companion and asked, 'Why are you doing this for me?'

He looked surprised. 'Because I said I would.'

'Is that all?' Cora thought she ought to find out before she was in too deep if there was a hidden agenda.

His eyes twinkled with amusement as he gazed across the table at her. 'What had you in mind, Cora? Do you imagine I'm going to make some outrageous demands on you in return, is that it?'

'Well, a girl has to be sure, you know!'

He burst out laughing. 'Good heavens, I'm really quite flattered, but you are mistaken. I just want you to live your dream and it so happens I'm in the position to help you do so, that's all. You have my word. Now tell me about the job.'

She told him about the interview and her concern about buying the necessary clothes and lack of coupons.

Joe put his hand inside his jacket and handed her an envelope.

'What's this?' asked Cora.

'I had wondered about this situation. I knew the dress code of the staff, so here are some clothing coupons, enough for two skirts and two blouses.'

She looked at him in astonishment. 'But are these yours?'

'Good heavens no! Just use them and leave it at that.'

She frowned as she looked inside the envelope.

'Now, Cora, these things happen during shortages. Everything has a price. It's common practice, you must know that surely?'

Of course she did. The black market was a part of life ever since the war began and it was still going on. Who was she to complain especially as it was essential to getting her job.

'Thank you,' she said and put the envelope in her handbag.

'Now for your living accommodation. I have found a small bedsit a couple of stations away on the Underground.

I thought it the best way to start, then when you're earning more money and know the city better you can move if you wish to.'

She was speechless for a moment. 'My goodness, you have been busy,' she said.

'When we've finished eating, we'll go and take a look.'

Although she was grateful, Cora suddenly felt as if her life had been taken over and she was a little uncomfortable about it, but what could she do? She was grateful; it saved her a lot of searching in a city she didn't know.

After their meal, Joe took her by Underground to Shepherd's Bush, then when they left the station within a short walk they arrived at a building. They walked up two flights of stairs and Joe stopped in front of a door, opened it and stepped back for her to enter.

It was a large room with a single day bed, which could double as a settee and a small round table with two chairs. Along one side, a draining board with small sink and a gas burner with two rings. A few pieces of crockery and plates were stashed away in a cupboard with a couple of small saucepans. There was a wardrobe, a dressing table with a mirror and a window overlooking the street. There was a small fire escape outside.

It was so compact and complete; she loved it and said so.

Joe looked delighted. 'I'm so glad. You can add bits and pieces to make it your own,' he said. 'You know, bed cover, cushions, the woman's touch.'

'How much is it a week?' she asked.

'Twelve shillings and sixpence. Being so small, the rent isn't expensive.'

Cora did a quick calculation. She could afford it with her salary and if she was able to make any commission, she'd be fine. Besides, she did have her savings to fall back on if necessary.

'Thanks, I can manage that. When do I see the landlord? I need to collect the key and I expect he'll need some rent in advance.'

Joe took a key out of his pocket and handed it to her. 'I've already seen him and paid a month in advance as a gift to get you started.'

Cora stared at him and said with some determination, 'That's very nice of you, but I certainly can't accept your offer. I'll pay you back. I have the money in the bank. As you know, I've been saving.'

Seeing the stubbornness in her eyes, he smiled and said, 'Just as you like. Send a cheque to my office.'

'How do I pay the rent?' was her next question.

He handed her a small rent book. 'A man calls round every Wednesday evening about eight o'clock. He calls on all the flats in the building.'

Taking the book from him, she said, 'I'd like to thank you for taking the trouble to help me. Without you, I'd still be struggling.'

'Not at all, young lady. I'm only too happy to help. Here are your keys, now is there anything else I can do?'

Anxious to be alone and look properly at her new home, she said, 'No. Honestly. I'll make a note of things I need then I'll catch the Underground to Waterloo.'

He walked towards the door. 'I've left a map of the Underground on the table. As you know, there's a station just along the road.' He shook her hand. 'Good luck, Cora. You know where you can reach me.'

When she was alone, Cora sat on the day bed and looked around. Although the room was fully furnished, it wasn't claustrophobic. She opened the window wide and listened to the sounds of the street outside. If she wanted, it would be easy to climb out onto the fire escape and sit with a cup of coffee at night after work. She was thrilled with her new home. When she was settled she would shop for a few bits to make it her own. Closing the window, she thought she could hardly wait, in fact she'd move in next week. That would give her time to get used to her new surroundings before starting work. But now she'd have to tell Belle she would be leaving and that wouldn't be easy. It was the only bad thing about starting her new life.

Chapter Seventeen

Belle was sitting reading the paper when Cora returned. She looked up at her friend expectantly.

'When do you start?' she asked.

'You were so certain I'd get the job, weren't you?'

'Don't tell me I'm wrong.'

Cora sat down opposite her. 'No. You were right; I start in three weeks' time.'

'Three weeks, why so long?'

'It'll give me time to settle in my bedsit.'

'Your bedsit? So you've managed to find somewhere already. That's lucky . . . or did Joe Keating find it for you?'

Belle was making her feel uncomfortable and Cora was annoyed because her friend was making her feel guilty when she had nothing to feel guilty about.

'Yes, he did and before you say anything else, I made sure there were no strings attached because I asked him!'

Belle grinned broadly at her. 'Good for you.' The tension between them faded.

'Well, I did listen to you, Belle. He thought the whole idea amusing and assured me there was no agenda, so you see, you were wrong. He said he just wanted to help me fulfil my dream.' She hesitated before continuing. 'I've decided to move up there in a day or two. It will give me time to settle in and get used to my surroundings.' Looking at Belle, she was suddenly overcome with emotion.

'I'm going to miss you, Belle. We've been through so much together.'

Belle looked at her with affection. 'Now listen to me, love, I'll miss you too, but Mr Keating is right, this is your dream. Your start to a new life and I want you to do it, honestly. I know what you've been through and you deserve a fresh start.'

'You could always come and stay,' Cora said, 'but I'll have to get a mattress for you to sleep on.'

'Let's not rush it, Cora. Get settled first. I can always come up for the day on a Sunday, after all.'

'There is one thing that worries me,' said Cora, 'what about *this* flat? As we shared the cost of it.'

'Don't give it another thought. I can afford the rent on my wages and overtime, plus I like living here. I may move to the Isle of Wight when the factory closes. Property prices are low with the war. You know, people moving who have lost husbands and such. I might pick up a bargain. Maybe I'll open a B&B.'

With a sense of relief, Cora chuckled. 'I can just see you doing that. You're a good cook and you like people.'

Getting up from her chair, Belle took out a half bottle of gin and poured them a drink each. 'Come on, Cora, love, this calls for a celebration. Southampton won't be the same without us!'

Whilst Cora and Belle were making decisions about their future, Hildy was doing the same. Milt had been given special permission to marry her before he was repatriated and to that end, they'd got a special licence and the marriage was to take place in a couple of days' time.

The preparation was manic. Her friends at the factory were preparing food to be served at a reception in a small hall hired for the afternoon. A couple of Milt's friends were going too. One as best man and together the two men would play at the reception. One on the piano, the other with his guitar.

Hildy's friends gathered in her flat with various items of clothing to make sure she would look like a bride. It was a hilarious evening with clothes being tried on and a variety of hats, and a few drinks to help them decide.

Milt had a twenty-four hour pass, then he had to return to the camp, ready to sail for the States, but as he said to her, 'At least I'll be leaving knowing my wife will be following eventually with the other GI brides.'

Cora had delayed moving to her bedsit for a couple of days as she and Belle had been invited to the nuptials. They enjoyed getting ready in their finery as all women do.

The sun shone, the bride looked wonderful, the groom proud, but nervous. It was a happy occasion and as the couple exchanged their vows, some of the small congregation had tears in their eyes, thrilled to see them standing together, knowing that so many didn't return from the war.

After the ceremony, confetti fluttered down, photographs were taken and they all walked to the hall together, laughing and chattering.

It was an informal affair, the gathering being small with their closest friends but Milt did give a speech.

'Today, I'm the luckiest guy alive! When I was posted to England, never did I imagine I would be returning to the States a married man. Hildy has made me the happiest guy on the planet and I can't wait to take her home. Thank you all for coming. I would now like us all to drink to my beautiful bride: to Hildy!'

Everyone stood, held up their glasses and in unison said, 'To Hildy!'

The bride was overcome with embarrassment, but at the same time she was delighted.

People gathered at the table to fill their plates with sandwiches and sausage rolls. There was a one-tier wedding cake, courtesy of the cook in the camp at Tidworth and later the two musicians sat and played.

Milt and his bride took to the floor as the music of 'The Anniversary Waltz' was played with everybody cheering.

Holding her close, Milt looked down at his bride. 'Hello Mrs Miller.'

She beamed at him. 'Hello husband. You know Milt, I think I'm living a dream and I'm scared to wake up and find it's not true.'

He lowered his mouth to hers and kissed her slowly and longingly. 'Believe me, honey, this is no dream, this is reality. It's what kept me going all the time I was in France. We are going to have such a good life together and when we grow old, we'll be sitting on our porch in the evening, remembering today and wondering, where did all those years go?'

'That sounds good to me,' she said and kissed him back.

Milt took a moment to speak with Belle when he told her how Jackson had saved his life. 'Without him, I wouldn't be here today. I owe him everything.'

It made Belle's day. 'Don't you worry about leaving Hildy,' she told him, 'we'll keep tabs on her for you.'

The following evening in the local paper, Olive Dickson nearly choked on her cup of tea as she saw a picture of a bride and groom with the headline:

LOCAL GIRL MARRIES HER GI

There was her daughter, Hildy, smiling at the camera, holding onto the arm of . . . that GI! The woman was incandescent with rage. How dare she get married without inviting her mother to the wedding! She looked again at the picture, but it only incited her anger even more. What would the neighbours think when they saw the picture? How was she to explain her absence? How could Hildy have done such a thing?

The following morning at her place of work, Olive faced question after question by her customers who had seen the photograph.

'Your Hildy looked lovely,' said one. 'Was it a good wedding?'

'Yes, lovely,' she replied and hurried off to serve another customer.

She managed to bluff her way through the morning until one of her neighbours walked in. There was no love lost between the two women. Her neighbour, knowing how she'd treated Hildy and had been a witness to Olive's angry tirade the day Hildy moved out, had been thrilled to see that the young woman had found happiness and would be free at last from her mother's controlling ways.

She waited until she'd been served and had put the vegetables in her basket, then as Olive handed her some change she casually said, 'Pity you weren't invited to your daughter's wedding, always a proud moment for any mother I always thought.'

The other customers looked up and listened with interest. Olive paled and pursed her lips. She glared at the woman.

'I thought she was making a mistake and said so.'

'Like you have done with any young man Hildy has ever taken home as I recall!' She gave a look of triumph as she said, 'But this time you lost. Well, I'm delighted for the girl, she deserves some happiness after the way you've treated her for years. Good luck to her I say.' She turned and walked out.

Olive saw the expressions on the faces of the waiting customers as they stared at her. There was such an air of hostility in the small shop that she couldn't face them. She turned and walked out to the back, took off her apron and left.

Hearing a lot of noise, the owner walked into his shop

from the storeroom and was greeted by several angry women all talking at once.

'Ladies, ladies, a little decorum, please,' he shouted and there was silence. 'Now that's better. Who was first?'

Whilst her employer was doing her job, Olive walked home, fuming. Trust that old hag from next door to interfere. How dare she make her look such a fool! How dare her daughter treat her this way, leaving her open to criticism.

Her mood wasn't improved the next morning when she arrived at work to discover she'd been fired.

Her boss was furious. 'You walked out yesterday without a word,' he complained. 'I heard a lot of noise in the shop only to find several very angry women, waiting to be served and no one behind the counter. Well, Mrs Dickson, that's not good enough. Here's your money and cards.'

As she made her way home, Olive wondered what she was supposed to do now. She had rent to pay and now she didn't have a lodger or a job. She'd have to find both – and quickly.

Chapter Eighteen

Belle was feeling lonely. After Hildy's wedding, Cora had packed her things and taken off to her new life in London. There had been an emotional parting between the women, Belle promising to visit one Sunday once Cora had settled, but as she watched her friend drive off to the station in a taxi, she felt bereft.

For years, she'd been surrounded by friends: fellow prostitutes when she was working the streets; Cora, who had become her closest friend. She had workmates in the factory, but they were just working associates. Now she had no one she was close to and she was unsettled. Even more so when there were rumours that the factory would soon be closing down and she came to the conclusion it was time for her to move on too.

To this end, she took a couple of days off, packed a small case and bought a return ticket for the ferry to the Isle of Wight. She planned to book into a B&B and look around at the price of property on the island to get some idea of what she had to face if she decided to move there as planned. She decided to start in Cowes, a good centre for tourists.

It was a balmy, sunny day and, once on board, she found a seat on deck and settled down for the journey. Halfway there, she walked down to the bar to order a sandwich and a gin and tonic. This really wasn't a bad way to spend her time, she thought, as she sipped her drink.

When she arrived at her destination, she wandered around the small streets of the town, thinking how very picturesque it was. She looked in the windows of several estate agents and was pleased to see there were many properties for sale, but as yet none that caught her eye. The prices varied, of course, and this was a popular centre for the yachting crowd who, no doubt now that the war was over, would soon be back sailing. There were those that could afford such luxuries, of course, and there were always moneyed people in the world.

She saw a notice for B&B at the end of the town and booked in for two nights. Then after having some lunch, she caught a bus to Shanklin and soon fell in love with the place.

Shanklin, with its narrow streets and thatched cottages, was everyone's idea of a perfect English village and Belle knew instinctively, that this was where she wanted to settle. She sought out the nearest estate agents and walked in.

The young man greeted her and asked her to take a seat at his desk. 'What can I do for you, miss?'

'I'm looking for a property to turn into a bed and breakfast,' she told him. 'Nothing too big. I'm looking for something with two or three bedrooms I could let.'

He showed her several on his books, but none of them appealed to her.

'Just a moment,' he said and went to pick up some papers from a filing cabinet. 'This house came in recently and we've only just put the file together.'

Belle looked at the double-fronted Victorian house and loved it, but she was sure the price would be beyond her.

'Why is this on the market?' she asked.

'It's a sad story,' said the young man. 'A family owned it, but the elderly couple died, then the son who lived there was killed in the war and his widow doesn't want to stay there anymore. Too many painful memories, you know. She wants a quick sale.'

Belle's heart began to beat wildly. Taking a deep breath, she asked, 'Any chance of looking at it now?' To her joy, he said yes.

As soon as she walked in the front door, Belle thought she'd come home. There was a feeling of tranquillity about the place. It was double-fronted with lovely old tiles on the hall floor, a sitting room to the right, a dining room to the left and behind a kitchen, utility room and outside toilet. Upstairs were three large bedrooms and a smaller room, which would take a single bed or a small double. There was a wardrobe and across the hall, a family-sized bathroom. On the landing was a good sized airing cupboard.

Apart from needing a lick of paint, it wasn't in bad shape.

'What are they going to do about the furniture?' she asked.

'Well, I know the lady is hoping to sell it with the house, otherwise it'll go to a sale room. Perhaps you'd like to see the garden?' he suggested.

They walked outside. The garden wasn't too big, Belle thought. It had a lawn, a few flower beds and a garage.

'Perhaps you'd like to look round on your own and get a feel of the place. I'll sit in the garden and wait, if you like?'

'Thank you,' Belle said, 'that'll be great.'

As she slowly wandered into each room, she pictured how it would look after she'd painted it. The furniture was alright for now and when she'd made some money she could replace it piece by piece. But would the price be too much?

They walked back to the office and she asked the question holding her breath, as she waited for the answer.

The young man looked at his papers. 'The lady is asking three hundred and fifty pounds,' he said.

'Right,' said Belle. 'Tell her I'll buy it lock, stock and barrel for three hundred . . . cash!'

He looked surprised. 'Well, Miss . . . ?'

'Newman, Belle Newman. I'm staying at this address in Cowes.' She gave him a card the owner of the B&B had given her. 'Call me when you've spoken to her and if she's agreeable and can give me a quick sale, she can have the money as soon as we exchange the deeds.' She rose from her seat. 'If you can find out by this evening, all the better. I'll be there after seven o'clock.'

The young man grinned at her. 'All I can say, Miss Newman, is I wish all my clients were as quick to make up their minds as you are. My life would be so simple.'

Belle laughed. 'Let's hope the outcome is successful for both our sakes.'

As she walked to the bus stop, she prayed that everything would work out. She wanted that house so much, she could hardly breathe. When she returned to her B&B, she told the landlady she was expecting a call and would be in her room.

To fill in the time, she tried to keep busy to give herself something to think about, but she was on edge and when she heard the telephone ring, she opened the door and waited.

'Miss Newman,' the landlady called.

Belle was down the stairs almost before she'd finished. Her hands shook as she took the receiver. 'Belle Newman speaking,' she said.

'Ah, Miss Newman, I've been in touch with the lady who owns the house, well, her mother actually. The owner is away and doesn't return until tomorrow, so I've left a message.'

Belle felt suddenly deflated. 'I see, thank you. Have you any idea what time she's due back?'

'Late morning and I've asked that she call me as soon as she walks in the door,' He chuckled softly. 'I know how much you want that house.'

'Thank you so much. I'll get a bus to your office, just in case and if the answer is no, I'll have to look around for something else.'

'Let's hope that won't be necessary,' he said.

Whilst Belle was trying to buy her dream house, Cora had moved into her new abode and was settling in, getting to know her surroundings. She was enjoying being alone in her own place, one that no longer was used for anything but her own comfort. She inspected the surrounding small shops and found the market. She loved to hear the banter among the stallholders and soon realised she was thrilled with her new life change.

She missed her friend Belle, of course, and in a funny way the shabby, dangerous streets of Southampton's docklands and the lowlife that crept around the area. But also the good people she'd known for so long.

The Underground was another way to get around and she was using it to discover the city. She walked in Hyde Park, stood in front of Buckingham Palace and took time to visit the Tower of London. All the places she'd read about, but had never seen. Using the clothing coupons that Joe Keating had given her, she bought two black skirts and two white blouses, all ironed, ready for her first day at work.

She'd encountered a few of the other residents that shared her building. There was an elderly couple on the ground floor, a young man on hers and an older gentleman whom she met at the front door one day. They'd all been friendly and said 'Hello,' or 'Good Morning,' which was nice. But tomorrow she started work.

She went to the shared bathroom and took a bath. Afterwards, she laid out her clothes for the morning, wisely choosing comfortable shoes which she polished until they shone brightly. Checking her purse to make sure she had change for the Underground and after tidying her room, she climbed into bed.

Chapter Nineteen

Belle took a bus to Shanklin just before noon and made her way to the estate agent's office, hoping for news about the house she wanted. The estate agent was on the telephone as she entered and he motioned to her to take a seat.

'I see,' he said to his caller. 'Well, if that's what you want to do. Will you let me know your position as soon as possible?' He listened for the reply and then said, 'Thank you. I'll wait to hear from you.'

He looked across his desk at Belle with pursed lips and a frown creasing his forehead.

'That was the lady who owns the house.'

Belle saw his expression and feared the worst.

'It seems now that she actually has an offer on the house she's got cold feet.'

'You mean she backed out?'

'Not exactly,' he paused. 'She just wants to go back and look around it and make doubly sure she's doing the right thing and she'll get back to me.'

Belle was devastated. 'Do you think she'll change her mind?'

'To be honest, I don't know. But I suppose you can understand her quandary. After losing her husband, the house holds too many memories, but, of course, in those circumstances, memories are all you have to cling to.'

'Yes,' said Belle. 'I can understand that, but nevertheless I need a house and that's the only one on your books that I like. I'll take myself off and see if I can find anything else just in case. I'll come back here and see you before I go back to Cowes, but I'm leaving for Southampton tomorrow morning.'

He rose to his feet and opened the door for her. 'I'll see you later.'

Belle walked away, thoroughly depressed. She felt sorry for the young widow, but she had to plan her own future.

She visited two other estate agents, but didn't like anything on their books. She went into a cafe for some lunch and eventually walked back to the original agent, keeping her fingers crossed that he would have some news for her.

He didn't. 'Sorry, Miss Newman, but I've not heard a word.'

Taking out a pen, Belle asked for a piece of paper and wrote down her address. 'I'm not on the phone,' she said, 'so you'll have to write to me and let me know the lady's decision.'

He promised to do so and she caught a bus back to the B&B and packed ready to leave in the morning.

In London, Cora had spent her first day at her new job. The manageress had been thorough, if not abrupt in showing her how she liked to work, where the stock was kept, and the way to approach the customers and how to help them in the fitting room, leaving the other assistant to attend to the shop, stepping in when she was required.

'Are there any questions you'd like to ask me?' she said at the tea break.

'Just one really,' said Cora. 'With the need for clothing coupons, how do you keep so busy?'

'I don't consider that's any of my business and certainly none of yours. We are here to give a service to the public and that's all.'

Cora felt like a naughty schoolgirl who'd been reprimanded by the head teacher and her cheeks flushed. Remembering how she'd been given such coupons, Cora assumed that the customers were in a position to buy what they needed. There was a price for everything really, especially in wartime. She'd seen that for herself in her previous life and here in this shop, no questions were asked, even among the staff.

The rest of the day was spent going through the clothes on show, familiarising herself with what was where, so she would look professional when faced with a customer. Eventually she made her way home.

Opening the window, she made a cup of tea and climbed out onto the fire escape where she settled and watched what was happening below. She found it fascinating, if not a little noisy, but as she discovered later, when the shops had closed and people had gone home, it was a reasonably peaceful place.

After cooking a meal on her two burners, she sat and

wrote to Belle, telling her about her day and hoping that Belle was doing alright. She described the flat and her perch outside the window and what she'd observed sitting there.

It's quite fascinating living here. Everything is so different to a seaport town. The air smells different and the pace is faster as everyone seems to be in such a rush. I can't wait for you to visit so I can show you around. I went to the Tower of London. You wouldn't believe the Crown Jewels!

She finished her letter, put it in an envelope and addressed it ready to post the following morning. Afterwards, she walked to the bathroom, washed, then climbed into bed. Tomorrow she was working on the shop floor and could hardly wait.

Hildy née Dickson, now Miller, had returned to work after her twenty-four hour honeymoon spent at the Polygon Hotel. Milt was ready to sail back to America and she was now listed as his wife and on the list of GI brides to be shipped across the Atlantic at a later date – as yet unknown. She kept fingering her wedding ring, still not used to the idea that she was now a married woman.

She'd arranged with the foreman to accept phone calls from Milt at certain times, so at least she could hear his voice, but today would be the last one, as the ship was due to sail for New York the next afternoon and the men would be boarding early in the morning.

Having been called to the office, she picked up the phone.

'Hello, this is Mrs Miller speaking,' she said laughing softly.

'Hello darling. This is your husband here. How are you?'

'Fine, wishing you weren't leaving so soon. I won't hear your voice again until I arrive in the States. Have you heard anything about that yet?'

'No, honey. There's a hell of a lot of troops to be returned first and then they can sort a passage for the wives, so it might be some time. We just have to be patient.'

'I know, it's just so hard.'

'Think of it this way: it'll give me time to get a place for us to live and get it all gussied up for when you come over.'

They talked for twenty minutes, then Milt had to go. 'Look after yourself, Hildy, I'll write often. I love you, darling.'

'I love you too and I'll write often.' She put the phone down, tears in her eyes.

The foreman looked at her and said, 'Take ten minutes and go and have a cigarette before you go back to your machine.'

Hildy just nodded, too full of emotion to speak.

The *Queen Mary*, still wearing her wartime grey paint – now nicknamed *The Grey Ghost* – pulled out of Southampton docks packed with troops. The public rooms had all been stripped of their finery and were now full of line after line of bunk beds.

Milt had told her there was no point in coming to the docks to see the ship sail as there were thousands of troops on board and little hope of him being on deck to wave goodbye to her. In one way she was relieved. It was bad enough to say goodbye over the phone, but to see the ship sail would have been even worse. Instead, she went to the pictures and lost herself in the story on the screen, blotting out her sadness. Then, when she went home she soaked in a hot bath and went to bed.

Hildy's mother was facing her own problems. Olive had no job, no lodger and no longer a daughter to bring in the money needed for rent and food. Olive had a little savings, but was having to use that to survive. She'd applied for several jobs unsuccessfully and eventually, out of necessity, had to take one as a cleaner in a local pub, which she thought was greatly beneath her. She'd placed another advertisement in the newsagent for another lodger but as yet no one had answered. This only made her more embittered as she knelt scrubbing floors, trying to clean the spilt sticky beer from the lino, washing the many glass cloths and polishing the long counter. She dare not complain because she needed the job too much.

Whilst Olive was hiding her discontent, Belle was trying to cope with her fear of losing the house in Shanklin she'd hoped to buy. It had been three days now and she'd not heard a word from the estate agent. She'd almost given up hope when at last she received a letter from him. She held her breath as she opened the envelope. Then she let out a cry of joy.

Dear Miss Newman,
I'm happy to tell you that eventually I've heard from
the owner of the house you liked and the good news is

that she's ready to sell. Can you give me a call and, if
you're still interested, I'll have the contract drawn up.
  Yours faithfully,
  John Pope

Interested? Of course she was still bloody interested! Belle rushed out of the house, down the road to the phone booth and dialled the number of his office.

'Mr Pope, Belle Newman here. Please go ahead. Let me know when to come over with the money and I'd like to move as fast as possible.'

He replied that he would do so and he'd be in touch.

Belle was delighted. At last she could start her new life. Well, in a few weeks when everything was settled, but in her heart she knew that until she held the deeds in her hand and paid over the money, she wouldn't feel safe. But tonight she was going to celebrate. Knowing that Hildy was feeling down, she invited her to join her that evening.

'We'll go and celebrate our new beginnings. What do you say?'

Hildy readily agreed.

It was quite a night. The two women went on a pub crawl. Halfway through the evening, Belle wisely decided they should eat, so they went into a cafe and then continued drinking until closing time, leaving the last pub, slightly unsteady on their feet.

Belle suggested they sleep at her place as it was nearer, though on arrival they almost fell through the door, so they had a cup of coffee and went to bed, waking in the morning with a fearful hangover.

'Remind me never to go drinking with you again,' moaned Hildy as she swallowed a couple of aspirins with a cup of tea. She nibbled on a piece of toast and held her head.

Belle was no better. It had been a long time since she'd felt so bad, but she said, 'Well, we had a lot to celebrate.'

'If I survive, I'll never drink again,' murmured Hildy as she poured another cup of tea. 'I don't fancy the noise of the factory machines today,' she added.

'Take some cotton wool with you and use it in your ears,' said Belle, handing some over.

When they walked into work, the foreman looked at them as they signed in.

'Bloody hell! What happened to you two?'

Trying to look dignified, Belle said, 'We went out to celebrate and had a few drinks.'

'A few? Looks to me as if you drank the bar dry. Are you able to work your machines safely? Now I'm being serious, girls.'

They both declared that they were. But it was a long morning.

Chapter Twenty

Cora had almost finished her first week in the dress shop and had enjoyed most of it. She loved looking after the ladies' needs and had been brave enough to suggest one or two dresses to customers who were wavering in their choice and had been successful. This had not gone unnoticed by the manageress, who was watching her new employee as she worked. As the customer paid her bill and left the shop carrying her wares, Cora earned a compliment.

'Well done, Cora. That lady went out of here a happy woman and the dress you chose suited her beautifully.'

This pleased Cora as she wasn't quite sure how to feel about her boss. Ever since she walked into the shop to be interviewed, she felt that Linda Franklin resented her being there. Why she should feel that way, she couldn't fathom, but at the end of the week just before the shop closed for business, the manageress was called to the phone. Cora overheard her conversation.

'Yes, she's doing well, thank goodness. I did have my

reservations when you first spoke to me, we'll wait and see how she does in the future.' She then listened to whoever was on the other end of the line. 'No, that's alright Mr Keating. Goodbye.'

Cora realised she had been the topic of this conversation. So that was it. Linda Franklin had taken her on against her will. No wonder she was abrupt and somewhat unfriendly. However, Cora thought, so far she'd seemed to please the woman, if that continued, her attitude towards her might change.

The following week, an elegant woman walked into the shop to collect a gown that had been ordered specially. Cora was sent into the changing room to assist her. The customer stared at her and Cora felt she was being unusually scrutinised, but ignored it, helping the woman into her gown, standing back, allowing her customer to inspect her image in the long mirror. She twisted and turned, until she was satisfied and Cora helped her out of her new purchase into her day clothes.

'Thank you,' the woman said, and stared at her once again, making Cora decidedly uncomfortable.

'Is there something wrong, madam?' she asked.

'No,' she answered. 'I'm just interested to see my husband's latest lost cause.'

'I beg your pardon?'

'Joe Keating is my husband,' she said. 'He's always taking someone under his wing.'

'Your husband was kind enough to help me find a job, as you obviously know,' said Cora softly. 'I am grateful for his help.'

The woman held Cora's gaze and said coldly, 'Don't be

too grateful.' She swished open the curtains and walked up to the counter to pay her bill, then left.

Cora was shaken. First, it was the surprise of meeting Mrs Keating; second, being termed a lost cause, but finally the inference that . . . what? Cora was confused. Was the woman suggesting that there was something between Joe and her? That made her angry. Her cheeks flushed and she walked out of the changing cubicle into the shop.

Seeing the consternation in Cora's expression, Linda asked, 'What's the matter?'

Standing in front of her employer, she was candid. 'I overheard your conversation with Mr Keating the other day, so I know you gave me the job because of him, but Mrs Keating insinuated that there was something going on between her husband and me and I can assure you, that it is not true!' Her indignation was very apparent.

Linda gestured for Cora to go with her into her office. Inside the room, she said, 'You are not the first girl he's asked me to take on, but they didn't stay for very long.'

'What do you mean?'

'Joe Keating moved them on to another job, after that I don't know. I've only heard the rumours.'

'What rumours?' Cora was beginning to feel uneasy.

'That he finds someone he can help and slowly he moves them to a better job and eventually they become his flavour of the month.'

'Well, that's not the case here!' Cora exclaimed angrily. 'I made sure of that before I accepted his offer. He thought my idea that he might have an agenda amusing and he assured me it wasn't the case.'

'Did he help you to find accommodation?'

'Yes.'

'Did he pay the first month's rent as a gift to help you out?'

Cora felt her shoulders tense. 'Yes he did, but I refused to accept it and sent a cheque to his office for the money.'

Linda looked surprised. 'Well, that's a first! Most girls were delighted.'

'Most girls . . . how many have there been?'

'Three or four that I know of.' She studied Cora closely, watching her reaction. Then she smiled slowly. 'This time I think he's made a mistake.'

For the first time, Cora felt her boss's attitude change. 'No one buys me, Miss Franklin. I am my own woman.' Then she suddenly realised what she'd said. Men had been buying her most of her adult life. She started to laugh at the irony of her remark.

'What's so funny?'

'Nothing really, only that Mr Keating is going to be disappointed, that's all.' Then she asked, 'If I do disappoint my saviour, for want of a better word, does that mean I'll lose my job here?'

This time it was Linda who laughed. 'Not if I'm satisfied with your work. Like you, I'm not for sale.' She walked to the doorway. 'I was just repaying a favour to someone. I could have said no, but he said he thought you would make an excellent saleswoman and in this instance I think he was right.'

When eventually she was alone in her bedsit, Cora sat outside on her fire escape. She went over the day's events in her mind. If Miss Franklin had taken on more of Joe's girls, what sort of favours was she repaying? Then remembering the clothing coupons Joe had given her, she wondered if that was how Linda managed to stay in business? Then she went over her time in the shop. She hadn't seen any coupons change hands, but had once or twice heard the final amount told to the client at the till and had thought it was wrong. She'd been sure that the garment they bought hadn't been that much, but being new didn't dare query it. Now it made sense. The extra might well have been for black market coupons.

She was about to climb back inside her room, when a cab drew up in the street below and she saw Joe Keating step out. She flattened herself against the wall out of sight, then quietly climbed inside and shut the window.

At the front door, Joe pressed the bell to Cora's room and waited. There was no answer. He walked away after glancing up at the closed window.

It was now late August and Belle had moved to the Isle of Wight into her new home. The fresh start made her feel years younger. It had been far too late in the season for her to consider starting her business and she wanted to get everything together and looking spruce before opening her doors to the public. With that in mind, she'd made a plan for each room and wearing old clothes and a headscarf, she began. Taking one room at a time, she started to paint the walls, which she thought easier than having to put up wallpaper.

At the end of the day, she'd get changed and walk along the seafront or on the beach, breathing in the smell of seaweed, sitting outside a pub with a glass of beer and a cigarette, chatting to the locals, getting to know her neighbours and making friends. She didn't know when she'd been happier.

Before she'd moved, she had spent a weekend in London with Cora, enjoying the sights and feeling like a tourist. She'd liked Cora's bedsit, knowing that eventually her friend would move on to something bigger when she was ready. She'd been told about Joe Keating and was concerned, but Cora brushed her worries aside.

'He's got the message, Belle. I've never opened my door to him. He's called a few times, but he's not been to the shop, so you see, you've no need to worry about me. I'm doing well. I'm earning a living and I'm happy!' Belle had returned home, knowing that when she had part of her new home, shipshape, Cora would come over for a holiday.

Meanwhile, on the other side of the Atlantic, Milt had been through the rigours of repatriation from his service overseas and being in the regular army, where others had handed in their uniforms and returned to civilian life, Milt had been given leave.

He'd returned to his parents' home in New Jersey to relax and enjoy being surrounded by his kin. They knew that he'd become engaged, but didn't know that he and Hildy had actually married. He showed his parents photos taken at the wedding and tried to describe their new daughter-in-law.

'She's a great girl! Bright, funny and I love her.'

His father, Gerry, a jovial man, placed an arm around

his son's shoulders and said, 'That's the most important thing, son, and I guess she feels the same about you.'

'We're longing to be together, Dad. She wrote to me often when I was away. It helped a hell of a lot and in time, she'll come over here to live, of course.'

His mother, Jean asked, 'Does she have any family back in England?'

Milt hesitated. 'Yes, her mother. The father left years ago.'

'Oh, that's sad,' she said. 'How does her mother feel about her settling so far away?'

'They aren't close,' was all Milt said. Then he changed the subject.

As she watched her two men chatting, Jean wondered about the background story of Milt's bride. It didn't sound too promising and like any mother she was concerned. Was there something in the girl's nature that could hurt her son?

That night Milt sat and wrote to Hildy, telling her of his return and his parents and how he couldn't wait to see them all together. He didn't tell her that he was trying to make up his mind about leaving the army and starting his own business.

The military had been his life and he'd been fulfilled, but having survived the war and now with a wife and eventually, he hoped, a family, he wanted a home, stability. In the army, you could be sent anywhere at any time. This was fine for a single man, but as a family man, he knew he wouldn't be happy. But what kind of business was his dilemma. He knew about weaponry, but he wanted to leave all that behind. He was able to command men so could handle staff, but the actual business itself eluded him. He would spend his leave searching the business columns, looking for ideas. He wanted everything to be settled before Hildy arrived in the States. But the army had been his life and he was finding it difficult to make a final decision.

Olive was far from settled. She was still scrubbing floors and cleaning at the pub, hating every moment, but she had to earn a living. She'd let her room to a young man who'd smoked heavily and drank to excess until she'd kicked him out after he came home legless and threw up his insides in her hallway. So now she was reluctant to try another lodger. She was having a tough time. She'd even contemplated visiting her daughter, trying to mend the rift between them, but she couldn't find the words to do so. She hated the man who had taken Hildy away from her – as she saw it – and she knew in her heart, she wouldn't be able to keep that resentment out of the conversation. It was too near the surface of her anger to stay hidden. Instead, she lived every day with a bitterness which fermented inside her until one day she was found on the floor of the pub, writhing in agony.

An ambulance was called and she was taken to hospital.

Chapter Twenty-One

Hildy was called to the foreman's office in the factory to be told that her mother was in hospital. Olive had her down as next of kin and had listed her home address, but she had the sense to know that at the time of her admission, Hildy would be at work and the hospital had called the factory.

'Sit down, love,' the foreman said when he saw the shocked look on Hildy's face. 'I took the number of the hospital and the name of the ward where your mother is, so give them a call and find out what's going on. I'll wait outside. Give you some privacy.'

With shaking hands, Hildy dialled the number, asked for the ward and enquired after her mother.

'Your mother is down in theatre at the moment, Mrs Miller. She has peritonitis and needed an emergency operation.'

'Is she going to be alright?'

'She's in the best hands so try not to worry.'

'When can I come and visit?' Hildy asked with mounting

concern. She didn't exactly know what peritonitis was except she knew it was serious.

'Leave it until this evening. That will give your mother time to come round from the anaesthetic. I know it's hard but try not to worry. It won't help your mother and it certainly isn't good for you.'

'Yes, I'll try and thank you.' Hildy put down the receiver and opened the door to let her foreman back into his office. She told him what had happened.

'Oh, Hildy, I am sorry, love. But it seems as if they've got it all in hand. After all, they didn't waste any time before they operated.' He looked at his watch. 'You only have fifteen minutes before your shift finishes so go and sign out now. Go home and make yourself a strong cup of tea. Try and relax.'

Once inside her flat, Hildy did put the kettle on, then lit a cigarette. Despite the difficulties she had with her mother, she was still concerned about her wellbeing. Hopefully the operation would be a success, but then Olive would have to come home to recuperate and there was nobody to look after her . . . except Hildy.

She sat on a chair in the kitchen and buried her head in her hands. She wouldn't have a choice; she would be duty-bound to take care of Olive. No way could she leave her to fend for herself – that would be inhuman. She knew what would happen then, she could almost write the dialogue. But not this time. No, she wouldn't let her mother take over her life again. She would wait and see the outcome of the operation and then she'd make her plans.

* * *

190

Later that evening, Hildy walked into the ward at the hospital and found her mother, laid back against the pillows, eyes closed, looking pale and older. It had been some time since Hildy had seen her and she was shocked at the fragility of the woman lying there.

What do you expect? she thought. She's just had an operation. She sat in the chair beside the bed and, leaning over, said quietly, 'Mum, it's me, Hildy.'

Olive could hear a voice, but it seemed so far away. Was it Hildy? It sounded like her. What was she doing here and where was here? Her mind couldn't or wouldn't make sense of what was going on. She slowly opened her eyes. Above her was a ceiling with strange lights. She was in a bed, but it didn't feel like her bed. There was someone sitting beside her. She tried to focus.

'Hildy. Is that you?' The voice was frail and childlike.

'Hello Mum. Yes, it's me. How are you feeling?'

Everything suddenly became clearer. She saw her daughter staring at her with a worried expression. Looking around, Olive then realised she was in a hospital as she saw the line of beds and the nurses walking by, tending to their patients. Then she remembered. The sudden agonising pain – then nothing.

'What happened? Why am I here?'

Taking her mother's hand, Hildy said, 'You collapsed and an ambulance brought you here. You've had an operation, Mum.'

Olive frowned. 'I have?' She tried to move and winced.

A nurse appeared at her side. 'How are you feeling, Mrs Dickson?'

'A bit fuzzy. I want to sit up,' she said.

The nurse helped to lift her higher up the bed, adjusting her pillows to make her more comfortable. 'There,' she said. She took a glass of water with a straw in it from the top of the locker. 'Just take a sip,' she said. 'A bit later you'll be able to have a cup of tea.' She smiled at Hildy. 'I'll bring you one too.'

Olive gazed silently at her daughter with mixed emotions. She was relieved to see her, but deep down she still couldn't forgive her for walking out and leaving her. All for a man. She gave a baleful stare at Hildy.

'Didn't expect to see you ever again,' she said curtly.

Hildy's heart sank. Nothing had changed. She looked at the pursed lips of the woman in the bed. She knew that expression so well and the belligerent tone of voice. But this time she was stronger and ready for any onslaught, although she knew that Olive was a sick woman and would have to be handled carefully.

'I could say the same, Mum, but when I heard you'd been taken to hospital, of course I came. Why wouldn't I? After all, you are my mother. Is there anything I can do for you?'

Olive tried to think. 'I need some stuff from the house. Clean nighties, a flannel and soap, toothpaste and toothbrush,' she said. 'It seems as if I'll be here for a while if I've had an operation. That's if it isn't too much trouble?' She couldn't keep the sarcasm from her voice.

Hildy chose to ignore it. 'If you give me a key, I'll get these things tonight and bring them in tomorrow.'

'The key was in my handbag. I don't know where that is,' said Olive.

Hildy looked in the locker beside the bed and found the bag. She took out the keys and put the bag back.

As she did so, Olive saw Hildy's wedding ring and pointed to it.

'How was the wedding?' she asked. 'I saw the pictures in the paper. Not a nice way to hear about your only daughter getting married, I must say.'

Hildy wasn't going to be drawn into an argument. 'I knew you wouldn't enjoy seeing me and Milt marry, so I spared you the experience,' she said and before her mother could respond, she stood up. 'I'll be in with your stuff tomorrow after I finish my shift. I'll be in during visiting hours in the afternoon.'

Olive was too tired to answer. She just nodded.

Hildy left the ward with mixed emotions. Naturally, she was sad to see her mother so unwell, but she wasn't going to let her get away with her snide remarks. She was amazed that Olive had the strength after an operation to still be so vindictive. She stopped at the desk and asked the nurse how long she thought Mrs Dickson would be in hospital.

'It's too soon to say. We will wait to see how she recovers. The doctor will take a look at her on his rounds tomorrow morning. We may know more then. But as far as I know, the operation was a success.'

Hildy let herself into her old home to collect her mother's belongings. After she'd packed a small case, she made herself a cup of tea and sat in the kitchen drinking it. She hated this house. It reminded her of the years she'd been a prisoner within its walls, pandering to a selfish and wicked woman and now it looked as if she'd have to return for a short time to do the same. Well, she would look after her, but she wouldn't become a permanent fixture again. With the money she was earning and the money that Milt sent her, she could afford to pay for help some of the time and that would allow her to retain her independence. Her mother wouldn't like that, but that's how it was going to be.

That night Hildy wrote to Milt and told him what had happened and her plans for her mother's recovery.

Obviously I have to see she's taken care of until she's fully recovered. But I'm going to hire someone to help so that I'm not my mother's only attendant. Then she'll realise that I now have a life of my own as a married woman.

A few days later when he read Hildy's letter, Milt frowned. He'd seen for himself the way Olive had manipulated Hildy in the past and was relieved that his wife had the sense to make this arrangement. He understood that Olive would need care at home until she recovered, but knowing her he guessed she'd hang it out as long as possible to keep a stranglehold of her daughter. Thank goodness Hildy was now able to cope with her, but he would be so happy when she was over here with him, being looked after herself for a change. He transferred some money into her bank account to help with the expenses.

* * *

194

The next afternoon, Hildy walked down the ward, carrying the case with her mother's things in it. As she stopped beside the bed, she was relieved to see that Olive looked marginally better than the previous day.

'Hello Mum, I've brought your things.' She started to put them away in the locker. 'You're looking better.'

Olive scowled. 'Well I don't feel it! I'm sore and didn't get much sleep last night. That woman over there was moaning all night long.' She nodded to the bed across the ward.

'I'm sure she couldn't help it,' Hildy ventured. 'What did the doctor have to say?'

'I'll be here at least for two weeks, maybe three. It all depends how I recover from the operation.' She looked slyly at Hildy. 'He said when I go home it's essential that I have someone to look after me. I can't be left on my own.' She waited for an answer.

Pulling up a chair, Hildy sat beside the bed. 'That's to be expected,' she said, 'you'll feel a bit weak for a while, but don't worry, I'll take care of that.'

The look of triumph on her mother's face didn't go unnoticed.

Hildy continued, 'I'll arrange for you to have daily help and in between I'll call and prepare meals for you. They will only need to be heated in the oven; we'll need to build up your strength until you're well enough to look after yourself.'

This wasn't at all what Olive was expecting. 'You won't be moving in to look after me?' she demanded.

'No, Mum. It won't be necessary. You'll be well cared

for at all times, so I don't want you to worry.'

The woman was speechless. Her carefully laid plans were being dismissed. She was convinced that Hildy would have had to move back and once again she'd be in control. She was outraged. Her cheeks flushed with anger.

'Well, I've never heard of anything so heartless!' she snapped.

But Hildy was ready for her. 'Not at all. You will have someone to clean your house, make you comfortable, wash you, help you to take a bath, make sure you eat well, and I'll pop in and check up on you and do my bit too. But I don't see the need to move in. After all, I have my own place now.'

Olive glared at her. 'I really don't know you anymore. Ever since you moved out, you've become hard. I suppose that's due to that man you've married.'

Hildy met her mother's angry gaze. 'That man has a name, he's called Milt and I've not become hard as you put it, but I now have a life of my own and I'm really happy for the first time in my adult life. You must accept the fact that you no longer rule me. The sooner you do, the better we'll get along.'

Olive leant back against her pillows and with a sneer she said, 'You've got it all worked out, haven't you? You think you know everything now you're a married woman.'

Knowing her mother so well, Hildy knew that Olive was about to give vent to her feelings and an argument was forthcoming. She stood up, put the chair back in its place and said, 'I have to go now, but I'll have a word with the nurse first. I'll be back tomorrow.'

'Are you sure you can spare the time?'

Hildy ignored the barb. 'See you tomorrow,' she said and walked away, stopping at the desk to check with the nurse on her mother's condition.

'Your mother will be here for about three weeks,' she was told. 'The operation went well and once the stitches are out next week, she'll be much better.'

'Then once she's allowed home, what then?'

'Obviously she'll be weak, but after a couple or three weeks' care she should be back on her feet.'

Hildy thanked her and left. She gave a wry smile as she left the hospital. Her mother was so predictable. But her plans for getting Hildy back under her thumb had been well and truly scuppered. *Well mother*, she thought, *you no longer run my life*. Those days were well and truly over and once Olive was at home, with someone else to look after her, perhaps at last her mother would finally get the message.

Chapter Twenty-Two

Whilst Hildy was sorting out her problems in London, Cora was enjoying life. She was working still in the same dress shop and earning good money. The bonuses she'd earned boosted her weekly wage. She and the manageress were getting along very well; she was making friends and slowly building a social life. But most important of all, Joe Keating had stopped calling at her flat.

Cora had become friendly with Simon Pritchard, the young man who lived on the same floor as she did. He was tall, athletic and good-looking. They used to meet coming in and out of the apartment building and eventually started going out together. He'd not been called up to fight due to a perforated eardrum, an injury he'd sustained playing rugby at school. Instead, he joined the Metropolitan Police Service as a constable. He was charming, great fun to be with and their friendship blossomed. Sometimes he'd meet her after work and Cora would be teased by her boss.

'Your police escort is waiting for you, Cora,' Linda

would say. 'Just be sure he doesn't have a Black Maria round the corner!'

Cora just laughed, thinking of the time in Southampton when she and Belle were arrested for soliciting and been driven off in one of them. But she was also aware that she did have a police record for that one occasion. Something she pushed to the back of her mind when she was with her boyfriend.

She was enjoying being courted by this upstanding young man. He treated her affectionately, but with respect and although his kisses were full of passion, he never let his physical longings get out of hand. Cora loved that. For so long she'd been paid to pleasure such longings, now she was being cosseted for a change. But as the weeks passed, she longed for more. She wanted to be held in Simon's arms, to be made love to and it was driving her crazy because she didn't want to spoil the image he had of her. Then one evening, she told him how she felt.

They had been to the cinema to see *Brief Encounter* with Celia Johnson and Trevor Howard. A tale of unrequited love between a married woman and another man. It was a poignant story and Simon teased Cora as they left the cinema with her mopping away tears.

They returned to their building and went to her flat for a nightcap. As she poured them a drink, they discussed the film.

'I think it was a shame that they had to part,' Cora remarked.

Simon looked shocked. 'But she was a married woman!'

'I know and you're right, of course, but sometimes

when you can't have what you long for, it can be hard to live with.' She sat beside him on the settee, putting their drinks down on a table.

He pulled her into his arms and kissed her. 'Now what on earth could you want and not have that would make you feel that bad?'

There was a benevolence in his tone as if he were talking to a child and she didn't feel anything like a child. She was very much a woman. A woman with needs. She gazed up at him and caressed his face, wondering what his reaction would be if she told him. Then taking a deep breath, she said, 'I want you. I want you to take me into your arms and make love to me.'

He was so surprised the smile disappeared. He looked at her with a puzzled expression as if he couldn't believe what he was hearing.

Cora watched him. She saw the consternation on his face as he eventually understood her meaning and was trying to deal with this unexpected request. He didn't know what to say.

Disappointed, more than a little embarrassed and having to cope with rejection, Cora rose from her seat and, heading towards the door, said, 'I think maybe you should leave, Simon.'

He got up slowly, staring at her as he walked towards her. Cora opened the door wide and stood back. 'Goodnight,' she said.

He hesitated, then he walked out of her flat. She shut the door behind him, wandered over to the table and drank her gin and tonic with one gulp, before going into her bedroom and getting undressed. Then she came back into the living room, lit a cigarette and drank Simon's gin and tonic.

Well, that's that, she thought. *I've really buggered up that relationship!* She was sad. She liked Simon so much and had hoped that in time, they may well have had a future together, but not any more. With a sigh, she went into the bedroom, turned back the bed covers and was just about to get into bed when there was a frantic banging on the door. Cora rushed out of the bedroom wondering what on earth was wrong, was the building on fire? She opened the door.

Simon stepped inside, slammed the door with his foot as he picked her up in his arms and marched into the bedroom, putting her down on the bed.

Leaning over her, he said, 'I can't possibly have you feeling as devastated as Celia Johnson because you can't have what you really want, can I?'

A broad grin crept across Cora's face as she gazed back at him. 'Absolutely not!'

Ever since their drunken evening together celebrating, Belle and Hildy had kept in touch after Belle moved to the Isle of Wight. Belle was aware of the relationship between Hildy and her mother so understood the difficult position her friend was in when Olive was rushed to hospital; now she was at home being cared for by private nurses and Hildy herself. Belle had called on her at Olive's home one day when she'd had to go to Southampton and had seen for herself how manipulative Olive was.

Hildy had confided in Belle. 'She's been home almost a

month now and I know she's so much better than she lets on,' said Hildy. 'She just won't let me go.'

Belle had an idea. 'I'll get a room ready for her,' she said, 'and next week I want you to pack a case for your mother. I'll come over on Tuesday and take her back with me for a week, then when she returns, you can tell her that she's now well enough to cope.'

Hildy didn't want to put Belle to so much trouble, but Belle was adamant. 'It's the only way you'll be free,' she insisted.

The next Tuesday, Belle arrived by taxi at Olive's front door. When she knocked, it was Hildy who opened it. She looked at Belle with a worried frown. But Belle just squeezed her hand and walked into the kitchen.

Olive was sitting by the range. She looked up and barely acknowledged the visitor and when Hildy picked up her overcoat and told her to put it on, Olive glared at her.

'I'm not going anywhere,' she snapped.

'Yes, Mrs Dickson, you are,' said Belle, heaving her out of the chair, taking the coat and forcing the older woman into it, leading her to the door. 'You are coming to stay with me for a week. Get some good sea air into your lungs, make you feel better. Come along!'

Before she was aware of what was happening, Olive was bundled into the waiting taxi, a suitcase in the front seat and the car on the move.

Belle chattered on, not letting Olive get a word in. 'You'll have a lovely time,' she said, 'my house is all ready now for next season and you'll be my first visitor to stay, but as my personal guest so you won't have to pay for anything.' The car pulled up by the ferry. 'Here we are,' said Belle and helped her out of the car and up the gangway.

'Come on, Mrs Dickson, we'll go straight to the bar and have a drink.'

Still in a confused state from the unexpected happening, Olive followed her and sat down at a table.

'What's your poison, love?' asked Belle.

'I'll have a gin and tonic,' said Olive, thinking to herself, *well, I might at least have something I want.* By now she began to realise how she'd been duped, but she was once again in charge of her faculties and she began to plot. She'd pretend to be more frail than she was. These two thought they had her beaten, but they were wrong. She'd show them!

But Belle was ready for her. After their drink, she took Olive up on the deck and found a sheltered spot for the two of them. Despite herself, Olive enjoyed the trip to Shanklin. The autumn day was reasonably warm and the sun was shining on the part of the ferry where they were seated and after a while, she closed her eyes and dozed off.

Belle looked at the sleeping figure beside her. Even in repose, the lips were tight and belligerent and she knew she'd have her work cut out for her during the following seven days, but she was determined to get Hildy out of her hole. The girl had done her duty as a daughter and was due a life of her own.

The ferry docked in Shanklin and Belle woke Olive gently. As they walked down the jetty to the taxi rank, Olive looked about her. She'd never been to Shanklin and was surprised at how pretty it was and she began to relax as they travelled to Belle's house. When the car stopped in front of the building, she was very impressed, although she didn't say so.

Belle paid the taxi driver, picked up Olive's case and walked to the front door. Opening it, she turned to Olive. 'Welcome to my home, Mrs Dickson.'

The tiles on the floor in the hallway shone and the house smelt of polish. The sitting room where Belle took her was cosy, well furnished and sunny. There was a vase of flowers on a table in the window and a fire laid in the hearth. For once, she was speechless.

'Come along,' said Belle, 'I'll give you a tour of the house.'

Now Olive was intrigued and willingly followed her. She loved the size of the house; it was bigger than any she'd ever been in before. The dining room looked posh to her eyes. The kitchen was large and upstairs the bedrooms were much bigger than any of hers. When she was taken into the one that was to be hers for the week, she was a happy woman. She suddenly thought she'd enjoy her stay here, but she wouldn't let on to her hostess.

But Belle wasn't fooled for a moment. She saw the look of avarice in Olive's eyes and immediately saw a way to handle this difficult woman.

'We can unpack your case later,' said Belle. 'Let's go downstairs and have some lunch.'

She prepared cold salmon she'd bought the previous day and made a salad to go with it, plus a glass of wine. Olive thought she was in heaven. Belle made a cup of coffee and then after said, 'Right, put your coat on and we'll walk along the seafront. We'll stop and have an ice cream before we come home.'

This time there was no argument from her visitor and Belle hid a smile.

They sat in deckchairs on the front and ate ice cream cones like a couple of children. Olive was quite chatty.

'I've only ever been to Cowes,' she told Belle, 'and that was years ago. I had no idea that Shanklin was so pretty.'

Belle told her how when she'd taken a bus there she'd fallen in love with the place. 'I'm hoping to have lots of tourists stay next summer. I shall advertise, of course.'

'Your house is lovely,' Olive said. 'I would think you'd do well.'

Belle was surprised at such a compliment. 'Well, thank you, Mrs Dickson. It means a lot to hear you say that. We'll go back when we've had this. You can put your feet up until dinner and then we'll sit and listen to the wireless. Tomorrow we'll get a bus and I'll show you some more of the island.'

'Oh I don't know if I can manage that,' Olive said. 'After all, I'm still recovering from my operation, you know, and today has been a busy one for me. I'm tired now.'

'Of course you are. But you see, after a good night's sleep you'll be fine. A bus trip isn't tiring, is it?'

Olive, now anxious to see more of the island, slowly agreed. 'No, I suppose not.'

'We'll stop off somewhere and have lunch, you'll like that,' added Belle as another incentive. Olive obviously enjoyed the good life and she wouldn't turn down an offer that included an outing to the fleshpots of the Isle of Wight, especially if she wasn't paying.

For the next few days, Belle took her guest all over the island, travelling by bus to see the sights. They stopped at the odd pub for lunch and occasionally at a hotel, sitting in deckchairs on the beach with a picnic, which delighted Olive. Belle was good company and eventually Olive forgot about being frail and indeed once or twice found herself laughing.

In the evenings before dinner, it was their habit to walk along the seafront and as the days progressed, Olive lost the post-operation pallor. Her cheeks filled out and the sun and sea breeze coloured her skin. She looked a picture of health and was walking spritely.

On the final evening, Belle took her to a local hotel for dinner and made sure that Olive had a couple of glasses of wine to put her in a mellow mood.

Belle held her up her glass. 'Cheers, Mrs Dickson,' she said. 'Thank you for coming to stay; I've really enjoyed your company. You know you really are a good-looking woman. I can't see you living alone for the rest of your life.'

With a frown, Olive asked, 'What do you mean?'

'You should get out and about when you go home, meet people. You could meet a nice man. Someone to share your life with.'

Olive stiffened. 'No, thanks! I did that once – never again.'

'Not every man is the same, you know. I was married

once, but I'm not against meeting another man and getting married again. Living alone can be lonely. You should think about it.'

'I don't know about that,' Olive muttered and Belle left the matter there.

The following day, Belle took Olive to the ferry and travelled with her to her house. She'd packed a bag with food she'd cooked and started to unpack it.

'Here you are, Mrs D. I made a couple of pies for you and there is some vegetables too to keep you going until you get to the shops yourself.'

'Hildy does my shopping or one of the nurses.'

'But you won't need them now, look at you. You're as fit as a fiddle! The sea air and stay on the island was just what you needed. Come on, let's have a cup of tea, I've brought some milk, then I'll be off.'

Belle let Olive make the tea and produced a couple of cakes. 'Here, just to finish off the holiday.'

At that moment, Hildy knocked on the door and Belle let her in.

'My goodness, Mum, you look so much better. You've got colour in your cheeks. The break has done you a world of good.'

Olive was just about to argue the point when Belle interrupted. 'Your mother is fine now, Hildy. You should see her walking along the seafront every evening and she's got her appetite back, haven't you?' She turned to Olive who couldn't argue after all the food she'd consumed at Belle's expense.

'Yes, Belle really looked after me,' she said reluctantly.

'I've bought some food to see your mother over a day or two until she goes shopping,' said Belle giving Hildy a knowing look.

'That's great,' she said.

Belle stood up. 'Well, Mrs Dickson, love, I'm off. I'm taking Hildy with me as we've a lot to catch up on. Thanks for your company, you take care of yourself now.'

Hildy, following Belle's lead, said, 'Well, I'm really happy to see that you've recovered. I'll pop in in a couple of days to see you.'

'What about the nurses?' asked Olive.

'Oh, I've cancelled them, Mum. After all, you're able to look after yourself now, thanks to Belle. The hospital said it would take about a month and obviously they were right.' She walked towards the door.

'Bye, Mrs Dickson,' said Belle, 'remember what I said about getting out and meeting people.' She gave her a knowing wink and left the house with Hildy.

Outside, Hildy looked at her friend. 'Bloody hell, Belle! What did you do? Mother looks a different woman.'

Belle started to laugh. 'Your mother is a snob, did you know that?'

Hildy shook her head.

'Once she saw my house, she changed. I took her out every day, we ate in pubs and the occasional hotel and she lapped it up. Soon forgot she was supposed to be ill. Now don't you let her try and fool you, she's completely recovered. Leave her long enough that she has to go out and do some shopping. About four days should do it.

Come on, let's go to the pub and have a drink to celebrate!'

'I don't know how to thank you, Belle.'

'Just one way. Don't let her take you for a ride again. Keep your distance, don't call too often and go on different days. Remember she's still the same devious woman.'

Olive, now alone, sat drinking her tea. She realised that her game was over; Belle had been too clever for her. But she had enjoyed her stay, she had to admit that. She got up and looked at her reflection in the mirror on the wall. Belle said she was still a good-looking woman. She turned her face this way and that and decided that indeed she didn't look bad. Her cheeks had filled out so her normally gaunt look had disappeared. Another husband? She wasn't too sure about that. But she had to accept that Hildy would soon be leaving Southampton to be with her husband and then she'd really be on her own.

She didn't want to continue washing floors in the pub, she'd look again for another job. Maybe another lodger. Belle had made her think. Having been out and about and enjoying herself on the Isle of Wight, she realised she needed to change her life, she'd go and buy the local paper and look again at the situations vacant. She didn't want to go back to staying within her four walls all the time so tomorrow she'd take herself off to the pier for a walk but now she had to unpack.

Chapter Twenty-Three

That evening, Cora and Simon were sitting in a pub having a quiet drink. He was telling her that something big was in the offing, but he couldn't tell her any more, except to say it would make the headlines in all the national newspapers if it came to pass.

Of course she was curious, but knew better than to question him. Simon was a dedicated policeman and was in the force for the foreseeable future. He was studying for his sergeants' exam at this moment. He did sometimes tell her little snatches of things that happened, but only minor things, usually about folk who had called out the police for silly things, like the woman who called because her husband came home drunk and was walking around the garden naked.

However, several days later Simon was able to tell her about the case.

'There are two brothers running a black market business in Southampton,' he said. 'But now they have tried to move their stuff to the city in co-operation with another London gang and have been caught red-handed. So we've been able to arrest several men. We're working with the Southampton police. It's a real feather in our caps.'

'Who are these Southampton racketeers?' Cora asked.

'The James brothers. They were into everything. Stolen petrol coupons, clothing coupons, foodstuff stolen from the NAAFI. And we found them selling sawn-off shotguns.'

Cora remained silent. She knew of the James boys who used the Horse and Groom regularly and were well known for their criminal activities. It had been rumoured that they had a couple of the police in their pockets and this had kept them out of jail. But she kept this information to herself.

'I'm off to your old town tomorrow,' he told her. 'I'm liaising with the police there so we can share all the information before the case goes to court.'

This made Cora nervous. Simon would probably be visiting the very places she used when she worked the streets and she didn't like the idea at all.

'That should be interesting for you,' she said and changed the subject.

Simon was kept busy the following morning once he'd arrived at Southampton police headquarters. He'd been out with a squad, searching various premises, where they had discovered the James brothers had stowed stuff away and were amazed at the amount of black market goods they'd uncovered. All of which had to be listed and labelled. At lunchtime they went back to the canteen for a meal.

Sitting next to one of the sergeants, he was asked, 'Is this your first visit to the town?'

'Yes it is,' he said, 'but my girlfriend, Cora, lived here.'

'Cora,' mused the sergeant, 'now that's an unusual name. I only ever heard of one before and that was the name of one of the brasses we arrested one night. Pretty young girl.'

'I best not tell her that,' laughed Simon, 'she wouldn't be very flattered.'

But when he returned to the station that evening to round off the day with his notes and report, the sergeant called him over.

'Here you are, lad, this is my Cora: as I said she was very pretty so I reckon your girl wouldn't be too upset if she looked like that. This Cora was arrested with her friend Belle.' And he handed over the files.

Simon looked at the picture and paled. Then he started to read the report, noting where Cora was picked up, the pub she frequented and her charge for soliciting in Canal Walk along with Belle Newman.

Fortunately the sergeant had been called away so was unaware of the havoc he'd caused. Simon put the file back on the desk and left the building. He asked the way to Canal Walk and the Horse and Groom. He was not in uniform so didn't cause alarm as he walked into the bar and ordered a half of bitter. At the bar, he looked round the room and saw a couple of women sat drinking, picking up clients and leaving only to return later. He was stunned and still couldn't quite believe what he'd discovered.

It was a quiet evening and he started talking to the barmaid, asking if she knew Cora. She did.

'Yes, lovely girl. Lost her parents and her home in the Blitz,' she informed him. 'Such a shame to see her on the game. That girl was far too good for the streets. Thankfully I heard she'd moved on.' She walked to the end of the bar to serve another customer.

Simon left, hailed a taxi and was driven to the station to catch a late train back to London. Tomorrow evening he'd arranged to take Cora out to the cinema.

The next night, Cora had changed ready for her date with Simon. They were going to the West End to see a film and out to a night club, as a treat he'd said, and she was looking forward to it. She made a cup of tea and sat waiting. Simon was late which was not unusual, he was sometimes held up due to some case or other.

In fact, her boyfriend was sitting in a nearby pub drinking half a bitter, trying to make up his mind as to the best way to bring up the devastating discovery of her past. He was finding it very difficult to believe. Cora had behaved like any young lady with morals when she was with him. Yes, their kisses had been full of passion, until that one night when she'd invited him into her bed and their relationship had become intimate . . . and now he'd been told she sold her body for money.

He sighed deeply and lit a cigarette. There could be no mistake – she had a crime sheet, for God's sake! He closed his eyes as if to shut out the fact. His girl – a prostitute? He'd taken many of those into custody in the past. It was part and parcel of their lives. They laughed, paid the fine and usually went straight back out onto the streets. How could Cora be involved in something so sordid?

Leaving his drink, he put out his cigarette and walked towards her bedsit.

Hearing his familiar knock on the door, Cora rushed to open it. 'Hello darling. You're late, is everything alright?' She leant forward and kissed him. He hardly responded, then walked past her and sat on her daybed.

Cora froze. What on earth was the matter with him?

'What's wrong, Simon?'

'Come and sit down, Cora,' he said, patting the seat beside him.

She did so and waited.

He looked her straight in the eye. 'I was talking to a sergeant in Southampton and I happened to mention you by name. He told me that he only had ever heard that name once before when a local prostitute had been arrested for soliciting along with her friend Belle. He showed me the files.' He waited for her reaction.

Cora felt sick. The very thing she'd been dreading had happened. There was absolutely no point in denying it, none at all. She straightened her back and met his gaze unflinchingly. She'd been down this road before with Hank Mason, but she'd not been in love with him. This time it was different.

'Yes, Simon. I'm afraid that's true.'

Although he knew that it was true, crime sheets don't lie, to hear Cora admit to it was devastating. He was speechless.

'That was during the war in another life. I came to London to put that all behind me and start again. Don't look at me like that, Simon, I can't bear it!'

'How do you expect me to look?' Now he was angry. 'I meet a girl, fall in love with her and discover she isn't at all who I think she is.'

Cora heard the words of love spoken and her heart was breaking.

'Don't you see, you idiot! How could I tell you? I love you too, I didn't want anything to spoil that.'

He just stared at her. 'But don't you see? It has spoilt it.' He rose from the daybed.

Cora sprang to her own defence. 'You haven't even asked me why. It wasn't something I did willingly, I can assure you!'

But he was walking to the door. He opened it and turned towards her. 'I'm sorry,' he said, then he walked out of her room.

Cora burst into tears.

When there were no tears left to shed, she left her bedsit and walked to the nearest phone box and rang Belle. When her friend answered, Cora broke down again and between sobs managed to tell her what had happened.

'Oh, Cora, love, I'm so sorry.' She was really upset because she knew how important Simon was to her and there was nothing she could do to change the situation.

'Can you take a few days off and come over here? A change of scenery will do you good and we can talk and try and sort out this mess. If Simon really loves you, he'll come back.'

Wiping her nose and sniffing, Cora said, 'I doubt that, Belle. You should have seen the look on his face when he left me. I'm not sure he'll ever get over it.'

'You'll just have to wait and hope, love. I'll get a room ready for you. Come over tomorrow. I'll see you then.'

She sat down and considered the situation. There was never a way to escape your past. Somehow, somewhere it came back to bite you. Always at the wrong moment. For women like her and Cora, it was a millstone they had to carry all of their lives.

Chapter Twenty-Four

Whilst Cora was trying to run away from her past, Hildy was planning her future. The first ship of GI brides was due to sail for New York in January and she had a berth booked. She'd had a medical, filled in pages of forms, showed her marriage certificate as proof and started to gather her things. In two months' time, she'd leave these shores for ever.

Her only problem was her mother. After Olive's stay on the Isle of Wight with Belle and now fully recovered from her operation, Hildy had taken Belle's advice and stayed away from her for a while, once she was convinced that she was well enough to look after herself.

Olive had found a new job in a Lipton's grocery store which she felt was much more fitting than scrubbing pub floors. She had managed to find another lodger, an older man, returned from the war and working in a local garage as a mechanic. He was quiet and kept himself to himself which suited Olive very well. Through judicious questioning of Olive's neighbour, Hildy had gleaned these facts and therefore had felt free once again, but now, she felt she ought to make an effort before she eventually sailed away. She was unsure how to go about it, knowing her mother's possessive nature. She didn't want to leave with any animosity between them and to this end, on Sunday morning she went to her old home and, holding her breath, knocked on the door.

Olive opened it and was taken aback when she saw Hildy standing there.

'Hello Mum. Just thought I'd pop in and see how you are.'

'Did you? You couldn't have been too concerned. It's been three months since I've been home and I've not seen much of you lately, but I suppose you'd better come in.' She walked away.

Hildy's heart sank. This wasn't going to be easy, but she felt she had to try.

'I thought we might have a cup of tea and a chat, that's all. You know, catch up.'

Olive looked at her with raised eyebrows. 'Really, how nice of you.' But nevertheless, she filled the kettle and put out two cups and saucers. 'Better sit down then.'

'You're looking well,' Hildy ventured.

'I'm alright considering I have to manage alone.'

Hildy ignored the remark. 'I heard you were working at Lipton's,' she said.

Olive glared at her. 'Has that mouthy woman next door been talking to you?'

'We bumped into each other in the street,' Hildy said. 'I was pleased to hear it.'

'Did she tell you I had a lodger too? Don't answer, of course she did. She's more interested in other people's lives than her own.'

She made the tea, poured two cups and pushed Hildy's over to her. 'So, what's the real reason for you calling today? It wasn't just for an idle chat, was it?'

There was no reason to lie so looking at her mother, Hildy said, 'I wanted to say goodbye really. I'm sailing to America in January.'

Olive's mouth tightened and she glared at her daughter. 'Going out to live with that man, well I wish you luck!' It was said with such venom that Hildy snapped back.

'That man is Milt, my husband and yes, I'm off to start my married life. And what's more, I can hardly wait.'

'Well, don't come running back to me when it all goes wrong that's all!'

Hildy calmed down. What was the point, it was exactly how she thought it would be. Olive was as vindictive as ever.

'You know, Mother, "that man" as you insist on calling him once told me he felt sorry for you.' She saw the surprise on Olive's face. 'Yes, he did. When I asked why, he said because you were such a bitter woman that you had missed so much happiness in life that he felt sorry for you.'

Olive's face flushed with rage. 'I don't need his sympathy or yours for that matter. I am perfectly happy with my life; I don't need anybody feeling sorry for me. Not him and certainly not you! Go and find out for yourself how difficult married life can be, then you might understand me better.'

With a sigh, Hildy rose to her feet. 'I'm sorry we have to part this way, Mum. I had hoped we could have parted as friends, but I can see I've wasted my time. Take care of yourself.'

She picked up her handbag and walked out of the house. At least she'd tried, from now on all she needed to be concerned with was getting ready to sail and she could do that now with a clear conscience.

Back in the kitchen, Olive sat staring into the fire. A bitter woman? Yes, she was, and with good reason. These youngsters think they know it all. Now Hildy had made her choice. Well, good riddance! But as she sat, knowing she'd never see her daughter again, tears filled her eyes and she sat silently crying.

On the Isle of Wight, Belle rushed to the front door, opened it and hugged Cora as soon as she saw her.

'Come in, love. I'll put the kettle on, or would you prefer something stronger?'

'Oh yes, Belle. A stiff drink would really go down well.' Cora followed her into the living room, sat in a comfortable armchair and looked around the room with its newly painted cream walls, comfortable furniture, cheerful curtains and potted plants on a small table. It was cosy and attractive.

'My word, you have been busy,' she said.

Belle handed her a drink and sat in another chair nearby. 'I've painted myself silly,' she said. 'The furniture is a bit old, but it will do until I make enough to replace it. How are *you*, love?'

With a shrug, Cora said, 'Much as you would expect. I've lost the man I wanted to spend the rest of my life with.'

'But you don't know that.'

'I think I do. If you had seen the look on Simon's face, you wouldn't have any doubts.'

'Did you ever sleep with him?' Belle asked in her usual straightforward manner.

Nodding her head, Cora answered. 'Yes, eventually. We took things slowly, I'm sure Simon thought that if he'd suggested such a thing any earlier, I would have been upset. In fact, it was me that asked him. Ironic, isn't it? I wanted to be courted, like any young woman. I wanted his respect as well as his love. Now I've lost both.'

'That's men all over,' Belle raged.

'Well, there you are.'

'Come on, let's go out to the pub, have a couple of drinks and get a meal. The sea air will do us both good and I've some interesting news to tell you.'

It appeared that Belle had received a letter from Jackson in New York and it had been forwarded on to her from the post office.

They sat at a table with a couple of drinks and Belle took out a letter from her handbag. She started to read the contents.

My dear Belle,

I hope you haven't forgotten about me? It's been a while, but as I told you, I was going to move to New York and here I am. I've got a job working in a hotel as a busboy. That means I help in the restaurant, clearing tables and setting them and assisting the waiters. The pay is good and we get our meals too. I have a small apartment with one bedroom with twin beds so another busboy and I share, which helps with the rent. We work different shifts so that means we have some private time and we get along just fine.

Gee, Belle, I wish you could see New York. It's a mighty fine city. They have an area here called Harlem where all we black folk hang out and listen to the music, where we are accepted for who we are. The city itself has so many different nationalities all living together that, here, there is no sitting in the back of the bus. How about that?

You would love the shops, honey. This city is a woman's dream. I really miss you, Belle, and think about you lots and the good times we had together and hey, I've got me a girl! She works in the hotel as a chambermaid and she's just lovely. It's early days yet, but I really like her so who knows?

I hope you meet someone real nice. You deserve a good man to take care of you, Belle. Write and tell me what you're doing. Are you still working building Spitfires?

You take good care now,
Jackson

Belle folded the letter and grinned broadly. 'My boy is doing just fine and I'm so happy for him. I hope he and his girl get married eventually – he'd be a great husband because he cares.'

'That's lovely news, Belle. I know how fond you were of him.'

Belle stared off into the distance, looking wistful. 'I'd like to find a man like that you know, Cora. I know I rejected the idea before, but being alone isn't a lot of fun once you stop working and the evening closes in. That's when you need male company with a man that cares about you.' She looked across at her friend and saw the pain reflected in her eyes. 'But, of course, you already know that.' She leant over and squeezed Cora's hand. 'Don't give up, love. He may come back, just give him time.'

Cora tried to make light of the situation. 'Just think, Belle. I could have been Joe Keating's mistress if I'd a mind to.'

'That would have been a big mistake!' Belle said, looking askance at her friend.

Laughing, Cora said, 'You should have seen the look on your face then, Belle. Come on, you know me better than that. I'm never cut out to be an old man's darling.'

With a mischievous grin, Belle said, 'Well, it would depend how old he was and how much money, then who knows, I might be tempted!'

'Bloody hell, Belle, you'd kill him off in a month.'

'Fabulous! Then I'd be a rich widow. Hey! It's an idea worth considering.' Then she doubled up with laughter.

During her visit, the two women decided that Hildy and Cora would spend Christmas with Belle. They wanted to see Hildy before she sailed and this seemed a perfect answer for all of them. Cora would be alone as would Belle so why not get together?

Prior to that, Cora was kept busy. The clientele of her shop seemed to be going to lots of cocktail parties and business was brisk. Simon hadn't contacted her at all, which broke her heart, but didn't surprise her. Now she was looking forward to Christmas.

The Christmas break arrived at last and Hildy, Cora and Belle sat down to their Christmas dinner, having already celebrated with glasses of wine whilst opening gifts, but the main topic of conversation was of Hildy and her future in America.

'Milt is going to meet me when the ship docks in New York. He's managed to take some leave from the army so we'll be on our honeymoon. We didn't have time before apart from one night at the Polygon Hotel,' she said.

'Oh how exciting,' said Cora. 'Where are you going?'

'We'll be staying in New York and in the summer we'll take off somewhere for a few days, but he wants to take me shopping. Imagine! New York and all those lovely shops!'

'And no clothing coupons needed,' Belle remarked. 'I'm so jealous!'

'I can't wait,' Hildy said. 'After all, I've nothing to keep me here. It'll be a whole new life, but I am a little nervous, I must confess,' she said, her smile fading somewhat.

It was strange, thought Belle, to see Hildy uncertain about anything. In the factory, she was so decisive and together. 'You'll be fine,' Belle assured her. 'Make sure you write and let us know how you get on.'

'Oh I promise I will. What about you, Belle, what are your plans?'

'I'll open for business at Easter,' she said, 'and hope to take bookings for the summer. It'll take a while to get established, but I'm ready for that.'

'Whatever, it'll be better than working in a factory,' Hildy said. 'At least you have your own home and that's a bonus. What about you, Cora?'

'I've no new plans, I'll stay put in London, working at the shop for the time being.'

Simon Pritchard spent the Christmas with his family in London. He tried to join in with the festivities and be cheerful, but he was missing Cora. No matter how much he tried, he couldn't forget her, nor her background.

During Christmas, Simon mulled over these facts, going over them continuously until his mother asked him if anything was wrong.

'No, Mum. Why do you ask?'

'Well, son, all through Christmas you've been somewhere else, not with us at all. What's on your mind?'

He apologised. 'I'm sorry, I'm just tired and we have a case that's hopefully coming to a head and I've been a bit preoccupied with that.' He put his arm round his mother's shoulders. 'That's all.'

It was a week after Christmas and Cora was back at work. The change of scenery and good company had gone some way to help her feeling of loss and loneliness. After all, she thought, if I survived the loss of my parents, I can manage without Simon . . . most of the time, but in bed alone at night, she longed to feel his arms about her, see him smile, hear his voice.

She didn't do a great deal in the evenings apart from go to a cinema and lose herself in the film that was showing.

Despite the fact that in her other life, she'd have walked into a bar alone – usually looking for punters without a second thought – now she didn't feel comfortable doing it. In winter it was too cold to sit out on the fire escape, so she either listened to the wireless or read a book. Sometimes out of desperation, she'd wrap up warmly and walk. She would go window shopping, pop into a cafe and drink coffee whilst watching people, but every time she saw a couple together, she felt alone and abandoned.

It was after such a walk one evening, she returned to her bedsit and stoked up the fire. Rubbing her hands together for warmth she then put on the kettle, hoping a hot drink would chase away the chill in her body. She was just about to pour the tea when there was a ring on her bell. She couldn't imagine who would be calling, but she walked out to the main door and opened it.

Simon stood there, his coat collar turned up against the cold.

'Hello Cora. May I come in?'

Chapter Twenty-Five

Cora was stunned to see Simon standing looking at her and for a moment she didn't move or speak, then she stepped back and opened the door wider.

'Come in,' she said and as she walked away, she felt her legs trembling. She never thought she'd ever see Simon again and wondered why he was here.

'I've just made a pot of tea, would you like some?' she asked for something to say as he followed her into her bedsit.

'That would be lovely, thank you. It's bitterly cold outside. Would you like me to put some more coal on the fire?'

'Yes, please,' Cora said. 'I've just come in and it needs building up again.'

She watched him as she poured the tea. In one way, it was wonderful to see him, but she couldn't bear it if he was offhand. He'd only break her heart again, just when she was beginning to get used to him not being around.

They sat at the table. 'How have you been? Did you have a good Christmas?' he asked.

'I'm fine and, yes, I did have a good Christmas; I went over to the island and stayed with Belle . . . and you?'

He gave the old familiar smile she knew so well as he looked at her. 'It was quiet, just with the family, but nice to have mum cook for me again.'

She took a deep breath. 'Why are you here, Simon?'

He sat silently for a moment staring at her, his gaze so penetrating she was almost mesmerised by it. She waited.

'Because I miss you. Not a day goes by that you are not in my thoughts. It's driving me crazy.'

'And?'

'I went to the Horse and Groom when I was down in Southampton.'

'Whatever for?'

'I just wanted to try and understand you, the life you used to lead – the reason.'

'You could have asked me,' she said sharply. 'You didn't have to go round Southampton to pry. I would have told you everything you wanted to know, but you didn't give me a chance. You made up your own mind – then you walked out.'

'I can see you're angry, Cora, and I don't blame you, but it was just a shock. It took me a while to get over it.'

'Really! And you a policeman. You of all people should know that sometimes things are not what they seem, but usually the people concerned have a right to defend themselves. You didn't give me that right, did you? You were judge and jury. Guilty, my Lord!' Getting up, she walked over to the window and looked out in an effort to calm down. She turned round.

'You said you loved me Simon, but it wasn't strong enough to try and understand me, was it? You know nothing about me. You know my body, but you don't know *me*!'

'I know how you lost your parents, your home and were left with nothing. I found that out in Southampton.'

She wandered back to the table. 'What else did you discover? That I was penniless, what I charged my punters? What services I offered? All you discovered, Simon, was how I survived. You didn't learn anything about what went on in here!' She thumped her breast. 'You didn't find out how much I loathed to feel a stranger's hands on my body, how I had to pretend to like what they did to me. How I lied to boost their egos. You know nothing!'

She was fighting back her tears. Tears of anger, tears for her lost years of innocence and her self-respect.

He could hear the anguish in her voice, saw the tears brimming in her eyes and was at a loss to know what to do. 'I'm really sorry, Cora. I didn't mean to hurt you, honestly.'

She took a handkerchief from her pocket and blew her nose. 'But you did, Simon, and you've no idea how much. You broke my heart.'

'Can you forgive me? Can we start again?' He reached for her hand, but she withdrew it from his touch.

She studied him, recognising the longing in his eyes. 'I'm not sure that would work,' she said quietly.

'Why ever not?'

'You would take me in your arms, make love to me,

but in the back of your mind, you'd begin to wonder how many men had done the same before you. It would destroy us.'

He didn't answer because in his heart he knew she spoke the truth and Cora recognised his reluctance and the reason for it.

'You see, I'm right. If you can't put my past behind you, we wouldn't have a chance.' She rose to her feet. 'I think it best that you leave, don't you?'

'Can't we be friends at least?' he asked.

'Simon, it's easy for friends to become lovers; it's much more difficult for lovers to become friends. Let's leave it like that.'

Simon was at a loss to know how to change her mind. As he gazed at her, he knew he still loved her, but he could see from the steely look in her eyes that Cora had made up her mind. He wanted to reach out to her, to hold her and convince her that things would work out, but she stood rigid before him and he had no choice but to leave.

Left alone, Cora sat at the table and finished her tea. *Funny old world*, she thought. She had wanted Simon so much, but when they had faced reality together the problem before them would have been too big to overcome. He was still too haunted by her past to make a future together possible. The realisation was hard to accept, but accept it she must and move on.

It was now January and Hildy was due to sail to America and a new life. She'd been moved to a camp at Tidworth with the other GI brides before being taken to the docks to start her journey. She was sailing on the *Queen Elizabeth* and Cora and Belle were there to see her off.

Bands played, streamers flew and, despite the cold, there was a festive air as those on the quayside sang songs. The railings on board the liner were crowded with women. Some waving, others crying and as Belle and Cora searched the faces, looking for their friend, they were in a panic in case they missed her.

'There she is!' yelled Belle and started waving madly whilst trying to point her out to Cora, who eventually saw her too. They shouted messages to Hildy who herself was yelling at the top of her voice, neither could hear the other in the maelstrom of sailing day.

Eventually the roar of the funnels filled the air, the band started to play 'There'll Always Be An England'. The stevedores let go the ropes after the gangways were taken in and the ship began to leave. Belle and Cora waved, tears streaming down their cheeks, still calling to their friend until it was time to leave.

'Come on,' said Belle, 'I need a bloody drink after all that.'

Half an hour later, the two women sat in a quiet corner of a bar with a couple of gin and tonics in front of them. They toasted their friend.

'To Hildy!' said Cora.

'May she live a happy life!' added Belle.

The two then started to catch up on each other's news. Cora told her friend about Simon's visit and the consequences.

'You sent him away?' Belle was surprised.

'He couldn't forget about my past, Belle. He even came here to Southampton, checking me out. Asking questions! That's a bit obsessive, don't you think?'

'Maybe it was because he loved you.'

'Don't, Belle. Leave it, please. I've made up my mind about Simon. He too is part of my past.'

Her friend remained silent, but she was sorry, knowing how much Cora had loved the policeman.

'Come on,' Belle said, 'let's get something to eat before I catch a ferry back to the island.' They left the bar in search of food.

Chapter Twenty-Six

Belle had settled well in Shanklin and was a happy woman. Having completed her house renovations, she started on the garden. With the help of a handyman, they had built a chicken house in the back and she'd purchased several laying hens, thinking the eggs would help with her catering and spread the rations. They had dug vegetable beds and planted potatoes, runner beans, onions, beetroot and carrots. It had been backbreaking but wholly therapeutic.

She had placed advertisements in local papers, in Southampton's *Evening Echo* and holiday magazines, announcing her opening at Easter and to her delight, she had already received bookings.

The local shopkeepers were now getting to know her and, with her outgoing nature, she'd achieved a certain camaraderie with them. The local butcher in particular had taken a shine to her and would occasionally slip her a bit of extra meat, which bode well for the future when she had guests. In return she would take him some eggs.

Cora would sometimes spend a weekend with her. After the busy city, the Isle of Wight was like a haven and she loved walking on the beach and, after their walk, finding a local pub and having a few drinks.

The pace was slower, the surroundings picturesque and Cora was beginning to find that London no longer held any excitement for her. She said as much to Belle one evening when they were at home having a quiet meal.

'Do you think I could find a job on the island, Belle?'

Her friend looked at her with surprise. 'Why?' she asked.

'Oh I don't know. It's so peaceful here. Frankly, I'm sick of the rush in London. Travelling each day by Underground, all the pushing and shoving in the mornings and at rush hour after a day's work. I get home and I'm exhausted.' She'd been shopping with Belle and enjoyed the chat with the shopkeepers. 'I don't really know anyone outside of work,' she continued and let out a deep sigh. 'Since splitting with Simon, I've pretty much kept myself to myself. A city can be a lonely place, Belle.'

Belle looked at her thoughtfully, she was fond of young Cora. They'd been through so much together and she, too, often felt lonely by herself in the evenings.

'Why don't you come and help me run the B&B? You could share my room. I could just about move another single bed in which would be a bit of a squeeze, but you could use one of the other rooms when it was free. I could do with a helping hand.'

'I couldn't possibly do that,' Cora said.

'Why ever not?'

'Because you don't know if you'll have enough business coming in.'

Belle laughed loudly. 'Oh ye of little faith! I'm already fully booked for Easter and I expect to do well in the summer. I thought I'd do afternoon teas too, outside in the garden if the weather is fine enough, if not, inside in the dining room. There are a lot of day trippers who come here. I can't manage that alone, I'd have to hire help. I can pay you a small wage and all your meals to start with and when we're busy and established, I'll pay you more.'

Cora started to smile. 'Oh, Belle! Really?'

'Yes, really. You will have to help with the cleaning, the cooking, the serving and the garden too. So you see love, you'd really be doing me a favour. What do you say?'

Cora jumped to her feet, rushed over to her friend, flung her arms around her and kissed her cheek. 'I say yes, of course!'

So it was settled. Cora would hand in a week's notice, pack her stuff and move in. They drank to their new arrangement. It worked for both of them. Belle had been concerned about managing if she was fully booked and now that was no longer a problem. She and Cora worked well together and shared a great affection for one another and so work would no longer be a chore, shared as it would be by two very close friends.

Cora's boss, Linda, was sorry to see her go, but when she heard her future plans she was delighted for her. 'If you find you don't like it there and it's too quiet for you, you can always come back, you know.'

Cora thanked her. 'That's really kind of you. I've enjoyed working with you and if you need a holiday, you know where to come,' she said with a grin.

The next two days were spent packing and cleaning the bedsit ready for the next occupant. When she'd given her notice to the rent man, she asked, 'Will the landlord soon find another occupant, do you think?'

'No idea, miss. As far as I know, the room will be advertised in a newspaper.'

She wondered who would be living in her bedsit next. She'd enjoyed her time there, she mused, as she finally packed her bag, called a cab and was taken to the train station. She was off to start another new life!

It was now Good Friday and on the Isle of Wight, Belle and Cora were preparing breakfast for their residents who had arrived the night before. Two couples, one with a small child who slept in a small cot that Belle had purchased for such an occasion.

The women had been busy, making soda bread as an alternative to the dreadful National loaf, plucking a chicken which Belle had killed, much to Cora's horror.

'I can't watch,' she'd said as Belle prepared to wring the chicken's neck and had fled into the house. But she was quite happy to sit and pluck it. They'd bought some fish from the local fisherman to serve for dinner on Friday evening and with the extra ration books, they'd be able to buy extra butter, bacon and meat.

Both were good cooks. They saved the fresh eggs for

breakfast and used the powdered eggs to make scones and a cake. The vegetable patch had supplied most of their needs. They were both thrilled to have a good start to the business.

After breakfast when their guests had vacated their rooms, they washed up the breakfast dishes, made the beds, cleaned the rooms and eventually sat down to a cup of tea and a bowl of porridge. Both were pleased with themselves.

'Do you think they were satisfied with the breakfast?' asked Belle with a worried frown.

'They were delighted!' Cora assured her. 'Both couples are nice; I don't see them being any trouble. Besides, why would they complain? The house is lovely, the beds comfortable and the food is good.' She poured another cup of tea. 'Relax, love, we're doing just fine.'

Belle started to chuckle. 'Who'd have thought it, eh? You and me, running a business. Bloody sight better than having to lay on our backs to earn a crust.' She looked at her friend. 'Do you ever think of those days?'

'No, never! I've locked every one of those days and nights away in a box never to be opened. That's my past; all I want to think about is my future.'

'Well, I do sometimes. It wasn't all bad. I met some nice blokes, most of them just scared of what lay ahead for them. Poor buggers, wondering if they'd come back alive or injured. Then, of course, I met Jackson. He was special. I'm really happy that he came out alive and now seems to have a good life. The rest I don't want to think about. However, love, let's remember, those days paid for our future and don't you forget that.'

'How could I? Without being on the streets, I would never have survived and look at us now.'

'Well,' said Belle with a grin, 'if we don't have enough customers in the summer, we could always open a brothel!' She doubled up with laughter.

'Belle! Don't even think of it,' Cora gasped, then she too started laughing.

As they only offered half board, they spent the rest of the morning finishing their chores and preparing the evening meal, then went for a stroll along the beach, breathing in the smell of seaweed and salt air. They sat in a beach cafe drinking tea and planning for the summer.

'I've advertised year round accommodation,' Belle told her friend, 'but I imagine from May onwards people will start booking, hopefully. July, August and September should be our busiest months, but if we're not booked up, serving afternoon teas will help with the shortfall.'

Cora cast an admiring glance in Belle's direction. 'I had no idea that you had such a good business brain.'

'Oh I've also had business cards printed and have put them in all the paper shops, you know in the window with all the adverts – and in Cowes. It's a favourite holiday place and hopefully if the B&Bs and hotels get booked up, we may pick up a few strays there, especially during the Cowes Regatta, which starts on the first Saturday in August, I believe. We might do well serving teas then. Loads of people come over to watch that and then they may decide to venture further.'

'Well, only time will tell,' said Cora as she went to pay the bill.

*　*　*

Belle's guests had left fully satisfied with their stay and, after cleaning the rooms and remaking the beds, she and Cora sat down with a cup of tea to read the latest news from Hildy. They'd received several postcards from her after her arrival in New York and her consequent move to a military base in Kentucky, now she'd written a letter.

Hello girls,

Sorry it's taken so long to write, hope you received my postcards, but as you can imagine, everything has been chaotic since my arrival. New York was fantastic and the shopping incredible! Milt really spoilt me. I have a whole new wardrobe of clothes, which is just as well as the other army wives would not have appreciated my utility English ones.

We are now living at the army base at Fort Knox. When Milt told me where we were headed, it reminded me of old cowboy films and I keep expecting John Wayne to ride in! It's not at all like that, of course. We live on the base in a housing estate set up for army families. I've met lots of the army wives. Most of them are friendly and being a GI bride makes me something of a novelty, which can be both enjoyable – and irritating. I sometimes feel like a specimen in a bottle! However, soon I hope to blend into the background when the curiosity wears off.

Milt is a great husband. He's such a strong character and I imagine as a sergeant he can be pretty strict, but the men seem to respect him for it. He's so kind to me and I know I made the right choice. He has been thinking about leaving the army and setting up his own business, but the army has been his life and he's so good at what he does, I wonder if he'd be happy. But no decision has been made as yet.

Life in America is so different and takes some getting used to. We are supposed to speak the same language as the Yanks, well don't you believe it, because we do not. But I'm learning. The yard is the garden. The pavement is a sidewalk, a lift is an elevator and a tap is a faucet. I know! Crazy, isn't it?

I'm not homesick because I'm so happy with this lovely man, but, of course, I miss my friends like you two. Glad to know you are in the B&B business and in such a lovely place too. Maybe if you make a bundle of money sometime in the future, you could come and visit me. That would be great, so save your pennies.

Take care and I'll write again soon.

Love,

Hildy

Belle put the letter down and smiled. 'Thank goodness everything seems to have worked out for her, after all. We must write back to her, let her know she's not forgotten. She took a chance sailing off to another country with a man she really didn't know well.'

'Yes, that is a relief,' Cora agreed. 'You hear of such terrible tales of those who were promised the earth to find it had all been a pack of lies.'

'Let's face it, you don't have to leave these shores to find that out. Men can do that anywhere.'

240

'Would you marry again, Belle?'

'No, love. Now if I did meet a bloke I liked, I would live with him, but that would be enough, then I could chuck him out if he didn't live up to my expectations.' She stood up and said, 'Let's go for a walk along the beach. We've earned a break.'

The two of them would not have been quite so happy about their friend Hildy had she written and told them the whole truth about her induction to army life.

On her arrival in New York, Hildy had been thrilled to be with Milt again and they'd had a great few days in the vibrant city on their delayed honeymoon. She'd been fascinated by all the sights and the shops and was looking forward to setting up a home for the man she adored. But when they arrived at Milt's army base in Kentucky, she found that things were different to how she imagined her married life and home would be.

As was usual for army wives, they all lived in houses attached to the regiment in the grounds of the military base. There was a definite division among the ranks. The homes of the officer's wives differed greatly from the ordinary ranks. The army set out classes and entertainment for the wives in an effort to stop them from being bored with army life and to try and keep them out of trouble. Boredom can lead to all manner of things, this the army had learnt over the years and the divorce rate was fairly high.

Their house on the base was already furnished, which had been a disappointment to Hildy. She had looked forward to choosing the furniture for their first home together, as she thought the interior of the house was bland

and characterless, but she kept such feelings to herself.

The other wives gave her a welcome party two days after she arrived to try and make her at ease having left her country as a GI bride.

As she had written to her friends, she did feel like a specimen in a bottle as she was questioned incessantly about her life back in, 'the old country'. Although why they called it that she often wondered when they had nothing to do with Britain and appeared to know so little about it.

They were unaware of the hardship the British people had suffered during the Blitz.

The fact that everyone had clothing coupons they found incredible and as for ration books and the meagre amounts of food allowed to each person for a week, they could hardly believe.

'Do you have television? Do you have beauty parlours? Do you know the Royal family? Do you have running water in your houses?'

On being asked this final question, Hildy smiled at the questioner and said, 'Good heavens, no. We have to wash in the sea. We are an island, you know, so we are never far away from any water.' For a while some believed her.

When she told Milt, he'd laughed but had warned her. 'Be careful, honey, we Yanks don't always understand the British sense of humour.'

Once a month, in a strict rota, each wife gave afternoon tea to all the others who inevitably turned out to see how one wife could outdo another. Hildy refused to be drawn into this and when it was her turn, she gave them a traditional English tea with cucumber sandwiches, home-made scones with jam and cream and a Victoria sponge cake.

The women were taken aback by its simplicity.

'This is how we do it back home,' she told them. 'This is exactly what the King and Queen have for their tea.'

For once they were impressed. Anything to do with Royalty or the aristocracy, seemed to impress them greatly, much to Hildy's amusement. They loved the scones, then they asked where they could buy the package mix to make them.

'They don't come from any package,' Hildy said and gave them the recipe for the scones and the Victoria sponge.

She supposed she'd get used to this way of life in time, but she was restless. It didn't take long to clean the house and do the laundry. So she bought a sewing machine and made new curtains and cushions to smarten up her house in an effort to make it her own.

Some of the wives thought this was amusing. 'You can buy all this stuff in the stores in town,' they said, but Hildy just smiled and said, 'I know, but I enjoy making my own and during the war we had to learn to make our own clothes.'

They didn't quite know what to make of this Englishwoman who'd arrived in their midst, but this didn't deter the indomitable Hildy. She just sat and wondered how these American women would have coped in similar situations if they had been bombed as she had been in Southampton and many other cities back home. She came to the conclusion that if their favourite beauty parlour had been decimated there would have been many who would not have survived. She chuckled at the very idea.

Back in Shanklin, Belle's happy existence took a nose dive after a visit to her local butcher. As he was wrapping her purchase, a man came out of the back of the shop and stared at her.

'This is my brother, Kev,' said Tom the butcher. 'He's been demobbed and is going to be working for me. This is Belle, my favourite customer,' he said.

Belle frowned as she looked at the stranger. He looked vaguely familiar, but she couldn't place him. 'Good morning,' she said.

'Good morning to you,' he answered, with a sly grin. 'Nice to meet you.'

Carrying her shopping home, Belle wracked her brains trying to place the man, but she couldn't and carried on with her daily chores.

Later that afternoon when Cora was at the hairdressers, there was a knock on the front door. On opening it, Belle was surprised to see Kev standing there.

'Afternoon, Belle. You don't remember me, do you?'

'No, I'm afraid I don't.'

He leant casually against the door frame. 'I was in the army during the war and stationed in Southampton. I used to drink in the Horse and Groom.'

Her heart seemed to miss a beat. 'Really?'

'Don't play coy with me, love. I was one of your clients. I went to your place a few times. Always came away satisfied.' He leered at her.

She became wary. 'Why are you here, standing on my doorstep?'

'I thought we could come to an arrangement, Belle. I'm sure you don't want it known that the owner of the B&B down the road used to be a prostitute. It would make a great deal of difference to your business and your standing.'

His arrogance made her angry and she wanted to slap him. She'd worked too hard to build her dream and she wasn't going to let this apology for a man spoil that.

'Arrangement? What arrangement?'

'I could call on you, say, twice a week and you'd show me just how grateful you are for my silence.'

She glared at him. 'You bastard! You think you're so very clever. Well, better men than you have tried to put me in a corner. Take your arrangement and shove it! You come bothering me again and you'll be very sorry.' She shut the door in his face. But her hands were trembling.

When Cora arrived home, she could see that her friend was upset. 'Belle, whatever is the matter?'

Belle told her about her visitor. Cora looked shaken. 'Oh my God! What are you going to do about it?'

'Frankly, I don't know, but if he does spill the beans, it could ruin my business. He's going to be a menace, holding such a threat over me. He won't leave it alone if I don't do as he asks.'

'You wouldn't!'

'No, I bloody wouldn't. If I did, heavens knows what else he'd demand. It certainly wouldn't stop at a bit of sex. I know his type. I just need time to think. He won't do anything in a hurry, it wouldn't pay him to do so. He's in a position of power whilst he can threaten me, so he'll not do anything yet.'

Cora realised the significance of the situation. All Belle's hard work and her life savings could be at risk through this creep of a man. How on earth were they going to be able to keep him quiet? How long would he wait and when he realised that Belle wouldn't agree to his demands, how long before her character was so besmirched that she'd be out of business? Then what? Would Belle be forced to sell up and start again elsewhere?

Knowing how devastating this was from her own experience with Simon, Cora cursed beneath her breath. Wasn't it ever possible for a person to leave a dubious past behind? Would it be forever something that would emerge only to ruin a life?

Chapter Twenty-Seven

During the following couple of weeks, Belle still shopped at the butchers as normal. She was determined not to let Tom's brother intimidate her and every time she walked into the shop she would try and be served by Tom – although Kev would sometimes get to her first. He was always polite, asking what he could do for her, but there was often an underlying meaning beneath his words.

Tom became aware very quickly that as soon as the two of them met in the shop, the atmosphere changed. His lovely, chatty and happy Belle became different. She was hostile towards his brother and he couldn't fathom the reason why. His brother was polite and didn't say anything out of line. It was a puzzle.

He questioned his brother one day after he'd served Belle and she'd left the shop.

'What have you done to upset my favourite customer?' he asked.

Kev looked surprised. 'Whatever do you mean?'

'It's obvious to me she doesn't like you. Why is that? Belle gets on with everyone . . . except you. I want to know why.'

Kev laughed. 'You're imagining it,' he said and walked away.

But Tom wasn't convinced and he was determined to get to the bottom of it.

Later that evening after the butcher's shop closed and Tom had showered and changed, he walked along the road until he came to Belle's house and banged on the door.

Belle opened it and was surprised to see her butcher standing there.

'Hello Tom. What are you doing here?'

'May I come in for a moment?'

Somewhat puzzled, she stepped back so he could enter. She took him into the kitchen and pointed to a chair beside a table. 'I'm just going to make a cup of tea, will you join me?'

'Thanks, that'd be lovely.' As she pottered about, he looked around the well-equipped kitchen, clean and tidy, with a delicious aroma coming from the oven.

Belle put the cups and saucers, then the tea pot on a tray and took it over to the table. 'Do you take sugar?' she asked as she poured the tea.

Shaking his head, he said, 'No, I gave it up when it was first rationed.'

Placing his cup before him, she handed over the milk jug. 'Help yourself.'

'Now, Tom, why have you called?'

'I want to know what's going on between you and my brother Kev?'

She was startled. 'Going on? There's nothing going on, whatever do you mean?'

'It's obvious you don't like him and I wondered if he's upset you in any way.'

Belle thought quickly. Tom mustn't suspect that she and his brother knew each other. That wouldn't do at all.

'I just don't like him, if I'm truthful. I think he's smarmy and I don't like him serving me.'

'And that's it?'

'What else could it be? I would prefer you to serve me in future.'

He seemed to relax and sat back in his chair. 'I admit he's not a likeable bloke. We never really got on as boys, but he came to me after he was demobbed with no job and asked for my help.' He shrugged. 'What else could I do?'

'Tell me about your brother,' she asked. 'You seem so different from one another.'

'He's three years younger than me and was spoilt by my mother. He was always in trouble at school. If it wasn't for my mum's intervention, he would have been expelled at one time for bunking off and stealing from the general store. She paid for the goods to keep from having the police involved.'

'Oh my goodness, what a worry for her.'

'As a teenager, he was always in fights. In fact, when he was called up we all breathed a sigh of relief.'

'And now?'

'We still don't get on. I don't trust him, if I'm honest.

249

I make sure I check the till carefully every night, but he's only got to make one wrong move and he's out on his ear.' He sniffed the air. 'My word, Belle, something smells good.'

She smiled at the compliment. 'I'm making a rabbit pie. Cora's gone to the pictures tonight and I'm alone. Would you like to stay for supper? I've got apple crumble for after.'

He beamed at her. 'Would I? I certainly would. After my wife died, I had to be chief cook and bottle washer, but although I'm a passable cook, there's nothing nicer than a home-cooked meal done for you.'

'Then that's settled. I'm glad of the company.'

When Cora arrived home later that evening, she was surprised to find the butcher and Belle sitting in the living room together, drinking coffee with a glass of brandy.

Belle smiled at her. 'Good film?'

'Yes,' she said. 'Humphrey Bogart and Lauren Bacall in *The Big Sleep*. He played Philip Marlowe. It was excellent – any coffee left?'

Tom rose from his chair. 'Best get home,' he said. 'Thanks Belle, I don't know when I've enjoyed a meal so much. Perhaps you'll allow me to take you out to dinner soon to repay your kindness?'

Belle actually blushed. 'Well, that's really not necessary, but yes, I'd love to. Thank you.'

As he walked to the door, he said, 'Don't you worry. Whenever you come to the shop in future, I'll make it my business to serve you.'

When Belle walked back into the room, Cora gave a

sly smile. 'So, what's been going on behind my back, Belle Newman?'

Looking a little embarrassed, Belle said, 'Absolutely nothing. He came to see me about his brother and stayed for a meal.'

'What about his brother?'

Belle told her what had transpired. 'Apparently he's always been a bad lot, which doesn't surprise me. Even his own brother doesn't trust him, but I'm still playing with fire.'

'How long before he makes a move do you think?'

Shaking her head, Belle said, 'I've no idea. But he'll get tired of waiting eventually and then I'll really have a problem.'

Cora sat wracking her brains trying to come up with a solution, but there was no way she could think of an answer and she was really worried that Belle's carefully laid plans for her future were to be ruined by this scumbag.

When Belle next entered the butcher's shop, Kev stepped forward, but Tom put his arm out to stop him. 'I'll look after Belle, thank you,' he said firmly.

Belle saw Kev's mouth harden in a fine line and he glared angrily at her, but she ignored him, bought her meat, handed over her ration book, paid and left the shop.

Kev tackled his brother. 'What was that all about?' he asked. 'I'm perfectly capable of serving *all* your customers.'

'You are, but in future I'll take care of Belle myself.'

'Fancy her, do you?' his brother sneered at him.

'Just get on with your work,' Tom snapped. 'That piece of lamb wants cutting into chops.'

Kev sauntered away, saying, 'Don't get too close to her, Tom. Women can be very devious.'

His brother just glared at him and turned to serve a customer who'd just entered the shop.

As he cut up the meat, Kev fumed. Had Belle said something to his brother? Then he thought she certainly wouldn't have told him the truth. She wouldn't want anyone to know of her past – but something had been said. He smirked to himself; there's more than one way to skin a cat. He would find a way to worry her until she had no choice but to meet his demands and once he had wormed his way into her bed, he would ask for a cut of her takings. Oh yes, he was on to a good thing if he played his cards right. He was a reasonably patient man if the end prize was a worthy one. He thought back to the days of the war when he was a client of the voluptuous Belle. He'd always left her feeling satisfied and looked forward to enjoying her again in the future.

'Haven't you finished yet?' Tom called. 'We haven't got all day!'

Kev stifled a retort. He didn't want to upset his brother because he needed a job and a roof over his head. Maybe later, he could move into Belle's home. That was a thought. He picked up the chops and placed them in the window.

Belle, sitting in the garden alone, was deep in thought. What if eventually Tom's brother did start telling folk about her past. Would it make a deal of difference? It would here among the locals in Shanklin, for a while anyway and she'd always be tagged with the label prostitute. The people who replied to her advertisements wouldn't know, but they might find out from village gossip. But if they were happy and satisfied with her home and food, would it matter?

She was trying to work out the percentages if the worst should happen. No way would she give in to his demands. She'd rather cut her own throat – metaphorically speaking, but how much would it cost her in revenue and self-respect. She knew she was well liked in Shanklin; she had always been gifted in dealing with people. Would it be a seven-day wonder? She gave a rueful smile. Tom would be disappointed to learn the truth, of course. Just like Simon. Pity, she really liked the butcher. Well, she'd just have to wait and see. She walked back into the house. From next week she was booked up and she wanted to sort out her menus.

Chapter Twenty-Eight

Simon Pritchard had been seconded to Southampton headquarters. The Met had sent him there to work in a different station to further his experience before he took his sergeants' exam. He was pleased with the move. Secretly he hoped to take the opportunity to meet up again with Cora. He'd deeply regretted the way that they had parted and he knew in his heart he still had strong feelings for her. After making enquiries, he had discovered she was in Shanklin, working with her friend Belle and on the first Sunday he was free, he took the ferry to the Isle of Wight.

Cora was sitting in the garden, drinking a cup of tea after cleaning the rooms and making the beds. Belle had told her to take a break whilst she did some paperwork before they started to prep the evening meal.

She lay back, eyes closed, breathing in the sea air, feeling the warmth of the sun on her face when she heard footsteps. Thinking it was Belle, she opened her eyes and saw Simon approaching. She felt the blood drain from her body with the shock.

'Hello Cora.' He stood in front of her smiling. 'What a lovely place you two have here. How are you?'

'Simon!' For a moment that's all she could say. Then . . . 'I'm fine, how are you? What are you doing here?'

He gestured towards a chair. 'May I join you?'

She nodded. 'Yes, of course.'

It was hot in the sun and he loosened his tie. 'I've been sent to work in Southampton for three months and I heard you and Belle were here, so I thought I'd come and see how you were getting on. I must say you look very well.'

'Thank you. Yes, we've been open for business since Easter.' She just couldn't seem to find the words to chat normally and everything she said sounded stilted. It was a relief to see Belle walking towards them carrying a tray of coffee. She put the tray down on a table and looked at Cora.

'Well, what a surprise,' she said beaming at her friend. 'I opened the door and this young man told me who he was and that he'd come to see you.' Her eyes twinkled mischievously.

Simon spoke up. 'I'm in Southampton for three months and it would have been a pity not to have looked for Cora. Nice place you have here, Belle.'

'Thank you. I fell in love with it when I was looking for somewhere to open a B&B. I knew this was the house and I was fortunate that it was on the market. Will you stay and have some lunch with us?'

Cora looked askance at her friend, but Belle ignored her.

'After all, we can't have you coming all this way without feeding you.'

Simon was delighted. 'How very kind. Thank you.'

'You stay here and talk to your friend,' she told Cora. 'Lunch will be in an hour, I'll give you a call.' With that, she left them alone.

Taking out a cigarette case, Simon held it out to Cora. She took one and he lit it for her. 'I've thought about you often you know,' he said quietly. 'I hated the way we parted.'

She didn't know what to say. Looking at him, he was as she remembered, but there was something different about him that she couldn't define.

He continued. 'I was a complete fool, I know that now and I've regretted it ever since.' He gazed at her, waiting for a response.

Cora was lost for words. She had put Simon out of her mind with her past, but now seeing him again, she was utterly confused.

'I don't know what to say to you, Simon. You coming here has taken me completely by surprise.'

'I'm hoping that you can forgive me for being so insensitive. I really didn't mean to hurt you, honestly.'

She didn't want to be reminded. 'Let's leave that behind, I don't want to talk about it.' She needed to get away from here and this intimate chat. It was too painful.

'Let's walk down to the beach, we have the time before lunch. Leave your jacket here and take off your tie, it's far too hot to wear it today.'

Belle watched them walk down the path from her kitchen window and smiled. Maybe, just maybe, things were looking up for Cora. She hoped so. She'd liked Simon immediately, but time would tell. Knowing Cora as she did, trying to push her would have the reverse effect. She would make her mind up in her own time.

The two of them walked along the beach and Cora took off her shoes and, walking into the water, paddled. She looked back at Simon.

'Take your shoes off and come in – the water's lovely.'

He did so, tucking up his trouser bottoms and joining her. 'This reminds me of my childhood when my parents would take me to the beach. We'd sit and have a picnic and, when I was really small, I would paddle in the sea with my mother.'

'And when you were older?'

'My dad taught me to swim. They were happy days,' then he suddenly remembered that Cora had lost her parents. 'Oh, I'm sorry, that was insensitive of me.'

'No, it isn't,' she assured him. 'I have my happy childhood memories too. I had sixteen years of things I remember and they are very precious. The rest . . . well, that we'll never know. But there are so many people who lost loved ones during the war. You eventually learn to live with it because there is no alternative. At least I had a happy childhood to remember.'

Smiling softly at her, he said, 'You are an amazing woman, you know. But I only realised that far too late.'

She heard the regret and the affection in his voice, but she wasn't ready to recall their happy times together, not yet.

'We'd best get back to the house,' she said hurriedly. 'Belle will have the lunch ready.'

They put on their shoes and left the beach.

* * *

'We went paddling, Belle,' said Cora as they walked into the kitchen. 'It was lovely, the sea was a bit cold but very refreshing.'

'When it warms up, we should go for a swim,' Belle suggested. 'Mind you, I'd have to buy a costume, I don't remember when last I wore one.'

'Me neither,' agreed Cora.

The lunch went well, with the three of them chatting away. Simon telling them about his work and impending exam. Belle gave him a tour of the house, which he really liked.

'You should do well, Belle,' he said. 'This is such a pretty village, the house is lovely and I can vouch for the food. Give me some of your business cards and I'll hand them round at the station.'

She beamed at him. 'Thank you, Simon, that's really good of you.'

They spent part of the afternoon in the garden until Belle said she had to prepare the evening meal. Cora offered to help, but Belle refused.

'I did most of it before lunch,' she said. 'Why don't you walk Simon to the ferry, by the time you come back I'll be ready for your help.'

It was said in such a way that Cora knew not to argue, so Simon thanked Belle for her hospitality and they left.

Just before he boarded the ferry, he caught hold of Cora's hand.

'I can't tell you how good it is to see you after so long and looking so well. May I come and see you again soon?'

As she looked at the smiling face that had meant so much to her, Cora relented. 'Yes, that would be nice.'

There was a look of relief in his eyes. 'Thank you, I'll call you.' He leant forward and kissed her cheek. 'Take care,' he said and walked up the gangway.

When she got back to the house, there was no time to chat, it was time to get the dinner cooked as their guests would soon return. It wasn't until dinner had been served and cleared that they sat down before doing the washing-up.

'Well?' asked Belle.

'Well what?' Cora answered.

'Oh for God's sake! How was it seeing Simon again and is he coming back? And by the way – I think he's lovely!'

Cora had to laugh at her friend's direct approach. Belle never did mince her words.

'Yes, it was good to see him – after I got over the shock. For one moment when I opened my eyes and saw him, I really thought I was going to faint.'

'How do you feel about him now?'

'To be honest, Belle, I don't know. I really loved that man and I guess I still do, deep down. But I was so hurt when we broke up. However, I have to say, he's softened a lot. Before, everything was either black or white in his eyes, but now . . . he seems more sensitive, which is strange really.'

'I don't think it's strange at all!' Belle exclaimed. 'You were hurt, but so was he – you seem to forget that and I can tell you that man is still in love with you. To me, it was as clear as day.'

'Well, I'm not rushing into anything. He asked to come again and I said yes. We'll see what transpires.'

Simon sat out on the deck of the ferry in the evening sun, feeling happy and relieved. When he arrived in Shanklin, he wasn't at all sure if Cora would even see him and then when Belle let him in the house and told him to find Cora in the garden he didn't know if she'd tell him to leave. He could see how shocked she was to see him and he held his breath for a moment until she spoke. Thankfully the afternoon went well and he was going to see her again.

He leant back in his seat and closed his eyes, remembering the happy days when they were together. The places they visited, the shows they saw and the times they slept together and were intimate. He longed for that relationship again. Her past didn't matter any more. He loved her and wanted to be with her, care for her . . . love her. Although he was still on shaky ground and he knew it. But she had said he could visit again. He could hardly wait, but he had the sense to know he'd have to step carefully and slowly.

Chapter Twenty-Nine

Hildy climbed off the bed where the army doctor had examined her, got dressed, and sat facing him as he smiled at her.

'Congratulations, Mrs Miller, you are about ten weeks pregnant by my calculations. When did you last have a period?'

She could hardly cope with the excitement she felt and told him the date.

'That's pretty conclusive. Congratulations! Have you told your husband your news?'

'No, I wasn't sure. You know, what with all the excitement of coming to the States, a new life, new husband, it could have been any of those things, but when I missed my second period, then I began to hope.'

'Well, now you can tell Sergeant Miller he's going to be a father.' He handed her a pile of leaflets and a small handbook. 'Here, take these home and read them; it'll give you lots of information about pregnancy. Come back and see me in a month, unless you're worried about anything.'

As she walked out of the clinic, Hildy was so happy she wanted to shout out her news. But there wasn't anyone around and she didn't know any of the wives well enough to want to share her news before she told her husband. It would have been lovely if she and her mother had been closer, but Olive would be the last person to be pleased for her and that was sad . . . but not for long. Milt was on leave from tonight and they'd planned to go to the Appalachian Mountains, where they'd hired a log cabin to spend a week up there, relaxing, walking, fishing and spending time together away from the base and the army. It was tonight when they'd settled in the cabin that she would tell him her news, she decided, and went back to their house to finish packing.

Later as she and Milt drove out of the base, Hildy let out a sigh of relief. Army life was all consuming and she could never get away from it with living there. Had they lived elsewhere, it would have felt so different. It was the only thing that Hildy regretted about her move.

'You alright, honey?' asked Milt, patting her knee.

'Yes, I'm fine. Oh Milt it's so good to get away, leave the army behind. To feel like a normal married couple.'

Laughing, he said, 'But we are a normal married couple!'

'Yes, I know, but you know what I mean, without the army intruding. Even having our own place to live, it's on the base, you open the front door and all you see are uniforms and jeeps. If we lived outside then it wouldn't feel that way.' Then she felt guilty, after all she married Milt knowing he was a military man.

'I'm not complaining, I guess I've not got used to it yet.'

'Never mind, darling, we have a week to put that life on hold. You'll love it in the mountains. I'll teach you how to fish. Eating freshly caught fish tastes so different you wouldn't believe.'

Hildy sat back enjoying the passing scenery, secretly hugging herself, knowing she had such news to tell this lovely man whom she loved even more with each passing day. He would be a great father. Strict if they had a son, teaching him to be a man, and kind and gentle if they had a daughter – as he was with her.

They eventually drove up through tall pine trees into the mountains and Hildy marvelled at the view. It was like being in another world, one she'd never seen before and one that took her breath away as she became aware of the force of nature.

Milt drew up in front of a log cabin, like those Hildy had seen in American movies, hardly able to believe she was actually there and, as they entered the huge sitting room, she was delighted to see the huge open fire, comfortable settees with colourful throws, a big basket of logs and another with fir cones, ready to put on the fire if they needed it.

The bedroom had a large double bed already made up with a patchwork quilt on the top of it. There was a big wardrobe and chest of drawers and bedside light either side of the bed atop of two small bedside tables.

'Oh Milt! This is wonderful. Just like all the old cowboy movies I've seen with the homesteaders living in the woods.' She looked at him and grinned broadly. 'Just tell me there aren't any marauding Indians around.'

He laughed at her delight. 'No, Hildy. Only bears.'

She looked horrified. 'Are you kidding?'

'No, I'm not. They are hereabout so we shouldn't leave any food outside, but don't worry; we could be here all week and not see one.'

They walked through to the kitchen which was well stocked with china, cutlery and cooking utensils. Milt put down a cardboard carton of food he'd bought at the army stores and Hildy started to put it away in the fridge in the corner. Then while Milt brought in the suitcase, she filled the kettle and made some coffee.

They sat outside in the fading light drinking the coffee and admiring the scene before them. There were other cabins in the area, he told her, but they were not in sight, which made the privacy for Hildy extra special. On the base the houses were all so close together, at times, Hildy felt everyone was living with her, part of her household.

As they sat together, Hildy asked, 'Would it be possible to rent or buy a place of our own outside the base?'

He looked surprised. 'I guess so, why do you ask?'

'It's just that I'd like to bring up our children in a house with a garden, little private shops, a civilian life. Don't get me wrong, Milt, I know that the army is your life and, although you did at one time think of leaving, it's what you were born to do and you do it so well. You wouldn't be happy away from it.'

He leant back in the chair. 'You're right, honey, it's what I do best, but if you want to move, we can certainly think about it when we have a baby.'

'Well, darling, I'm afraid we'll have to start thinking about it right now. We don't have time to waste.'

He nearly choked his coffee.

'Hildy, are you saying you're pregnant?'

'Yes, you are going to be a father sometime in December!'

He leant forward, took her in his arms and kissed her. 'Hildy, that's marvellous!' He kissed her again. 'Are you alright? Did the doctor say everything was fine?'

Chuckling, she assured him she was. 'Pregnancy isn't an illness, Milt. It's quite normal, you know.'

He just looked at her. 'You have made me the happiest man alive,' he said. 'Come on inside, it gets chilly in the mountains at night. I'll light the fire and we'll cook a meal, then we can sit and decide on a name for our child.'

'For heaven's sake, darling, there's plenty of time.'

'I know, but just indulge me here. We can both make suggestions. After all, we may have quite different ideas.' He was like a child who'd been given a new toy she thought and was amused by it.

After consuming steak and a salad, they settled by the fire, nestling close and started discussing names. At the end of the evening they still couldn't agree and decided to do the sensible thing and buy a book of names and try again.

As they lay in bed, Milt placed his hand gently on her stomach. 'If it's a boy or a girl, I promise you, I'll take care of it and you for the rest of my life. You want to move out of the base, then that's what we'll do.'

Hildy didn't know she could be this happy as Milt made love to her, whispering how they would spend the rest of their lives together with the family they planned. The house he would buy for them, the holidays they would take, how they would bring up their children and eventually in the twilight of their years, how they would sit on their porch in the evening with their grandchildren and reminisce.

The following morning after taking a shower and eating a hearty breakfast, Milt drove her to a nearby lake and tried to teach her how to cast a fishing line. It took a while, but eventually she managed and was delighted.

They put their rods in special holders and sat drinking coffee from a flask until Hildy saw her line jerk. 'Oh my God! I've caught a fish!' She jumped to her feet. 'What do I do? Help me, Milt.'

He stood behind her showing her how to let the fish run and to suddenly tighten the line until they pulled the fish to the shore and Milt caught it in a net.

'Well done, darling! I'll make a hunter out of you yet.'

He, too, soon had a bite and by the afternoon they had a nice catch to take home. On the way, Milt slowly stopped the car.

'Look,' he said, 'over there.'

Hildy looked in the direction he was pointing and to her dismay and eventual joy, she saw a brown bear and two cubs, walking among the trees. They sat and watched, Hildy fascinated by the sight. This was something to write and tell the girls about.

'The most dangerous thing for anyone who comes across a bear and her young is to get between them, you remember that.'

She looked at him in surprise. 'Milt Miller, I will never ever be in that situation – that I can promise you. I make sure I look out of the cabin window every time you or I go outside. If I saw a bear, you wouldn't see me for dust!'

He laughed. 'I guess we have some time to go before you become at home in the mountains.'

'Not true! I feel perfectly at home . . . in the car or in the cabin.'

Their week in the Appalachians was idyllic and when it was time to pack up and go home Hildy let out a deep sigh of regret. It had been so good to have Milt to herself twenty-four hours a day, but duty called. However, now she had something to plan for, but when she was unpacked the first thing she would do was write to Belle and Cora. They were the closest thing she had to a family and she could hardly wait to share her news.

What a shame they weren't here with her. They would have had such a good time together. Hildy started to chuckle. She couldn't imagine Belle living in the woods for one moment, she loved being surrounded by people. The solitude of the mountains would drive her crazy. Now Cora would probably settle better, she was so very resilient.

With those thoughts, she sat down to write to them.

Chapter Thirty

Both Cora and Belle were delighted to receive a long letter from Hildy and when they read she was going to have a baby, they were thrilled for her.

'How bloody marvellous!' Belle said. 'I did hear in the factory she had a difficult time with her mother and they didn't part friends. Shame. But she'll be a superb mother.'

They read on about her trip to the mountains and seeing a bear and her cubs.

'It's a different world out there,' Cora remarked as she poured a cup of tea. 'Think back to our earlier days when we all worked together, all our lives have changed and who would have thought it. Hildy married, you and I here . . . and you too, with a man who's interested in you.'

'What are you talking about?'

'Tom the butcher, of course. He fancied you from the moment you walked into his shop. I reckon you could be on to a good thing there.'

'Now you're being ridiculous!' Belle retorted, but her cheeks flushed as she spoke.

Cora noticed but decided not to tease her friend further. Tom seemed a decent bloke and Belle could do worse.

It was the next evening that Tom and Belle had a date for dinner. He'd booked a table at a restaurant in Cowes which had been recommended to him by a customer, and, as he showered and changed, he hoped that Belle would approve. He straightened his tie, put on his jacket and walked downstairs.

Kev was sitting in an armchair, reading the evening paper and he looked up as Tom walked into the room.

'Going somewhere special?' he asked.

Tom put his keys in his pocket, walked to the door and said, 'Yes, I'm taking Belle Newman out to dinner so don't lock up before I get back.'

Kev's eyes narrowed as he watched his brother leave. The last thing he needed was for Tom to get cosy with that woman. He had plans of his own for her. Perhaps it was time to put a bit of pressure on her. Stop her getting cocky.

Completely unaware of the situation between his brother and Belle, Tom called at the house to collect her and Cora invited him in to wait.

'She won't be long,' she told him and they chatted away until Belle came downstairs.

Tom got to his feet. 'Belle, how lovely you look.'

'Well, thank you. You scrub up pretty well yourself!'

'Sorry, Belle, that I have to take you out in my butcher's

van in your finery, but you understand with petrol rationing and all . . .'

'Don't be silly!' was all she said.

Cora looked at the pair of them and hid a smile. 'Now remember, Belle, home no later than eleven o'clock or I'll lock the door on you.'

Belle grinned broadly at her. 'Yes, mother! Let's go, Tom, before she gets completely carried away.'

Cora watched through the net curtains and saw Tom hold the door to the passenger seat open for his companion, him fussing, making sure she was comfortable. What a nice man and she hoped that something would come of this. She deserved a happy future just as much as their friend Hildy. She crossed her fingers as she watched them drive away.

The evening in Cowes went well. The restaurant was comfortable, the food was good and Tom and Belle were at ease with each other. He told her how he'd worked with his father and taken over the business when he retired and how consequently, it was left to him in his father's will.

'I think the old man would have been proud of me to see how well we're doing,' Tom said.

'How did your brother take the news that you inherited the business?' Belle asked.

'He wasn't around much and he had no time for our father. In fact, the only times he came to see him was to ask for money.' Tom's eyes flashed angrily.

'Yet you took him in when he was demobbed.'

'I thought I'd give him one last chance. He could be a fine butcher if he wanted to be, but he just does as much as he has to, to keep his job, if I'm honest. We have never had anything in common even as youngsters.'

Belle didn't question him further.

After they ate, they decided to take a stroll along the front. The evening was reasonably warm and there were other people walking too. Tom took her hand, which to Belle felt quite natural. They sat on a bench overlooking the sea, talking about the coming Cowes Week in August which would find the town crammed full of yachtsmen and the crowds who came to watch the races.

Belle confessed that she'd never been on the island at that time and Tom suggested they come together. 'It's quite a sight, Belle, you must see it at least once. The place is buzzing. It's quite a festival.'

As they walked back to the car, Tom said, 'I can't tell you how pleased I am that you came to Shanklin, Belle. You've certainly made my life more cheerful. I so look forward to you coming into the shop, but it would be nice to continue meeting away from business. What do you say?'

She smiled at him and said, 'I would love that, Tom. It's nice to get away from work and spend time in good company.'

'My sentiments exactly!' he said.

When they arrived back at Belle's house, Tom walked round to her side of the van and helped her out. He looked at his watch.

'Five minutes to eleven. You just made it in time!' They both laughed. Tom drew Belle into his arms and kissed her gently. 'Thank you for a delightful evening. It's been a long time since I took a beautiful woman out to dinner.'

'It was quite a change for me too,' she replied, 'and I look forward to the next time.' She reached up and touched his face. 'You are a good man,' she said as she leant forward and kissed his cheek.

Cora was sitting in the kitchen drinking a cup of cocoa, when Belle walked in.

'No need to ask if you had a good time; you have a glow about you,' she said.

Belle dismissed her remark. 'It was the brandy and the sea air, but we did have a nice time. Everything alright here?'

'Yes, no problems. All our residents are in bed. I've laid up the tables for breakfast. Do you want anything to drink?'

'No thanks, love. I'm off to bed.'

'I'll come up with you then.' Cora put out the lights and they left the kitchen.

It was late on the following Saturday when Belle was tidying up a few papers she'd been working on and Cora had gone to bed when the front doorbell rang. She looked at her watch. Ten-thirty, who would possibly be calling this late? Perhaps it was someone looking for a room. Well, she was fully booked so they'd be unlucky. She opened the door.

Kev stood there, an alcoholic grin on his face. He pushed past her and walked into the kitchen.

She followed him. 'How dare you come charging into my house uninvited? Get out!'

He leant against the kitchen sink and sneered at her.

'Now, Belle, that's no way to greet an old friend,' he said, slurring his words. 'I've come to discuss our arrangement.'

She was livid. 'First of all, you are no old friend and we do not have an arrangement!'

The smile faded and he glared at her. 'Not yet we don't, but if you know what's good for you, you'd better change your mind. After all, my sanctimonious brother would be shocked to know he dined with one of the most popular prostitutes that ever walked the streets of Southampton.'

'You bastard! There is no way I'd let you into my life and certainly never into my bed. You'd better get that fact through your thick head.'

His tone was menacing as he stared at her. 'You are the one who's thick, my dear, if you think I'm going away. I'm holding a great hand of cards, remember that. I can ruin you, now that alone is worth a good night's sex.' He lunged forward and grabbed her, forcing his mouth on hers, his hand on her breast.

She pushed him away with such force he nearly fell and grabbed at the sink as Belle picked up a large kitchen knife and held it at his throat.

Her eyes glittered with rage as she held the knife. 'Don't ever think I wouldn't have the guts to use this if pushed. All I would have to say was that you attacked me and in my own defence I picked up the first thing that came to hand.' She pushed just a little harder and the point of the knife punctured his skin and a drop of blood oozed forth.

'You bloody mad woman, put that down before you do something you'll be sorry for.' But she saw the fear in his eyes as he spoke.

'Your brother would be furious if he knew you came in

here and tried to rape me,' she said. 'You'd be out of a job then. No money, no home.'

'Rape you? I didn't bloody rape you!'

'Who's to know? It would be your word against mine. After all, I may have been on the game but at least I was earning a living, whereas you've been a waster all your life. Your brother would testify to that.' She stepped away from him, but still pointed the knife at him.

Kev put his hand to his throat and saw the blood. 'You fucking bitch! You cut me!'

'Just be careful I don't bloody castrate you if you come bothering me again. Now get out!' She jabbed the knife towards him as she spoke.

Cursing beneath his breath, he staggered to the door and out into the night.

Belle closed the front door and leant against it. She was trembling now that she was alone. The terrible thing, she admitted to herself, was the fact that she was sorely tempted to use the weapon she'd been holding. That scared her more than the devious Kev.

She walked back to the kitchen and threw the knife into the sink. Then she poured herself a stiff gin and tonic, lit a cigarette, took a large swig of the drink and sat down. *Bloody hell*, she thought, *that was very dicey*. The outcome could have been disastrous. Kev could have tried to rape her and then she might have been tempted to . . . it didn't bear thinking about. But had she scared him enough? As long as he was around, he was a menace. She'd have to do something about it – and soon.

* * *

Kev staggered along the road, cursing. That bitch Belle had stabbed him. 'Fucking lunatic!' He had been taken by surprise at her reaction and was mad at himself for being outfoxed. Well now she'd really pissed him off and he would make her pay if it was the last thing he did. She may well have had the upper hand tonight, but she had no idea who she was messing with.

He let himself in the side door of the shop and climbed the stairs to his bedroom. He stripped off his shirt and vest, went to the bathroom and swilled his face with cold water. Then putting his mouth under the running tap, drank, quenching his alcoholic-induced thirst – all the time planning his revenge.

Chapter Thirty-One

The answer to her predicament came from an unexpected source when Simon came to call a couple of days later. He'd been sent over to the island on police matters and when it was finished he'd called to see Cora, but she was at the hairdressers. Belle invited him in and made him a sandwich and a cup of coffee.

'You'll have the neighbours talking after seeing you here in uniform,' she teased. 'They'll think I've been up to no good.'

'And have you?' he asked with a grin.

Belle frowned and hesitated as she thought about the night that Kev had called and therefore took some time to answer. 'No, of course not.'

He studied her for a moment then asked, 'What's bothering you, Belle?' She began to deny it, but he intervened. 'Belle, I've been interviewing folk for years, I know when they are not being truthful or have something to hide. Now I'm your friend, what's worrying you? Perhaps I can help.'

She then told him the whole story even about pricking Kev's throat with a knife, enough to make it bleed. She looked at him, eyes wide with horror. 'I was *so* tempted, Simon!'

'But you didn't do it. However, we can't have this man threatening you. I could have him up for blackmail and intimidation at least. How about I go and pay him a visit? Perhaps seeing me in uniform may be enough to frighten him of the consequences.'

'Do you think so?'

'We could give it a try.'

'One other thing, Simon. I didn't tell Cora any of this as I didn't want to worry her.'

He looked at his watch. 'Don't worry about that, this will be between us. Look I have to go, give Cora my love and I'll be in touch with her this evening. Now what does this man look like and where is the butcher's shop?'

Simon walked along the parade of shops and saw Harrison and Son above the frontage of what was obviously a butcher's shop and entered. There were two men behind the counter and Simon recognised the man he was seeking from Belle's description, but it was Tom who stepped forward.

'Afternoon Constable, what can I do for you?'

'Afternoon, I'd like to have a word with your brother if you don't mind . . . in private.'

Tom looked surprised – but not nearly as much as Kev.

'Yes, of course,' said Tom. He looked at his brother with a frown but only said, 'Take the constable through to the back room.'

Simon followed Kev into a room where big fridges were housed with a large chopping block standing in the middle and a sink on one side. It was here that Kev stood.

He glared at Simon. 'What do you want to see me for?' he demanded.

'Intimidation and blackmail, for openers,' Simon said firmly.

'What? What the bloody hell are you talking about?'

'I'm talking about your visit to Miss Belle Newman last Saturday night.'

'What's that bitch been saying?' Kev's face flushed with anger.

'I'm told you were drunk and forced your way into her house, then threatened and molested her.'

'What a bloody pack of lies! Yes, I called on her, we knew each other during the war. I was just renewing our acquaintance,' he blustered.

'Don't lie, Harrison. I know why you went there. You threatened to tell everyone about her past unless she did you favours, like sleeping with you as a price for your silence, then you tried to force yourself on her.'

'Your Belle Newman is no bloody angel, did she tell you that too?'

'She didn't need to, I know of her past history and if I have to, I'll be looking into yours before I arrest you. Today you get off with a warning, but if you trouble Miss Newman again I'll have you. Understand?'

'Did she tell you she knifed me?'

'Where? Show me.'

Kev pointed to his throat. 'Here!'

278

Simon examined his neck closely. 'Funny, I can't see a thing. I'll be keeping tabs on you, so make sure you keep out of trouble!' He turned and went into the shop.

'Thank you,' he said to Tom with a nod, then he walked out.

As Kev was about to go back to the shop, Tom grabbed him by his shirt front and pushed him back into the room. 'You bastard! I heard what you did. Now you can go and pack your bags. I don't want to ever see you again.'

With a derisive laugh, Kev glared at his brother. 'You would put her before me – your own flesh and blood – that whore? Because that's how we met in the war. Your special lady was a common prostitute!'

Tom hit him with a clenched fist and sent him flying backwards onto the floor.

'Whatever she was, she's a better human being than you'll ever be. Now pack your bags and get out. I'll give you a week's wages and a week's holiday pay, but don't ever come near me again. Clear?'

'Crystal!' snapped his brother as he removed his white overall and threw it on the floor.

Tom walked back into the shop, fuming, but a customer walked in and his expression changed. Smiling, he said, 'Good afternoon and what can I get you?'

Upstairs, Kev was thrusting his clothes into a suitcase, muttering to himself. 'You bitch! You've cost me my job and my home, you bloody well are going to pay, Belle Newman, and that constable can go take a running jump!'

He put on his jacket, walked downstairs and marched into the shop. 'I've come for my money!'

Tom handed over a small pay packet and just glared at him.

'You're making a big mistake,' he said glaring back. 'She'll take you down too if you keep seeing her.'

'Get out!' Tom said quietly.

'You'll see that I'm right,' Kev said as he walked out into the street.

That evening after the close of business, Tom went upstairs and poured himself a glass of beer, then he sat and in his mind, relived the revelations of the afternoon. He was pleased to be rid of his brother, he'd never felt at ease with him around, but the reasons behind his going were still a shock. Firstly the fact that Kev had called on Belle and attacked her, but secondly at discovering Belle's background. That had really taken him by surprise – but strangely, it didn't seem to matter. Everyone had a past of some kind. The Belle he knew was an entirely different woman, one that he really liked. Hard-working, charming, funny. She'd slaved so hard getting her place together for her business and he admired her work ethic, having worked hard himself . . . unlike his no good brother. No, that waster wasn't going to spoil his friendship with her in any way.

The same evening the telephone rang and Belle answered: it was Simon.

'Belle, before I speak to Cora I want you to know I

called on that man and read him the Riot Act. Hopefully you won't be troubled any further, but listen, I've met his type many times. Just be vigilant. Make sure you lock your doors and windows at night . . . just a word of warning. You can't be too careful.'

'Thanks, Simon, I'm really grateful. Just a minute, I'll call Cora.'

Kev booked himself into a B&B on the outskirts of Shanklin, intent on making Belle pay for his dismissal from his job and home. He went to a nearby pub and ordered a sandwich and a pint of beer, which he took outside and sat in the garden of the pub, scheming.

He was wasting his time spreading rumours about her, he needed something instantaneous. Her business was the thing that was most important to her, it was the way she earned her living – the very thing she'd taken from him. Well, he'd now do the same to her, he decided. An eye for an eye, as the Bible said. He drank up and made his way to a tobacconist where he bought several bottles of lighter fluid.

It was getting late and Belle was tired. Her guests had left that morning and Cora had helped her strip the beds, clean the rooms and remake them for their next clients who arrived two days hence, which gave them a short break. Cora had then taken a late ferry to Southampton to meet Simon and stay overnight.

After checking the rooms, locking the doors and windows, Belle sat in the kitchen having a cup of tea and a cigarette. She was looking at her ledger, assessing her takings and smiled with satisfaction. Even halfway through her first season, she was making money. All her efforts had paid off. The money she'd earned in her earlier profession had bought her her dream. She was a success. Every man who'd paid for her services had paid for the house she loved and she didn't regret any of it.

Washing up her cup and saucer, she checked that the back door was locked, turned out the lights and went upstairs, thankful that tomorrow she could spend an extra hour in bed if she had a mind to.

Across the road, Kev sat, hidden from sight. He waited until the house was in darkness, gave Belle time to fall asleep, then he crept over the road, clutching a small bag in his hand. He smiled as he withdrew an old cloth from the bag and soaked it in petrol, and then he did the same with two more. Walking round the back of the house, he broke a small window, lit the cloth and threw it inside, followed by another. He watched as they erupted into flames, and then he did the same at the front door, pushing the burning rag through the letter box. He watched for a while, making sure that the fire he'd planned had worked, then he left.

Belle was restless. She'd dozed off for a while, but something woke her. She listened, but all was quiet. She turned over but couldn't get comfortable. In the end she sat up, plumped her pillows and was about to lay down, when she sniffed the air. What the hell was that smell? It was as if something was burning. She got up and opened her bedroom door and saw the smoke. Fortunately the floor in the hallway by the front door was all flags of stone but upon them, near the door, something that looked like a heap of cloth was burning. She opened the front door, picked up an umbrella from the stand and flicked it outside, then she saw flames through the open kitchen door. She rushed to the phone and called the fire brigade then made her way to the kitchen. Her cupboards were burning. She filled a washing-up basin with water and hurled it over the flames, but she knew it was too far gone for her to cope so she fled into the hall, closing the door behind her as she heard the sound of the fire engine approaching.

The men hustled her outside whilst they tackled the fire in the kitchen. Nearby neighbours came out to see what was going on and comforted her.

'How did it start?' asked one.

'I've no idea,' Belle told them, but in her heart she knew.

The police car drew up and two constables stepped out and walked over to her. They took down her details and asked her what happened. They searched for the piece of rag she had tossed out and realised that the fire was deliberate.

'Have you any idea who would have done such a thing, Miss Newman?' asked one.

'Oh yes, I have a very good idea.'

A few hours later, it was deemed safe for Belle to enter the house. The police accompanied her into the kitchen. The sad sight that greeted her brought tears to Belle's eyes. As far as she could see, the cooker was intact, most of her crockery and cutlery which had been housed at the other end of the room were fine, but the cupboards by the back door were burnt as well as the door. The walls were black and the smell of smoke was thick. She would have to cancel her bookings until it was fixed. She thanked the firemen profusely.

'Just doing our job, miss. We're just pleased that you woke when you did, or the consequences could have been so much worse.'

She took the police into the front room, leaving the front door open to let out the smell of smoke and she said, 'No one is going to walk in unannounced with a police car outside!'

She gave them a statement and told them everything she knew about Kev Harrison. How she first met him, how he'd threatened her. She mentioned that Simon Pritchard had called on him to warn him off, but she was convinced that Kev was behind all of this.

They said they'd go to the butcher's shop and question him. They advised her to try and get some sleep and that they'd be in touch.

She showed them out and went back to the kitchen, trying to estimate the damage now she'd calmed down. The cupboards would have to be replaced and the back door which was badly scorched. The whole kitchen would have to be painted as well as the hallway where the walls were black from the smoke. She would be out of business for at least a couple of weeks, she estimated – and that was only if she could get everything done quickly.

'You bastard, Harrison!' she uttered as her anger rose deep inside her. Apart from the damage he'd caused, she'd had to give the police details of her past, so now it was no longer a secret. Would it come out? Of course it would, if they could prove he did it and the case went to court. It would be in the papers and she was sure the headlines wouldn't be pretty.

While Belle was trying to sort out her troubles, Tom had opened the door of his flat in answer to the loud knocking. He was surprised to see two policemen on the doorstep and even more so when they asked to see Kev.

'He no longer lives here, I fired him yesterday. Why are you looking for him?' When the police told him, he said, 'You'd better come in.' He then told them about Simon's visit and what he'd overheard which was the reason he'd told his brother to leave.

'Do you know where he is now?'

'I've no idea, but if the fire was only hours ago, he must still be on the island.'

'Have you got a picture of your brother?'

Tom found one and gave it to them. 'He's been in trouble all his life,' he told them.

'Don't worry, Mr Harrison, we'll soon find him and then we can take him in for questioning.'

'Is Miss Newman okay?' he asked anxiously.

'Well, she's upset as you can imagine, but not physically hurt, she's more annoyed she'll lose business until she gets her place fixed up. Understandable. Shame, she seems a nice woman.'

'Yes, she is,' Tom agreed.

When he was alone, Tom fumed. He had no doubt who was behind the fire. Kev had been spiteful as a child when he couldn't get his own way. This was typical of him, but to have gone to such lengths . . . Belle could have been killed and if she'd had visitors, they too . . . the police didn't mention anyone else was in the house, perhaps she was on her own. He dressed quickly, went along the road to Belle's and knocked on the door.

Belle, in her dressing gown, opened it and when she saw Tom standing there, she burst into tears. He stepped forward and took her into his arms, then he took her into the living room and made sure she was unhurt.

'I'll have to find people to redo my kitchen, Tom. I can't open until it's all put right.'

'Now you take yourself off to bed, love. I'll sort all that out. I'll be round first thing in the morning. No, you are not to worry, you hear?' He managed eventually to persuade her to go to bed and walked home fuming about his brother.

At seven-thirty the next morning, Belle opened her door to find Tom standing there. When she saw him, her eyes filled with tears and she couldn't speak.

Tom stepped inside and took her into his arms. 'There, love, let it all out. You've had one hell of a shock.' He patted her back, talking softly to her trying to comfort her. When she'd stopped crying, he said, 'Right, show me the damage.'

He saw at once what needed doing. 'Fine! I'll have some men come in this morning to take down the cupboards and paint the walls. Tell me the colour you want and we'll do that and the hallway.'

She was overwhelmed at his kindness and tried to thank him.

He took her hands in his. 'We both know who was behind this and so you must let me help you. I insist. Have you any visitors now?'

'Fortunately not, but I've cancelled the next lot who should have come tomorrow. I've managed to book them in elsewhere.'

'So how long before the next lot come?'

'Ten days, but I'll have to get in touch with them too.'

'No, you won't. I'll make sure everything is done in time for them. Come on, Belle, where's your fighting spirit?'

Despite everything she had to laugh. 'Right now, I really don't know.'

'That doesn't sound like the woman I know and admire.' He drew her into his arms. 'Come on, my bloody brother isn't going to spoil your business, not if I've anything to do with it.'

She looked up at the man who was holding her tight. She liked and admired him too, but he wouldn't feel the same if he really knew her and she felt she owed him the truth.

'There are things about me you don't know, Tom,' she began, but he interrupted her.

'I know all about your past, Belle, I overheard the conversation between Kev and the policeman. I know he was blackmailing you and why and, as far as I'm concerned, that was then and this is now.'

287

She didn't know what to say for a moment. 'You are an extraordinary man, Tom Harrison.'

'As are you an extraordinary woman, Belle Newman.' Then with a chuckle he said, 'Can I use your phone? I want to get a workforce in here today.'

Chapter Thirty-Two

Whilst Belle was coping with her drama, Hildy was dreaming of the time she and Milt would leave the base and set up home on their own, ready for the birth of their first child. This fact she had kept to herself. It was her turn to give the monthly tea to her small group of army wives, who were aware of her pregnancy, but that was all they knew.

She made a selection of sandwiches, fairy cakes and a fruit cake decorated with crystallised fruits and nuts. She'd grown to like most of the American women, yet hadn't made any close friends, not that it had really mattered. She had taken her time to try and become acclimatised to their way of life, but she found a few of them very loud and brash. Some of them, she knew, couldn't understand her reticence; others thought her English ways quaint, but were intrigued by the difference. Today she hoped would be the last time she'd have to entertain them en masse.

To her surprise and delight, everyone had brought some small gift for the forthcoming baby and were anxious to give her advice about motherhood and so the afternoon passed happily.

As they were leaving and she was thanking them for their gifts, one said, 'You're welcome, nearer your time, we'll give you a shower.'

Hildy looked startled. 'Why would you want to wash me?'

This caused much amusement. 'No, Hildy, it's what we call when someone is having a baby. It's a sort of party where we all bring gifts to celebrate the coming birth.'

'But you did that today!'

'Today was just a gesture . . . you wait and see, then you'll understand.'

After they'd all left, she took the dirty dishes into the kitchen. With a shake of her head, she muttered, 'I'll never understand these Yanks!' When Milt came home, she'd tell him about today and her faux pas about having a shower – that would amuse him – but later as he walked through the door, she saw his expression and was dismayed. Something was wrong

'Milt. What is it?'

He took her hand and led her to the settee. 'I'm afraid our plan to move will have to be put on hold for a while, honey.'

'For goodness' sake, why?'

'I'm being shipped out to Germany next week.'

'You what?' She couldn't believe she was hearing this. 'For how long?'

He held her hands even tighter. 'Three months.'

'Can I come with you?' It was her first thought.

'I'm afraid not, Hildy. You'll have to stay here, but at

290

least you won't have to worry. You'll have all the medical care you need for you and the baby and the other wives to support you.'

Tears filled her eyes. She was devastated. She'd had such plans, making a home of their own, being together in a different environment and now this . . .

'Oh Milt!' It was all she could say.

He gathered her into his arms. 'I'm disappointed too. I was so looking forward to fulfilling our dreams, but it only means they are on hold. When I return we will move, but the fact that I know you'll be here on the base when I'm gone means I don't have to worry about you being in a house alone somewhere else, should anything go wrong. Here you are protected. Problems of any kind will be taken care of by the army.'

Hildy had the good sense to know he spoke the truth. In many ways it was her safety net. The army took care of their own – as did all the services. That much she had learnt. Looking at her husband, she could see his concern etched on his face, she didn't want him to leave her this way. She knew how bad it was for the men to be shipped out anywhere with family problems on their mind, Milt had told her about this and the effect on the men many a time.

She hugged him. 'Never mind, darling. Three months will soon pass and you'll be back before we know it.'

His look of relief was her reward. But as he slept beside her that night, silent tears trickled down her cheeks. If only Cora and Belle lived nearer. Suddenly, for the very first time, she was homesick.

* * *

When Cora had returned from her trip to Southampton to find the house full of workmen and smelt smoke, she was horrified, even more so when Belle had explained what had happened. But she soon got down to work as there was so much to do. All the linen was sent to the laundry because the smoke had filtered into the linen cupboard. All the rooms had to be aired. They polished furniture until it shone, washed and hoovered every carpet, washed every surface with bleach until in the end all anyone could smell was fresh paint.

The police had called. They had checked all the local hotels and B&Bs and Kev Harrison had been found as he was just about to leave his. In the room was a bag and inside, several empty cans of lighter fuel and the remains of torn cloth, which matched the charred remains of the one Belle had tossed out of the front door. They traced the shop where he'd purchased the fluid and the man remembered him buying it. Harrison had been arrested.

Although Belle was pleased he'd been caught, it meant there would be a court case and her past would be laid bare for all the locals to see. She only prayed it wouldn't make the national papers.

Tom had been on hand every day after work, making sure everything was done properly and quickly. He'd helped to fit and hang the new front door that had been badly charred, moved appliances in the kitchen and he made Belle laugh, for which she was more than grateful.

When Cora had told Simon what had happened, he came over to Shanklin and gave a statement to the police about his visit to Harrison and he took a few days off to lend a hand as well. Consequently the house was finished earlier than was expected. The four of them sat round the table after a sumptuous meal that Belle had insisted on cooking in her new kitchen.

Tom opened a bottle of champagne and filled the glasses, holding his up he made a toast. 'To the future!'

They all echoed, 'To the future!'

Belle looked at Tom and said, 'I couldn't have done this without you. Thank you.'

'Yes, you could love – but it would have taken longer!' They all laughed. 'At least now you won't need to cancel any more bookings.'

'Well thank goodness for that, as I'll need the money to pay for all the work that's been done.'

'No you won't, Belle, it's all been settled.'

'But you must let me pay you back,' she insisted.

'No, that won't be necessary. My brother caused all the damage and I feel it's my place to put it right,' and as he saw she was about to argue, he said, 'I can afford it, love, and it would give me great pleasure to do so.'

Belle was overcome. 'I don't know how to thank you.'

He grinned broadly. 'You can invite me to another meal sometime; you're a great cook, you know.'

Simon rose from the table and said, 'Cora and I will clear away and wash up, why don't you two push off into the living room and take a break?' When they had done so, he said to Cora, 'Do you think there's something going on between those two?'

With a chuckle, she said, 'Not yet, but I live in hope.'

He put his arms around her and pulled her close,

kissing her gently. 'I too have hope, am I being foolish?'

She placed a finger on his lips and said, 'Let's wait and see shall we?' Then she turned back to the sink and started the washing-up.

During the two days spent in Southampton with Simon, they'd resumed their intimate relationship after an evening out when they'd had dinner and several glasses of wine. On their return to Simon's flat he had said if she wanted she could sleep in the spare room, but he'd looked at her and added, 'But it would seem such a shame when we could curl up together. I so want to hold you and if that's all you want, then that's fine.'

But as she looked at him, Cora knew that wouldn't be enough. She wanted him to make love to her. His attitude had changed and he was once again the man she loved. She took him by the hand and led him into his bedroom without saying a word.

When he came over to the island to help, they'd shared a bed in one of the guest rooms, but as yet she didn't want to commit to anything further. The future would take care of itself.

The rest of the summer sped by. Belle was fully booked which kept her and Cora busy, but she was able to take time out to go to Cowes with Tom to watch the yacht racing. The town was packed with people, the bars were full and there was an air of festivity that was infectious and Belle felt she, too, was on holiday.

Tom was a great help to her in her business. He was able to supply her with meat on ration and sometimes a bit extra, which certainly helped with the succulent meals she served. Many of her guests had booked again, which delighted her.

She and the butcher spent time together in the evenings. He would either come to her place and sit drinking coffee or wine, or they would go out for a drink to a local pub so Belle could get out for a break. Their friendship blossomed. They exchanged kisses and caresses, but Tom waited for Belle to instigate more and she didn't, so he didn't push her.

'I am a patient man, Belle,' he would tell her. 'I can wait, but I want you to know that I want you in my life any way you choose. But I also want you to know, I want us to be together – permanently.'

Belle knew that he'd fallen in love with her and she with him, although they'd never said so, but she was concerned that when her case came to court, if they had made a public commitment, he and his business might be harmed by association and she would never let that happen, not after he'd been so good to her. But he was unaware of this.

'Let's just take things slowly,' she said.

It was now October, the season was over and the island returned to normal. But for Belle, her troubles were just beginning. The case against Kev Harrison was due to be heard in the Southampton law courts and she'd been summoned to be a witness. She was dreading it. Tom also had been called, in case his testimony was required as he was there when Simon had called to see his brother – when Belle realised she was mortified. Tom would be drawn into it one way or another.

She told the butcher how sorry she was when he called at the house that evening.

'I didn't want you mixed up in my past which will soon become public knowledge, I'm *so* sorry.'

'For heaven's sake, Belle! You seem to forget it was *my* bloody brother who set light to your house, of course I'm involved.'

'Yes, I know, but you aren't accountable for your brother, and by going out with me after everyone knows how I earned my living can only be harmful to your reputation and then maybe your business.'

'Do you think I give a damn? It will be a nine-day wonder anyway. You forget, love, how people have warmed to you since you came to Shanklin. All the shopkeepers like you because you talk to everybody. They won't care, why should they?'

'But the women might.'

He smiled. 'Indeed, they might gossip about it for a bit, only because they'd be curious.'

'Perhaps I could open a course. I could have classes in my house; I could make money during the winter that way.' Her eyes twinkled as she looked at him.

Tom burst out laughing. 'You're joking but I bet if you did it, you'd have a few takers!' He put an arm round her shoulders. 'No matter what, love, you and I will overcome anything that anyone throws at us. Right?'

'Right!' She looked at his smiling face and said, 'Tom Harrison, you are a wonderful man.'

'Then, Belle, that makes us a great couple and when this is all over, we have some serious decisions to make.'

'Do we?'

'You know damn well we do.' He pulled her to him and kissed her until she was breathless.

When eventually he released her and she'd recovered, she said, 'You could give a few lessons yourself, Tom.'

He grinned broadly. 'You are such a naughty lady, Belle Newman!'

Chapter Thirty-Three

It was the first day of the court case and Belle had been advised by the solicitor for the Crown Prosecution to book into the Dolphin Hotel for a couple of nights so that she'd be on hand if she wasn't called the first day. Tom had done the same. They had caught an early ferry and taken a taxi to the law courts. Here, they were asked to sit in the corridor until they were called.

Tom took her hand in his. 'Take a deep breath, Belle. You have only to tell the truth, that's all.'

'He's right, Miss Newman,' the solicitor said. 'I will lead you and you just answer my questions without trying to add anything. In my questions I will be bringing up your previous occupation. Keep it simple. Understand?'

'Yes, but what about when I'm cross-questioned?'

'You do the same. Harrison's solicitor will try and discredit you, be prepared for that, but don't get angry. Keep a cool head and your answers brief.'

* * *

Inside the court room there was quite a buzz as the reporters from the local paper sat waiting as did members of the public who'd read about the case and were curious.

Kev Harrison was led up the steps to the dock, followed by two policemen and was told to sit down for the moment. He scowled and looked round the room, glaring at everyone.

'All rise!' demanded the clerk of the court as the judge made his appearance. Harrison was nudged in the back and told to get to his feet, which he did reluctantly.

The judge took his seat and everyone sat, except for Harrison, who remained standing.

'The Crown versus Kevin Harrison.'

The morning was taken up by the evidence from the policeman who'd come to Belle's house as the firemen were trying to put out the fire. He told the judge about the damage that had been done, how they searched for Harrison when they suspected he might be the culprit and what they found when he was discovered. The fingerprints on the cans of lighter fuel matched those on the letterbox of the front door of Belle's house and a small window frame at the back, where a pane of glass had been broken and Harrison had thrown in the lit rags.

Harrison's solicitor tried to discredit the findings without success and was told by the judge to move on. The policeman left the witness box and the fire chief was called. He gave the report on his findings and the conclusion that this was definitely a case of arson.

Belle was the next witness to be called.

She had dressed for the occasion wearing a neat brown

costume, white blouse and a small brown hat with a feather in the front, brown leather gloves and matching shoes and handbag. She looked every inch a lady which was her intention, knowing that her past would be brought up and she didn't want in any way to appear bawdy or common.

Holding the Bible in her hand, she read out the oath, took a deep breath and waited.

The solicitor stood up and smiled at her trying to help her relax a little.

'You are Miss Belle Newman, owner of Loxley House, run as a B&B in Shanklin on the Isle of Wight?'

'I am.'

'Do you know the prisoner in the dock?'

'Yes, I do.'

'Tell me how you first met.'

'It was just before D-Day in Southampton. I was working as a prostitute and he was one of my clients.'

'Did you know him well?'

'No. I didn't remember him at all until I saw him earlier this year, working as a butcher in his brother's shop and thought he looked familiar.'

'Did he make himself known to you?'

'Yes, he called at the house one evening, reminded me about our earlier meeting and then tried to blackmail me.'

'In what way?'

'He suggested that to buy his silence about my past, which if it was known could ruin my business, he would visit me twice a week for sex. I refused and he threatened me again. I told him in no uncertain terms where to go and shut the door on him.'

'Did he leave you alone after that?'

'For a time, but he would always try to serve me in the butcher's shop and make me feel uncomfortable. It was obvious there was a tension between us and eventually his brother started serving me instead.'

'Did he call on you again?'

'Yes. He was drunk one night and came to my house. When I opened the front door, thinking it might be someone looking for accommodation, he pushed past me and walked into the kitchen.'

'Please tell the judge what happened.'

'Mr Harrison once again threatened to blacken my name and when I refused to accept his offer of sex for silence, he grabbed me, kissed me forcibly and grabbed my breast.'

'What did you do then?'

Belle looked over at Kev with distain as she answered. 'I pushed him away and picked up a kitchen knife and pointed it at him. That stopped him.'

'Did you use the knife on him, Miss Newman?'

'No, sir. But I did threaten to castrate him if he touched me again!'

There was a sound of laughter in the court, but the solicitor cast a warning glance at Belle and she realised she'd not kept her answer brief and to the point as she'd been told.

'Did Mr Harrison leave then?'

'Yes, sir. He swore a lot and told me I'd pay for this.'

'Did you see him after this visit?'

'No, I didn't.'

The solicitor then asked her to tell the judge what

happened on the night of the fire and she did so. The solicitor thanked her.

'No further questions, My Lord,' he said and sat down.

Harrison's solicitor stood and faced Belle. 'How many years did you work as a prostitute, Miss Newman?'

The other solicitor stood up. 'Objection! This has absolutely nothing to do with the fire. My learned friend is just trying to cast aspersions on Miss Newman's character.'

The judge agreed and told the solicitor questioning Belle to move on.

The solicitor knew he hadn't a hope of getting his client off, the evidence was ironclad, the only hope was to plead for his client's state of mind.

'Did Mr Harrison appear deranged in any way?'

'No, sir. He was very drunk, but he knew exactly what he was doing.'

'But when you refused to agree and you pulled a knife on him, didn't he become agitated?'

'No, sir. He was just scared in case I used it.'

He questioned her further trying to insinuate that she'd provoked Harrison, which she denied. She answered further questions and was concise in her answers until eventually, Belle was allowed to step down from the witness box. He then addressed the judge.

'My Lord, my client served in His Majesty's service during the war, fighting for his country. He came home without any money or a home until his brother offered to take him in. He was still suffering mentally from his experiences in the war and therefore was not in his right frame of mind when he threatened Miss Newman and then tried to set fire to her house.'

He sat down, knowing that this was as weak a plea as could ever be offered.

The Crown Prosecution leapt from his seat. 'My Lord this is complete fabrication. Kevin Harrison is in complete control of his faculties. He is a man without principals and saw an easy way to make money. When that didn't work, he decided to get his revenge. He knew exactly what he was doing.'

'Do you have any witnesses to call?' the judge asked Harrison's solicitor.

'No, My Lord.'

Kev was livid. 'I want a different solicitor! That man is an idiot and I'm going down because of him,' he yelled.

The judge glared at him. 'Silence! You will be going down, as you put it, because it has been proven without a doubt that you set fire to this house. Fortunately for you, Miss Newman escaped or you might well be standing in front of me on a charge of murder! It is obvious to me that you knew exactly what you were doing, you are a danger to the public and perhaps your time in prison will convince you of the error of your ways. I sentence you to five years' imprisonment.'

Kev went white and his legs gave way. The two policemen standing in the dock held him up and eventually led him away.

Tom walked Belle away from the courthouse and to the nearest pub where he ordered two large gin and tonics.

They sat together, relieved that the unpleasantness was over, but Belle was wondering about the fallout and said as much.

'That could be my business down the drain, Tom.'

'I don't think so for one moment. There was only reporters from the local paper there – no nationals – I made sure of that and as I told you, love, it'll be a nine-day wonder. This season's over, by Easter next year, who's going to remember?'

She was comforted by this. 'Of course, I hadn't thought of it that way.'

'There you go! You ought to shut up the house for a week and go away. Take a holiday, recharge your batteries.'

'That's a nice thought but at this time of year where on earth would I go?'

'Does it matter about the weather? Go to a nice hotel, have someone wait on you, cook your food, clean your room. Relax. Sit and read a book, have a couple of drinks.' He paused. 'If you don't want to go on your own, I'll get someone to run the shop for a week and come with you.'

She looked at him in surprise. 'You'd do that?'

'Yes, of course I would. I've not had a break for a couple of years, but there's a friend of mine, John, a good butcher who helps me out when I have to be away on business, I could get him in.'

She beamed at him. 'You're a good friend, Tom, I don't know what I'd have done without you since the fire.'

'For a bright woman, you can be really dumb at times!'

'What?' She looked at him and chuckled. 'No one has ever told me that before.'

'Oh for God's sake, Belle! You must surely know by now that I'm in love with you!'

She didn't know what to say. Yes, she'd wondered, especially lately as her own feelings for this lovely man had grown, but she'd learnt in the past from her dealings with men that there was usually an agenda and hadn't wanted to let her own feelings surface in case she was disappointed.

'Say something, Belle, don't just sit there. At least tell me if I have a chance with you.'

'It would be a stupid woman who would let such a fine man as you get away! I'm not that dumb!'

His laughter echoed round the bar and folk looked over to see what had caused it. They saw the big man lean over and kiss the woman he was with and were delighted to see her kiss him back.

'How about Bournemouth? We could drive through the New Forest, stay a couple of nights in Lyndhurst, then on to Bournemouth for the rest of the week. What do you say?'

'That would be wonderful. When do you suggest?'

'I'll get in touch with my friend this evening, see when he's free, then I'll come round and let you know. When we have the dates we'll inform the police and they can keep an eye on the house.'

'I'll have to cancel my bookings at the Dolphin Hotel,' she suddenly remembered. 'I booked in for two nights.'

'Me too. I'll do it from here if you like. The landlord won't mind if I use the phone I'm sure,' and he went up to the counter then off into another room. He soon returned and sat down.

'There, all sorted.'

Belle sat back enjoying the feeling of a man taking care of her. For so long she'd had to manage life alone. Being Belle, she had just got on with it, but she remembered telling Cora how lonely she was and now it appeared that life was going to change and she loved the idea. She would write to Hildy and tell her all that had happened and that at last she, too, had a man in her life. All it needed now was for Cora and Simon to get together and the three of them would have found happiness.

Chapter Thirty-Four

Hildy was having a hard time. Milt had gone to Germany and she was now alone on the base. A wife of one of the officers had called on her, a charming woman who told her it was part of her job to make sure all army wives were being taken care of – especially those whose husbands were deployed abroad.

'Believe me, Mrs Miller, I know how it feels, I've been there. It's part of being an army wife.' She then told Hildy that classes were held for those women who were pregnant and suggested she went along.

'Having your first child is daunting and you'll be with other women who are in the same position as you. There is a nurse there to advise you on everything to do with caring for your newborn. They even have a life-sized doll so you can practise bathing a baby!' She laughed. 'I know that sounds ridiculous but believe me after doing so a few times, the first time you have to bath your child, it doesn't seem quite so scary.' She gave Hildy a printed list of various activities arranged for the wives: a book club, one for quilting, a choir. 'Do you sing?' she asked.

Hildy burst out laughing. 'Certainly, but out of tune I'm afraid.'

'Have you been to see the doctor?'

'Yes. I've to see him in a month unless I'm worried.'

'Good. Now here's my number, you can call me if you have any queries or concerns.' She rose to her feet. 'Please don't worry, Mrs Miller, there's no need to be lonely here whilst your husband is in Germany. Don't shut yourself away; it's not good for you.'

Several other wives called over the next few days, which was a surprise and a delight and suddenly Hildy didn't feel so alone. An army vehicle drove some of them into town for a shopping spree, picking them up several hours later. She found it was fun and she was getting used to their joie de vivre and became a little less reticent herself.

When the mail was delivered, she read the letter from Belle with relish as it brought her closer to home. But she was shocked at what had transpired – the fire, the court case – and was even more surprised on reading the enclosed cutting from the local paper where she learnt of Belle's colourful past which the reporter had detailed. She was very familiar with Canal Walk and the area where the prostitutes worked, in fact it was such a familiar sight it became the norm, especially during the months leading up to D-Day and after.

Hildy was not judgemental. To her mind, knowing the hardships suffered ever since the war had been declared, where everyone had to do the best they could to survive, she felt the girls were perfectly entitled to earn their money their own way. But when she thought more about it, she wondered how they could have sex with a stranger? It must have been a hazardous occupation, but she knew Belle, she knew she was a strong woman and no doubt her hard-earned money had bought her the house on the Isle of Wight. She was happy for her. At least she was away from the mean streets of Southampton, living in Shanklin, a beautiful, quiet, middle class area which could not have been more different.

She smiled as she read on about Belle's planned holiday in Bournemouth with Tom. She hoped for Belle's sake something good would come from this liaison. Then she opened another letter, this time from Cora who also told her of the fire. Hildy was surprised when she read that she was back in touch with Simon. Through an exchange of letters, Cora had briefly touched on her earlier relationship with the policeman but Hildy had sensed there had been more to it than her friend had told her, now she was going to spend a few days with him when Belle closed the house.

Hildy made herself a cup of coffee and sat digesting the news from England. It seemed romance was in the air for both her friends and she was happy for them. She pulled a face then chuckled. There was no romance for her with Milt away, but her baby was growing within her and she filled her time planning for Milt's return, thankful that it would be a couple of months before the birth. He wrote regularly, telling her of his time in

Germany. How he missed her and how much he was looking forward to returning and becoming a father.

Life here in Frankfurt isn't a bundle of laughs. There is a charged atmosphere; the Russians are not the friendliest of people. We make our own entertainment. We play baseball and go to the movies, that's about it. But I tell myself it's not for long. When I return we'll see about getting somewhere away from the camp and try to live a more normal life in our own little world.

Hildy read the letter several times, drinking in every word. She would write and tell him about the class for expectant mothers and how the other wives had rallied round as she knew that would please him. She told him also about the baby clothes she'd bought, but not knowing if the baby was a boy or girl, she'd kept the clothes white and pale lemon. When they eventually moved, they could set up a room as a nursery. To this end, she'd already made a list of things she'd seen when she'd been shopping with the other wives and sometimes when she'd ventured into Louisville alone.

She smiled to herself thinking how by now she'd settled into the American way of life, visiting the beauty parlour, having her hair done and sometimes a manicure to fill her day. She read the books on childcare that she'd been given at the maternity class, preparing herself as best she could to be a mother. She bought knitting wool and patterns to make matinee coats, booties and bonnets, which helped her to while away the time.

* * *

Back on the Isle of Wight, Belle and Cora had cleaned the house from top to bottom, turned off the gas and electricity, locked all the windows and the door, then piled into Tom's car and headed for the ferry. They would part company in Southampton.

Simon was going to meet the ferry. He'd taken a week off so that he and Cora could be together. They planned to go to London where they would behave like a couple of tourists, visiting Madame Tussauds, the Tower of London, Westminster Abbey – and shop. Simon had also bought tickets for a West End show.

When Cora visited him, she stayed at his flat and their relationship had grown closer. When they were together, they were like a married couple, but as for a future together, neither had broached the subject. Simon was soon to take his sergeants' exam and of course Cora had been busy working with Belle. Both had been content with this way of life, neither had wanted to rock the boat and perhaps spoil what they had.

When the ferry docked, Tom drove off and when he saw Simon, stopped the car so that Cora could transfer her luggage and leave them. They then went their separate ways.

As they drove out of Southampton and down to the New Forest, Belle was at last able to relax. The October day was cool, but bright and they enjoyed the vegetation of the forest, delighted at the sight of the ponies, grazing beside the road, slowing down to let some amble across the road, unfazed by the traffic. They eventually booked into a hotel, handed over their luggage and made for the bar.

They sat at a table in the window, overlooking the garden. Tom picked up his glass and spoke.

'To a good week and us,' he said with a smile. 'I can't tell you how happy it makes me to sit here with you, away from everyone, on our own at last.'

With a chuckle, Belle clinked her glass with his. 'Who'd have thought it? I'm really looking forward to this break. I don't remember when I last had a holiday.'

'Ah well, my dear, things are going to change from here on in. Both of us deserve to enjoy life. We've both worked hard for it, after all.' He sipped his drink. 'Don't know about you, but I'm starving, let's take our drink into the dining room and eat.'

Afterwards, they went for a walk around the shops in the main high street. They took their time and meandered to a part of the forest near the hotel, sitting on a bench watching the ponies and other visitors. They stopped for a coffee, and then went back to the hotel and up to their room. Here, Tom drew her into his arms.

'It's been a while since I made love to a woman, Belle, so I might be a bit rusty!'

She kissed him back. 'Let's find out, shall we?'

They undressed and climbed beneath the sheets, cuddling into one another, feeling the warmth of their naked bodies close together, kissing and caressing and eventually having sex. Belle relished every moment, knowing that here and now, the man on top of her was there because he loved her, that to him she was special. He was kind and considerate to her needs as well as his own.

As they lay together after, she kissed his cheek softly. 'If that performance was when you are rusty, I can't wait until you feel competent.'

Tom laughed. 'You are so good for me and I'm so relieved that I pleased you.'

They slept for a couple of hours, had a shower then went downstairs, stopping in the bar for a while until going along the road to a restaurant they had seen earlier.

Belle asked Tom about his late wife.

'We knew each other from our school days,' he began, 'then went our own way until one night at a dance we met up again. I courted her for a year, then we married. My dad was alive then and I worked in the shop with him until he died, then as I told you, he left me the business. We would have liked a family, but it didn't happen and after several tests, we found that my wife, Ann, was suffering with cancer of the liver.'

'Oh, Tom, I'm so sorry.'

'Yes it was a bad time and then I lost her. She was a good woman; she didn't deserve to die like that, but that's life. I've been a widower for five years now. I've never looked at another woman until you walked into my shop.'

'But, Tom. I'm not a good woman! Not like your wife.'

'How can you say that? You have a good heart; your past doesn't make you a bad person. You didn't commit any crime! You're everything I want, isn't that enough?'

She was overcome. 'Are you absolutely sure?'

He caught hold of her hand. 'I've never been more sure of anything in my life. I love you, Belle, and I'm a lucky man to have found you.'

'Will you stop it!' Belle cried. 'You'll have me in tears in a minute.'

He chuckled, 'For heaven's sake, don't cry. People will think I've been unkind to you. Here, have another glass of wine, you'll feel better!'

On their first evening in London, Simon and Cora went to the Victoria Palace Theatre to a variety show.

On the Sunday morning, they walked through Petticoat Lane. As they got there, Simon warned Cora to keep a tight hold of her handbag as pickpockets were notorious in the area. They walked up and down looking at the various stalls, listening to the banter of the stallholders trying to attract customers to buy their wares. They ate cockles from one and chips from another. They looked at the antique stalls and finally made their way to a pub for a drink.

They were pleased to be out of the cold and undid their coats so they'd feel the benefit of them once they left to explore further.

'That was fun,' said Cora as she sipped her beer.

'It's great to get away,' Simon said, 'and it's so good to be able to spend time together without having to worry about ferries to get us home.'

'That's about the only inconvenience of living on the island,' she agreed.

He looked thoughtful. 'Would you mind coming back to the mainland to live in the future, Cora?'

She looked puzzled. 'Why would I do that?'

'Well once I become a sergeant, I want to have my own

place and I'd hope you'd come and live with me.' He saw her consternation and added, 'I'm not asking you to live in sin with me, darling, I'm asking you to marry me.'

She was so surprised that all she could say was, 'Oh, Simon!'

He looked amused. 'Is that a yes or a no?'

'But what about Belle? How could she manage without me?'

'Cora! I can't believe you said that. Are you going to turn me down all because of your friend? She can hire someone.'

The girl was flustered. 'No, of course not. I'm sorry; I was so taken by surprise.'

'You still haven't given me an answer and now I'm really worried!'

'Oh, Simon, darling, I'm so sorry, of course I'll marry you.'

He pretended to wipe the sweat from his forehead. 'For one awful moment I thought you were going to turn me down.'

She leant forward and kissed him. 'However . . .'

'What?' Now he did look worried.

'I need to be with Belle when she opens at Easter, just to make sure that her business isn't in trouble after the court case. I know she'll be worried and frankly so am I.'

'That's not a problem,' Simon assured her. 'We need to get Christmas out of the way and it'll take time to find a place and plan a wedding, and you've yet to meet my parents.'

'Oh dear,' she said, 'yes I suppose I must.'

Laughing, he protested, 'You needn't look like that, they won't eat you, they're really decent people.'

Grinning broadly, Cora said, 'Yes, I'm sure they are. Oh my goodness, I didn't think our few days away were going to be quite so exciting. I wonder how Belle and Tom are getting on.'

Chapter Thirty-Five

Things were not going well in Bournemouth. Belle and Tom had been there for several days, walking, talking, making love, enjoying each other in every way. They were happy together until that night as they were climbing into bed and Tom had taken her into his arms.

'God, Belle, I don't remember when I've enjoyed myself so much. We are having such a good time, I always knew you were the woman for me and these days spent together have proved it. Now all we need to do to make it perfect is to get married.'

He felt her stiffen in his arms.

'No, that wouldn't do at all,' she said firmly.

He could hardly believe what he'd heard. 'Why on earth not?'

'I tried marriage once before and I didn't like it.'

'When was that?'

'A long time ago when I was young and foolish. I said I'd never marry again. I'll be your lover, Tom, but I won't be your wife.'

317

'You told me you loved me.'

'And I do. I want to be with you, but not as your wife.'

He sat up in bed and stared at her. 'That doesn't make any sense, Belle.'

'It does to me! I've been on my own too long. I don't want to give up my independence. I know how you said you wanted children, but I never did. Besides, I'm too old now to be a mother.'

'How old are you?'

'Thirty-four and that's a question no man should ever ask a woman, Tom Harrison!'

'Under normal circumstances, I would agree, but this is different. You are still of childbearing age.'

'There you go! You still hanker after a child and I don't want to be a mother so we're not as well matched as you seem to think.'

He was lost for words and got out of bed. Lighting a cigarette he sat in a chair and faced her. 'Marriage doesn't mean giving up your independence; I like that part about you, you're a strong woman. That's great.'

She shook her head. 'Marriage changes people, I'm happy the way things are between us, let's leave it at that.' She turned away from him, pulling the sheet up under her chin.

Tom was at a loss for words. He put out the cigarette, climbed into bed and put his arm over Belle, but she lay still. He put out the light and lay beside her, unable to understand her reasoning.

The following morning over breakfast, for the first time, there was a feeling of tension between them. The jollity that

318

had been central to their relationship was no longer there.

Belle looked at him and said, 'I think we should go home.'

He didn't argue. They packed their bags, checked out of the hotel and drove back to Southampton and the ferry.

When finally Tom pulled up outside Belle's house, he got out of the car, picked up her case and began to walk to the door.

'I can manage,' Belle snapped.

He glared at her. 'You will unlock the door and I'll take a look around to make sure everything is as it should be – then I'll be on my way.'

He made a thorough search of the house and when he was satisfied he returned to the kitchen and Belle. 'No problems anywhere,' he said, 'so I'll go.' He pulled Belle to him and kissed her hard and long. 'I will see you very soon,' he said. 'This is not yet over.'

Belle watched him drive away with a heavy heart. He was a fine man and she did love him, but she liked being her own woman, not having to answer to another for anything. She wanted to earn her own money and be in control of her life. And, yes, she did want him around, keeping her company, sharing her bed – but marriage? That was a step too far. She was also concerned that her colourful past was now public and knowing men as well as she did, she knew that if they were married, some man was bound to bring up her past one evening, no doubt in a derogatory way, even if it was in a joke and she couldn't embarrass him like that. No, it wouldn't be fair.

* * *

Tom drove home slowly, giving himself time to think. He'd saved his petrol coupons for the trip and saw he still had some petrol left in the tank. As he put the vehicle away, he was still confused. He couldn't believe that Belle had turned marriage down, not after they'd had such a great time. He knew they were good for each other, but how the hell could he convince her? What was she afraid of? He wasn't a controlling man. He gave a wry smile. He couldn't envisage anyone controlling Belle. She was a feisty woman and he liked that. He let himself into his flat thinking he'd leave her alone for a few days, give her time to settle down and then he'd call on her.

Two days later, Cora returned from her break in London, full of tales of where they'd been and what she and Simon had done. Belle listened intently, pleased for Cora but when she was asked how her trip to Bournemouth had been, she was somewhat reticent in her answer.

Cora stopped her chatter and looked at her friend. 'What's wrong?' she asked.

'Nothing,' Belle said tossing her hair back, 'we had a good time; it was lovely.'

'But what?' Cora persisted, 'there is a "but". I know that tone of voice.'

Her friend sat down by the kitchen table. 'Tom asked me to marry him!'

'But that's wonderful, I hope you said yes?'

'No, I didn't. I refused his offer.'

There was silence, then Cora asked softly, 'Why, Belle? He's such a lovely man and he thinks the world of you.'

'I know that and I really like him, but I am too independent to be tied down.'

'That's a load of bloody rubbish! You love him, I know you do, he would make a great husband. You've told me how lonely you are at times, how you want a man to sit with in the evenings, to look after you. Tom would do anything for you and you know it!' She stopped her railing and studied her friend. 'There's something you're not telling me. What other reason do you have?'

'How can I marry him when everyone knows about my past? Someone is going to bring it up. How do you think he'll react when they do?'

'If it's a bloke he'd probably punch out his lights.'

'Exactly! And don't forget the women. The men would probably think he's on to a good thing, but the women . . .'

Cora could understand her point of view, hadn't she been down the same road with Simon? But when she'd discussed it with him, he said people soon forget and in time no one would remember anyway.

'Have you told Tom about this?'

Belle shook her head. 'Of course not.'

'That's hardly fair, is it? He's offered to spend the rest of his days with you, how do you think he feels? Devastated is how. He has a right to know why you really turned him down.'

Belle ran her fingers through her hair in despair. 'Yes, I suppose he does. When I see him, I'll tell him.'

Cora didn't think it was the right time to tell her friend

about her engagement and her future plans, instead she said, 'Right, I'm off to unpack and have a bath. I'll see you later.'

The following morning, Belle left the house to shop for food. After leaving the grocery store, she walked into the butcher's shop. She needed some sausages and, after thinking over the conversation she'd had with Cora, had decided to invite Tom to her house to explain her fears. The shop was full and she stood at the back of several women, waiting her turn.

'Nice to see you back, Tom,' one said.

'Thank you. I took a break and went to Bournemouth.'

'Yes, I saw you driving off with that woman, Belle Newman,' said another.

A third woman joined in the conversation. 'I read about her house being burnt and the court case. Sorry to hear about your brother. Especially after you gave him a home.'

Belle saw the tightening of Tom's jaw as his smile faded.

Before he could comment the first woman spoke again. 'Imagine her being on the game! You never know who your neighbours are, do you?'

Belle stepped forward and into sight. 'You don't have to worry, my dear, I have a new career now so you won't have to worry about your husbands calling on me!' She stormed out of the shop.

Tears of anger stung her eyes as she hurried back to her house. All her fears had erupted that morning, now surely Tom would understand that they could never marry.

After Belle's exit, the three women were flushed with embarrassment and indignation at Belle's outburst and

322

they twittered like a lot of birds in an aviary after being disturbed.

Tom glared at them. 'That remark was uncalled for,' he told the woman who'd made it. 'Miss Newman's past is nobody's business but her own. She is here to run her B&B and she works hard to do so.' His icy look stopped the gossip.

'Right, who's next?'

Early that evening Tom called on Belle, who opened the door, looked at him and said, 'You'd better come in.'

He followed her into the kitchen and watched as she poured them both a gin and tonic. She handed him a glass and said, 'Sit down, Tom.' When he was seated she stared at him and said, 'Now perhaps you'll understand why it isn't possible for me to be your wife.'

He spoke softly. 'You would let a bunch of village gossips spoil the happiness we could have together? That's not the woman I know. *She* was there this morning giving them hell . . . where did she go, Belle?'

'Oh I can still stand up for myself and don't you forget it – and I'm prepared to take them all on if I have to, but I can't have you embarrassed because of me.'

'Don't you think that is *my* decision? Yes, there would be a few who would not be able to miss the opportunity in the beginning, that's the downside of human nature but don't you understand in time, it would all be water under the bridge?'

She sat sipping her drink, thinking. 'Perhaps you're right, so let's wait a while until that water dries up. There's no rush. Let's give it time.'

He could see she was adamant. 'Very well, if that's the way you want it.'

She walked round the table and sat on his knee, running her fingers through his hair. 'That's settled then.'

He put his arms around her and kissed her. 'You are going to give me so much trouble, but Miss Newman, know that you've met your match!'

Laughing she said, 'I wouldn't have it any other way.'

Chapter Thirty-Six

Back at Fort Knox, Milt and his men were home from Germany and all their wives were overjoyed, none more than Hildy. She had cleaned their home from top to bottom, baked some cakes and was in a state of nervous tension until he walked through the front door, carrying a large bunch of flowers.

Flinging herself into his arms, she kissed him until he could hardly breathe.

'I must go away more often,' he teased.

'Like hell you will! That was the longest three months of my life.'

He held her away from her looking at her swollen stomach and, placing a hand on it, asked, 'How's the baby?'

'Fine, absolutely fine. I think it's a boy the way it kicks me.'

'How are you, darling? Are you going to the doctor regularly?'

'Of course, don't fuss, I'm fit and well, just very lonely.'

He put the flowers on the table and said, 'How about

making your old man a cup of coffee then we can sit and catch up with each other's news?'

Soon they were sat at the table, cutting into one of her cakes and drinking the welcome brew.

Milt sat looking at his wife. 'God, I've missed you,' he said. 'The days seemed never-ending.'

'For me too, but the other wives have been great. We go shopping together and to antenatal classes . . . you should see me bathing the doll.'

'Bathing a doll?' he looked bemused.

'Yes, it's the same size as a newborn baby, so when ours is born, I'll feel competent.'

Shaking his head slowly, he said, 'I can't imagine you being anything else but competent, Hildy.'

'Oh I don't know about that, I've never been a mother before.'

'Nor I a father, but we'll be great, you'll see.'

He then told her about being in Frankfurt, how the country was trying to build itself again after the war. 'We are so lucky here in America,' he said, 'you've lived through the same devastation as Germany, but here, apart from the troops who have been involved, civilians have no idea.'

Hildy laughed. 'I do know. When I was asked about the war in England and told the wives about the Blitz and the rationing and clothing coupons, they found it hard to understand. But thank heavens for that, enough folk have suffered.'

She told him the news from England, the fire and the court case, but didn't mention Belle and Cora's past; it was their business after all.

* * *

326

The following weeks passed by as Milt and Hildy returned to their normal lives on the base. They had decided to wait until the baby was born and then look for their own house as Hildy was so near her time.

The other wives had arranged their shower for her, which was a revelation. So many lovely gifts: clothes, nappies, soft toys, a bassinette. She was overwhelmed by their generosity and thanked them profusely.

These they brushed aside. 'We army wives stick together, Hildy,' one said and she realised how true that was, knowing that without their company when Milt was away, her life would have been very different.

One morning when she was alone tidying the house, Hildy doubled over from a pain that was so bad she cried out: then her waters broke. For a moment she was in a panic, knowing that the wives living either side of her had gone into town. She managed to crawl to the phone and rang the duty office. When she told the soldier on the end of the line what was happening, he told her not to move, he'd send someone over.

Within minutes, a doctor arrived with a nurse. He examined her carefully and, looking at the nurse, said, 'We need to get her to the hospital now!' He picked Hildy up in his arms, put her gently in the back seat of the car with the nurse beside her and drove swiftly to the camp hospital, where she was put into a bed and undressed. Milt was summoned quickly.

He was outside the ward, walking up and down, waiting for someone to tell him what was going on. He'd been told his wife had been taken into hospital, but that was all. However, there had been something in the voice of the caller that worried him.

Eventually a doctor came to see him.

'Sergeant, we have examined your wife and we think the baby is in trouble, so we need to give your wife an emergency caesarean section and she's being prepped for surgery now.'

'Can I see her?'

'Yes, for a moment. Try and calm her if you can, she's worried naturally.'

Milt was taken into the ward as Hildy was about to be wheeled to the theatre, he walked beside the trolley, holding her hand.

'Take a deep breath, darling, and relax. Everything's going to be just fine.'

'What about the baby, Milt?'

'Baby's fine too, just enjoying a bit of drama, so it's bound to be a female. I'll be here waiting for you. I'm not leaving this building, you hear?'

She gave a wan smile. 'I hear.'

He watched as they took Hildy into the theatre. A nurse told Milt to go to the waiting room. 'We'll come and see you after the operation, Sergeant. Your wife's in good hands, I promise.'

Milt went through all kinds of hell as he waited. He'd been in war zones, seen men killed and had never been as scared as he was right then. His thoughts were driving him crazy. If anything happened to Hildy or the baby, he didn't know what he'd do. He'd brought her away from friends and her homeland and now – was she in danger? Were they going to lose the baby? He walked up and down, unable to settle. He chewed gum until his jaws ached.

Eventually, to Milt it felt a lifetime, the doctor emerged from the theatre and came over to him. 'Congratulations, you have a daughter,' he said.

'My wife?'

'She's fine. She'll be a bit sore for a while, but she's okay.'

'The baby?' Milt asked.

'Your child had the cord twisted around her neck, that was the trouble; we've put her in an incubator and are monitoring her all the time, but her chances are good. She's just had a hard time making it into the world.'

The relief flooded through Milt and he felt sick. The doctor went to the water cooler, filled a cup and handed it to him.

'Here, Sergeant, drink this and sit for a moment, I don't want another member of the family collapsing on me.'

Milt thanked him and downed the water in one go. 'I didn't realise that childbirth could be quite so dramatic!'

The surgeon laughed. 'Fortunately normally it isn't. I know, I've four children.'

'I'm not at all sure I can put my wife – or me for that matter – through this again.'

Putting a hand on his shoulder, the surgeon said, 'Don't let this put you off, an only child is a lonely child. I know: I was one. We'll let you know when your wife is back in the ward and you can sit with her. She's still under the anaesthetic, so she won't be awake for some time, but we can take you to see your daughter.'

'Oh thanks, that would be great.'

'She has some breathing apparatus helping her at the moment, but in time she'll be breathing on her own.'

Milt was taken into a room and led over to a small incubator with a nurse attending. She smiled at Milt.

'Come and meet your daughter, Sergeant Miller.'

He looked down at the tiny figure through tears as he saw the breathing apparatus in her mouth. She looked so small and vulnerable. He looked at the nurse.

'Is she going to make it?'

'Oh yes, she will, we just have to hope that with a little care and attention she'll not suffer any problems with her breathing in the future. We'll know pretty soon. She looks a fighter to me, Sergeant, so try not to worry.'

Another nurse came in. 'Your wife is back in her ward, Sergeant Miller, if you want to join her.'

He took one last lingering look at his daughter and then went to find Hildy.

Sitting beside the bed, he gazed at the sleeping figure of his wife, saw the paleness of her skin, the dark circles under her eyes and he wanted to weep. Taking her hand, he kissed it.

'Oh honey, I didn't want to put you through this,' he said quietly. 'I've been to see our little girl and she's beautiful. Don't you worry now, she'll be fine.' He paused, wanting to say so much more, but to find the words was difficult as he was so overcome with emotion.

'I love you so much, Hildy. I am so lucky that we met and now we have a child. How amazing is that! You scared the hell out of me, honey, and I'm not sure I'll ever recover, so don't you dare do it again, you hear me?'

Her eyes flickered. 'Milt?'

He stood up and, leaning over her, he kissed her cheek. 'I'm here, honey, and I ain't going nowhere.'

He felt her gently squeeze his hand and saw her smile softly, then with a sigh, she slept.

A nurse came into the room, took Hildy's temperature, checked her pulse and looking at Milt said, 'She's fine Sergeant, she's sleeping off the anaesthetic, she'll wake in her own time. Can I get you a coffee? You look as if you could do with one.'

'Thanks, that is a great idea.'

Milt sat beside the bed until eventually Hildy came to. She was still a little woozy but she smiled at him. 'Hello,' she said.

'Hello honey. Gee, I'm so pleased to see you awake.'

She frowned. 'The baby?'

'She's doing just fine, I've seen her and she's perfect. She's in an incubator at the moment, but not for long. The cord was round her neck, so they're just taking precautions, making sure she's okay.'

At that moment the surgeon walked into the room. 'Ah I see you're awake, Mrs Miller. Now you're not to worry about your daughter, she's in good hands. Tomorrow, we'll put you in a wheelchair and you can see for yourself.' He smiled at Milt and left them alone.

Eventually the nurse sent Milt home.

'You look worse than the mother,' she chided. 'Go and get something to eat and go to bed. Both your women will be fine, you can come back tomorrow afternoon.'

He drove back to the house, poured himself a stiff

measure of bourbon and drank it. He searched in the fridge for something to make a sandwich, as he realised he was hungry. In his mind was a picture of his newborn child in an incubator with the breathing apparatus and he felt the tears wet his cheeks. Lighting a cigarette, he left the house and walked around the perimeter of the camp until he felt calmer and in control, before he went home.

News spread among the men of the new arrival and Milt was congratulated and teased all the morning and by the time he left to visit the hospital in the afternoon, he was loaded down with flowers, fruit and magazines sent along by the wives.

To his surprise, Hildy was sitting in the chair beside her bed.

'Well, honey, that looks a good move. Are you alright?'

She grimaced. 'They got me out of bed this morning,' she said, 'and I walked a little, it is uncomfortable but when they take out the stitches, I'll be fine.'

At that moment a nurse arrived with a wheelchair. 'Come along, Mrs Miller, we are going to see your baby.' She helped Hildy into the chair and wheeled her to the room where the baby was. Hildy peered into the incubator.

'Oh Milt, she looks so frail!'

He put a hand on her shoulder. 'She's going to be fine, honey.'

The nurse walked round and opened a section of the incubator. 'Here, hold her hand.' Then she left them alone.

Hidly took the small fist in hers and stroked it, cooing and talking softly.

'Hello little one, I'm your mother and your dad is here too. You are so beautiful and I can't wait to hold you. You get better soon so we can all be together.'

The nurse returned. 'She'll be fine, don't you worry. We have to get you fit enough to cope with a new baby too, so let's go back to your room and put you back in bed.'

When she was settled, Milt handed over all the goodies and flowers that he'd been given. Hildy was overcome with such kindness and said so.

'Well, darling, the base is a kind of family – we all help each other.'

'It was like that back home in the Blitz. It's amazing how people pull together.'

'Now, of course,' said Milt, 'we have to choose a name for the baby. Any ideas?'

'Yes, as a matter of fact, I would like to call her Hope. Don't ask me why, I just like the name and we have such hopes for her future. What do you think?'

'Hope Miller . . . yes, I like it.' He chuckled. 'I was warned by my men who were fathers that choosing a name caused so many arguments with their wives, but look at us. Wait 'til I tell them, they won't believe it!'

'Next time you come in, will you bring me two airmail letters so I can write to the girls and tell them the news?'

'Of course. I wonder how they're getting on.'

Chapter Thirty-Seven

It was mid December and the Isle of Wight was now devoid of all visitors, which was always appreciated by the locals. Visitors were essential for business through the summer and autumn, but afterwards, everybody could breathe and enjoy the island for themselves.

Belle took the opportunity to buy a few new pieces of furniture to replace the old, washed the light summer curtains ready for next season, checked all the bed linen and washed the blankets with Cora's help.

By now, Cora had told her friend of her engagement to Simon – now a sergeant – and they had a celebration of their own with a bottle of champagne. But Belle still was adamant that she wasn't going to marry Tom. Despite the fact that now no one spoke about the court case and her past. As Tom had predicted, it was old news and forgotten. He didn't press her but she knew he was disappointed.

They spent time together and every weekend he stayed with her, arriving on Saturday night. When the Sunday papers were delivered, they made breakfast and took their food and papers back to bed and read them. Then they would make love, have a bath, get dressed and go out to lunch later, at whichever restaurant they fancied. It was a cosy and happy existence.

Folk knew of their relationship and were used to seeing them together, wondering if ever they would make it permanent. That was the only gossip in Shanklin these days.

Simon wanted Cora to spend Christmas with him and meet his family. She was dreading it. By now she was wearing his ring, but hadn't met her future in-laws yet.

'What if they don't like me, Belle?'

'Oh for goodness' sake, why on earth wouldn't they? Anyway, you're not marrying them and, thank God, they don't live locally so you won't have ma-in-law on your doorstep. Anyway, you're not getting married until the spring, so you've still got time to get to know them.'

'That's another thing,' Cora said frowning. 'They expect to have a big wedding when Simon gets married and I definitely do not want that!'

'Does Simon know how you feel?'

'Yes and he's fine about it, but I think this visit could be difficult if the situation is mentioned.'

'Right!' Belle stared at her friend. 'This is what I suggest, but feel free to say no. I will take the place of your parents. You can marry in the local church here, invite a few friends, limit how many they can ask and come back here for the reception. How does that sound?'

'That sounds absolutely marvellous! I don't have many friends to ask. Sadly Hildy can't come. All I want is the folk who are important to me, that's what a wedding should be about, not masses of people.'

'Then I suggest you put this to Simon before you go away. He'll back you up, I'm sure. Are you seeing him this weekend?'

'Yes, I'm going over on Friday night, coming back on Monday. I'll have a word then.'

Cora took an afternoon ferry and did some shopping in Southampton before meeting Simon at his flat. They had planned to go to the cinema, but it was raining hard so they decided to stay in. They bought fish and chips to save cooking and whilst they ate, Cora brought up the subject of the wedding and Belle's plan.

'That's extremely generous of her,' Simon said when he heard the news. 'She's a good friend, you're lucky to know her.'

'Yes, I am but what do you think, will your parents go along with it?'

He gazed at her with affection. 'Darling, it's your day; you must do as you wish.'

'Well, it does mean that your parents will have to stay over on the island and any guests they may ask. That may cause a few problems.' She looked uncertain.

'Then they will have to make a decision, they come or they don't.' He put his arm round her shoulder. 'Don't worry. As long as we get married that's all that matters.'

But as they went to bed, Cora was still fretting.

* * *

The following week the girls each received a letter from Hildy with the news of Hope's birth and the difficulties that she'd encountered, but the news was good; the baby was breathing on her own and they hoped to bring her home in a week's time.

'Poor Hildy and Milt, what a worry. But thank God it's all worked out in the end,' Belle said as she put the letter down. 'It's times like that that you need your family and she doesn't have anyone but us and we're too far away to be of any use.'

'She said as much in my letter,' Cora said. 'She really wished we were there, she felt quite homesick in the hospital; but she's fine now she's home with Milt. She says he's a good man and is looking after her really well.'

'She made a good choice, thank heavens. I wonder how her bitch of a mother is? She's a stupid, selfish woman, who didn't appreciate what a good daughter she had.'

'Well, they say you reap what you sow,' Cora murmured, wondering what kind of harvest she would have over Christmas.

It had been difficult wondering what gifts to take to Simon's parents. Cora had saved her sweet ration to buy a box of chocolates for Mrs Pritchard and after Simon said his father liked the odd cigar, she'd bought three, which were encased in silver containers and made them look a bit special. She'd bought Simon a watch, knowing the one he wore was old. Rationing made life very difficult at such times. She'd used some of her clothing coupons to buy

Belle a splendid silk scarf in shades of purple and lilac and some tobacco for Tom who smoked a pipe occasionally.

Simon and Cora caught a train to take them to Coulsdon in Surrey where the Pritchards lived. As they sat in the taxi from the station, Cora looked with interest at the mixture of modern housing and old cottages and it was in front of one of these that the taxi stopped.

Simon paid the driver, squeezed Cora's hand and said, 'Relax, darling, it'll be fine.' He picked up their cases and walked towards the door, which was opened before he got there.

A woman with brown hair, greying at the sides, walked towards them. She was neatly dressed in a pale grey twinset and pearls. She hugged her son and stretched out her hand to Cora and kissed her cheek.

'How nice to meet you at last, come inside into the warmth. Arthur is putting the kettle on.'

They walked straight into a cosy living room with an open fire that was burning brightly, with a pile of logs beside it. Christmas decorations were hung across the ceiling and in the corner a Christmas tree, with fairy lights and glittering baubles. There were two easy chairs either side of the fire and a settee opposite. The floor was tiled with rugs scattered around. It was warm and inviting and Cora felt herself relax.

'What a lovely room,' she said.

'I'm glad you like it, my dear. Here, give me your coat – sit down and get warm.'

At that moment a tall gent walked in carrying a tray of

tea and a plate of home-made biscuits. He smiled at Cora.

'Hello, sorry, can't shake hands at the moment but I'm sure after your journey you could do with a cuppa.'

'Thank you, that's very welcome, it's chilly out.'

Cora listened as the family caught up with their son's news. They were thrilled he'd got his sergeant's stripes, then there was various news of other family members and Cora began to wonder just how many of them there were. It was now making her very nervous as her allocation for their guests was not a long one.

Eventually the conversation turned to the wedding in the spring.

Mary Pritchard turned to Cora. 'Such an exciting time for a girl,' she said. 'I remember mine. I had four bridesmaids and a pageboy. It was before the war, of course, so food was not a problem. We had a lovely reception at the Grange Hotel. Fortunately they had a large dining room.'

Cora's heart sank. 'Well, things are very different now; our wedding will be very quiet in comparison. We're getting married in Shanklin and my dearest friend, Belle Newman, is giving the reception in her house.'

Mary frowned. 'Is that the lady you live and work with in the B&B?'

'Yes, that's right. With extra tables in the dining room for the occasion we can accommodate about twenty people at a push.' She saw Mary frown and added, 'You see, I have no family, my parents were both killed in the Blitz and I'm an only child.'

'Oh my dear, I'm so sorry. However did you manage on your own?'

Cora looked across at Simon for help.

'She worked, Mother, but I'm sure Cora doesn't want to talk about those days. We both want a small intimate day with our closest friends and family. After all, the ceremony is what is important – not the reception.' His voice was firm and defied argument.

'Yes, you are right, of course.'

'Nearer the time, I'll send you all details, hotels where you can stay, etc.,' Cora said, hoping that would put an end to the discussion.

Mary rose to her feet. 'I must look at the fish pie,' she said. 'Thank goodness that fish isn't rationed, without it I don't know how we'd manage.'

'Who is giving you away, Cora?' asked Arthur.

'Tom, our local butcher, he's Belle's boyfriend – a really lovely man. When I asked him he said he would be honoured, wasn't that nice?'

'Indeed and correct. It is an honour and I'm looking forward to seeing you both walk down the aisle. Frankly, my dear, a small wedding is much more enjoyable. In fact elopement to my mind is even better!' he started laughing. It was infectious and Simon and Cora joined in.

Mary walked back into the room. 'What's so funny?' she asked.

'I'm telling these two they should have eloped – it's so much easier.'

She looked horrified. 'Arthur! How could you?' She turned and walked back into the kitchen, which made them laugh even more.

* * *

Christmas went well in Coulsdon after all, despite the fact that Simon and Cora had been given separate rooms. He'd laughed and said, 'My parents are old-fashioned, just go along with it.'

They went to the carol service on Christmas Eve and on Christmas day, had a turkey with all the trimmings and a Christmas pudding which Mary had made.

'I've been saving the ingredients all year for this; I've even made mince pies.' It was all delicious, washed down with wine Simon had brought and a bottle of champagne to finish the day with.

Gifts were exchanged. Mary had made a nightdress case for Cora and a sweater for Simon with some wool she'd unpicked from another garment. 'Make do and mend' was a watchword during such days. Arthur was pleased with his cigars and Mary delighted with her chocolates. Simon wore his new watch and Cora opened a velvet jewellery case he gave her to discover a gold bracelet. She was thrilled.

As Simon's parents climbed into bed that night, his mother remarked, 'That was a good day, thankfully.'

Arthur looked at her and asked, 'Did you have doubts about it?'

'Oh I don't know, dear. I was worried about meeting Cora which is only natural, after all.'

He cuddled up to his wife. 'She's a lovely girl and they are really happy together, so relax.'

'I'm a bit disappointed about their wedding plans, if I'm honest.'

'Now listen to me, Mary, it's their wedding and I think it sounds delightful. You know I can't abide big weddings full

341

of people you don't see except at weddings and funerals. It'll be just fine.'

She said no more but two days later, when her guests had gone and she was having coffee with a close friend of hers, she once again spoke of her disappointment.

'Cora's friend Belle Newman is giving the reception in her B&B as Cora hasn't a family. Not quite what I had in mind.'

'Times are different now, Mary,' said her friend. 'Before the war, there were no restrictions, today there are so many for the young to cope with. It'll be fine, you'll see.'

In Shanklin, Belle and Tom had decorated the house within an inch of its life as Belle loved to celebrate the festival and they had invited two couples to join them for Christmas day. They'd started with champagne and nibbles then sat down to enjoy one of Tom's turkeys with stuffing and vegetables. Belle had put chestnuts in with the sprouts and added carrots and peas, plus a Christmas pudding for dessert. They were all stuffed after the meal and put the plates to soak in the kitchen, before moving to the living room to recover with coffee and a glass of brandy.

'My goodness, Belle,' said one man, 'you certainly can cook, no wonder you're booked up. I've a mind to book in for a week myself!'

'And I'll come with you,' said his wife. 'It would be a joy not to have to cook for you for a week.'

On Boxing Day, Belle set out a cold buffet and she said, 'I flatly refuse to cook two days on the trot, so help yourselves or go without!'

In the evening, they sat playing cards until it was time for bed.

Tom took her into his arms and kissed her. 'Thank you for a lovely Christmas, darling. I so enjoyed it as did the others.'

'Me too,' she said. 'I just love to look after people.'

'Well, I've no complaints,' he said and held her closer.

She chuckled softly. 'I know what you're after, Tom Harrison.'

'And what could that possibly be?' he asked as he buried his head in her ample bosom.

Chapter Thirty-Eight

Cora had gone to London to see her old manageress at the clothes shop where she'd worked. She'd called Linda telling her of her impending wedding, inviting her to come over for the ceremony and added the fact that she needed a wedding dress. 'Can you help me?' she'd asked. Linda was overjoyed at her news and said indeed it would be her pleasure and they'd arranged an appointment.

As Cora stood outside the shop and looked in the window, she recalled the thrill of her first job here after leaving the streets of Southampton and her old employment. It had been the start of the life she'd strived and suffered for and, of course, it was in London she'd first met Simon. For a fleeting moment she wondered what had happened to Joe Keating, was he still collecting waifs and strays?

She entered the shop and Linda greeted her warmly. 'Cora! How well you look, it's so good to see you. Come through to my office and we'll have a cup of tea and a quick catch up and then we'll look at some dresses.'

Cora told her all about Belle and their business and of Simon.

Linda grinned broadly. 'I remember teasing you about his Black Maria. I'm so pleased it worked out in the end. Now I have some good news for you. I've managed to find a couple of dresses. They're not new but worn only once. You know how difficult it is these days but they are your size and I'm sure you'll like them. Come with me.'

In one of the cubicles, Cora saw two exquisite wedding gowns hanging and caught her breath. 'Oh, Linda, these are haute couture.'

'I know, both by Norman Hartnell.'

'I couldn't possibly afford either of these!'

'I want you to try them on and, if you like one of them I'd like it to be my wedding present to you.'

With eyes wide with surprise, Cora looked at her old boss. 'I couldn't possibly . . .'

Linda interrupted her. 'Please, Cora, I want to do this for you, it would give me so much pleasure. Come on, try this one first.'

It was beautiful and fitted perfectly, but they both agreed the second one was better. It was fitted, plain, high-necked with small pintucks down the bodice, plain sleeves and a full skirt with a small train. The simplicity of it showed the skill of the cutter and the style of the designer. It looked what it was: a piece of art.

Linda left the cubicle and returned with a small tiara and veil. She placed it on Cora's head. 'You know they say that a bride in her regalia always looks beautiful and that certainly is the case. Just look at your reflection in the mirror.'

Cora looked. Who was that girl? She felt like a film star. 'Oh, is that really me?'

'Indeed it is. You make a stunning bride. Now I've found a pair of plain matching satin shoes, so put them on.'

They fitted. Cora laughed as she said, 'Cinderella, you shall go to the ball!' And twirled round, arms out, veil flying out behind her.

'Oh Linda, will it all disappear at midnight?'

'Absolutely not! Now take it off and I'll pack it up for you.'

As she watched Linda pack the dress in tissue paper and a box, she asked, 'Do you still see anything of Joe Keating?'

'No,' Linda said. 'I don't know what happened to him. His wife doesn't come here any more either.'

'Maybe she eventually put her foot down about his philandering.'

Cora arrived home late that evening having managed to catch the last ferry and could hardly wait to show Belle her wedding dress. They unpacked it and hung it on a hanger.

Belle was speechless. 'Bloody hell, Cora, Hartnell is the Queen's dressmaker!'

'I know. Wait until Simon's mother sees me in this, it will take the wind out of her sails. She thinks my wedding is very underwhelming, this will show her!'

'I'm only sorry I won't be serving caviar.' They both doubled up laughing.

The wedding day arrived. Simon, his parents and their few guests had arrived the night before and had been booked into a nearby hotel. Belle and Cora had been baking and cooking for a few days, freezing some of the food to be defrosted and warmed on the day of the wedding. The tables in the dining room were laid with pristine cloths, small floral decorations in the centre, and then there was a two-tiered wedding cake that Tom had procured, on a side table. He refused to tell them how he'd managed that in these days of rationing. All he said was, 'It's not what you know, but who you know!'

The church was beautifully decorated with flowers, an organist was at the ready and the bell ringers. Several of the locals had planned to watch at the church gates as they all loved a wedding.

The hairdresser had come to the house early that morning to see to Belle and Cora and it was time to get dressed. Belle helped Cora into her gown and headdress before slipping into her own outfit, a dusty pink lace dress she'd had packed away for years but had taken out to the cleaners, worn with a new hat and matching shoes and bag.

The two women stood side by side in front of a long mirror and looked at each other's reflection and smiled.

'Bugger me!' Belle exclaimed. 'Would you ever believe it?'

At that moment Tom arrived. The front door was opened by one of the waitresses Belle had hired to serve the food.

'Anyone at home?' he called.

'Up here, Tom!'

He walked into the bedroom and stared at both the women who were facing the door waiting for his reaction.

He stood open-mouthed for a moment. Then he smiled.

'My goodness me, I'm with a couple of film stars. Belle, you look wonderful, very classy. But you, my dear Cora, are the most beautiful bride I've ever seen, I swear. What a stunning gown. Come here.'

He held her carefully and kissed her cheek. 'I'm going to feel like a king walking you down the aisle.'

Belle poured them all a glass of champagne. 'Here's to the future,' she said and they drank.

In the hotel, Mary Pritchard was getting dressed, fussing about, muttering about a reception held in a B&B, getting more irritable by the minute until Arthur shut her up.

'Enough!' he cried. 'I've lived with you all these years and didn't realise just how much of a snob you are.'

His wife looked startled. 'What do you mean?'

'If a mere B&B isn't good enough to hold a reception in your eyes, I suggest you stay in the hotel and we'll go without you.'

'But this is my son's wedding!'

'*Our* son and just you remember that it is *Simon's* wedding day and not yours. You will behave and if you dare show any sign of resentment or disrespect for the woman who's giving the reception, we will leave! Do I make myself clear?'

It had been many years since Mary had seen her husband so angry and she knew she'd overstepped the mark.

'Yes, very clear.'

'Then put on your hat and gloves and let's go; the car's waiting.'

The organist was playing quietly as the guests arrived, one side for the groom, the other for the bride. On Cora's side there were only a few people. A few friends she'd made, Linda Franklin and a partner and Belle in the family pew.

Simon was at the front waiting, fiddling with his watch strap, next to his best man, hoping that his bride wouldn't be late as he was already a nervous wreck. His parents in the family pew on the opposite side of Belle and Mary were trying hard to look happy.

The bride arrived only a few minutes late. The organist started to play the bridal march and the congregation stood.

At the door, Tom squeezed Cora's hand. 'Ready, love?'

She nodded. 'Ready.'

'Then smile, darling, you're going to your wedding, not your bloody funeral!'

That made her laugh and she relaxed.

They walked slowly down the aisle and Cora saw Simon turn, look at her and smile. She looked at him all the time until she reached the altar, so she didn't see the look of surprise on her mother-in-law's face as she saw the striking gown, but Belle did and she hid a smile.

When the ceremony was over, the wedding party gathered outside the church to have their photographs taken. They moved to the lawn and stood beneath trees for more and eventually the wedding carriage drove the couple to the reception.

Belle had slipped away to be there when they arrived, overseeing everything. Champagne was on ice, canapés ready and waitresses stood with trays as the few guests walked in.

To her great surprise, Cora saw caviar on toast on one tray. Belle saw her expression and catching her eye, she winked.

Simon introduced his bride to some of his relations, then took her into a quiet corner, pulled her close and kissed her. 'Darling, you look stunning, I'm such a lucky man.'

'Yes, you are and don't you forget it!' she teased. Then she saw her mother-in-law approaching.

Mary kissed her cheek. 'Wonderful dress, my dear. Where did you buy it?'

'In London, I have a friend who deals in haute couture,' she said smiling, trying not to feel just a little triumphant at her coup.

Eventually they sat down to the wedding breakfast: salmon and hollandaise sauce, followed by roast chicken with all the trimmings and fresh vegetables and crème brûlée for dessert.

Tom whispered into Belle's ear. 'You are a magician to have seen to all this. The dining room looks splendid, as good as any high-class hotel and the food is delicious. Well done!'

She smiled her thanks at him. 'I did it for Cora,' she said.

After the meal, the best man made an amusing speech about the groom and how he'd made the best arrest of his life when choosing his bride. Simon gave his speech, thanking the guests for coming, thanking Belle for providing the wedding breakfast and, turning to look at Cora, he added, 'I look at this beautiful lady and wonder just how I managed to persuade her to spend the rest of her life with me. I intend to make sure she never ever regrets her decision.'

As the day ended, the wedding guests departed. Simon and Cora were to spend the night at Belle's, catching a ferry the following morning, then taking the train to Devon for their honeymoon. The four of them, Simon, Cora, Tom and Belle sat drinking champagne when at last they were alone.

'I can't thank you enough, Belle,' Simon said. 'Today was just perfect. It was small and intimate, just as a wedding should be and I'll always be in your debt.'

'What rubbish!' she exclaimed. 'I loved doing it. Now Tom and I will clear these glasses, everything is done in the kitchen, so I suggest you two go to bed, you've a long train journey ahead of you.'

Cora hugged her friend. 'Thanks, Belle, it was all that I ever wanted, thanks to you.' Tom helped her wash the glasses and they sat in the kitchen for a moment, talking about the day.

Belle was laughing. 'Well, Mrs Pritchard senior certainly got a surprise today,' she said. 'I know she wasn't impressed that her son's wedding reception was to be in a B&B, I'm not a fool, but you should have seen her face when she was offered caviar!'

'Yes, I was so lucky to be able to get that, a friend of mine had jars put away for a special occasion and he was kind enough to sell me a few.'

'It must have cost you, Tom.'

'It's only money, love, and Cora was worth it after what she's been through. She'll be fine with Simon – that boy's a diamond and he'll take good care of her.' He drew Belle into his arms. 'Did today change your mind about marriage?'

She looked puzzled. 'I'm all for marriage, Tom, just not for me. Come on, let's go to bed. I'm tired, it's been a long day.'

He knew further conversation on the subject would be useless so he followed her up the stairs.

Chapter Thirty-Nine

As Simon and Cora left to start their new life together, Hildy had at last moved out of the army base with Milt and Hope, now five months old and fully recovered. They had rented an unfurnished house in Louisville, not too far away from Fort Knox and she had been busy setting up her own home, choosing furniture, making cushions and enjoying being away from anything military. She was a happy woman.

Milt was thrilled to see her eyes shining with delight when he came home and she showed him yet another innovation. They had painted one room and turned it into a nursery for Hope and Milt tended the small garden at the weekends if he was off duty.

Hildy and Milt invited some of the wives and husbands she'd befriended to a barbeque. Milt did the cooking, while the men talked and drank beer; the wives came to see her new abode and fuss over the new baby. Some had been a little envious, others were content with military life on the base, but were happy for her. She remembered how they'd helped her when Milt had been in Germany and was still glad of their friendship. The men teased Milt, saying living on the base wasn't good enough for him any more. He'd laughed and said they were absolutely right.

Hildy would take Hope out during the day, becoming familiar with her surroundings. Milt had taken them down the Ohio River on a paddle steamer which had been a thrill to watch the paddles swish as they turned in the water and she couldn't help but think how different it was to the Isle of Wight ferry in Southampton.

Milt had teased her telling her how in bygone years tribes of American Indians had ranged in the area, trying to fight off the people who were taking over the territory, but assured her that they were now living in civilised times.

She punched his arm in fun. 'I know that!' she retorted. But she had been horrified to learn that many years before, Louisville had been the centre of the slave trade and when she'd told him how shameful that was he surprised her by telling her that slave trading went on in her own country many years ago. She had no idea.

They had decided to rent the house, rather than buy. When Milt retired then they would buy their own property wherever they decided to settle, but that wasn't imminent and they hadn't given too much thought to it yet.

She wrote regularly to the girls. Belle was still running her business with outside help now that Cora was again based in London, married to Simon and working, but hoping to start a family of her own. They all exchanged photos. Hildy had been thrilled to see the ones of the wedding and had sent several of Hope and herself and postcards of Louisville, so her friends could get some idea of where she was now living. Hildy's one regret was that her friends couldn't see her daughter for themselves. But her in-laws were coming to stay and she was looking forward to that. At least she felt as if she did have some kind of family. She had given up on her mother after her final visit before she left England. But as she gazed at her daughter asleep in her cot, she did sometimes wonder if Olive saw her granddaughter, would she have changed her bitter attitude? Then she would dismiss it from her mind.

Milt had promised Hildy that when he eventually retired, they would take a trip back to Southampton and visit her friends and she looked forward to that, but she'd become slowly integrated into the American way of life and was no longer homesick – nostalgic maybe for what had been and her roots, but life in America was good for her and her family and now she had her own place, she was content.

Her in-laws were kind and were thrilled with their granddaughter. They visited occasionally and sent parcels for Hope, nevertheless Hildy was pleased they didn't live too close, she knew from her own mother just how controlling mothers could be, but at least Milt's was different in that respect. Hildy just felt more secure with their relationship being long distance. She sometimes thought this was being selfish, but that was the way she liked it and Milt was happy with the situation too.

The year seemed to speed by. Belle was kept busy and was fully booked throughout the summer. She served afternoon teas in the garden in good weather and in the dining room when it was wet. She'd earned a good reputation and her visitors made return bookings, which delighted her. She had now a small team of local women to take Cora's place and was making a good living.

Tom was still running the butcher's shop and was always on hand if needed for a leaking pipe or any other dilemma that Belle may encounter – and they were happy together. Marriage was no longer mentioned and the locals now accepted their relationship as normal.

It was a Friday night in late October that things changed. There had been several days of heavy rain and there had been roads flooded, but Tom insisted on making his deliveries.

'People rely on me, Belle,' he told her when she voiced her concerns. But she always fretted when the shop closed and Tom was on the road in the dark. Then one evening she answered the telephone and all her fears were confirmed. Tom had been involved in an accident and had been taken to the cottage hospital. She called a taxi at once.

Belle paid the taxi driver and ran into the hospital, heading for the reception where she asked which ward Tom was in, but she was told that he was in the operating theatre. The ward sister was called and, seeing Belle's distress, took her into the waiting room and sent for a cup of tea, then she sat beside her.

'Mr Harrison has a broken leg, fractured ribs and dislocated shoulder,' she told Belle. 'But he's suffered some trauma to the head and we're investigating that at the moment.'

Belle suddenly felt icy cold. 'What does that mean exactly?'

'Mr Harrison is in a coma and we're monitoring him constantly. But it could have been much worse.'

'Worse? Bloody hell, it sounds serious enough to me! Sorry, Sister, didn't mean to swear.'

The woman smiled. 'That's alright, I've heard it all before and you're worried, but he's in the best hands.'

'He's not going to die, is he?'

'No, he's not going to die, I promise. He looks a pretty strong man to me and fit too, which helps. Now you just sit here, when he comes out of surgery and recovery, I'll come and get you.'

Belle tried to settle but once she'd drank her tea, she walked up and down wondering just how long she'd have to wait. When she did sit down, she was overcome with emotion. If she lost Tom, she didn't know what she'd do. He'd been a part of her life for so long now that she took his presence for granted. Oh my God! He wouldn't be able to run his business. Suddenly she realised that she'd have to sort out that problem – and quickly. There was a public phone box down the hall and she rang John, the man who used to take over from Tom when he needed coverage.

She got through and arranged for him to open up in the morning with a spare key that she had and carry on until they knew exactly the situation. He'd collect the key from her early the next morning. Then she rang Cora.

The relief of hearing her friend's voice was such that Belle burst into tears, then she told Cora what had happened.

Cora was shocked at the news. 'Oh God, Belle, is

there anything I can do? Do you want me to come over?'

'No, love, but thanks for the offer. Obviously Tom will be in hospital for some time and I've covered his shop. I'll let you know what happens after I've seen him and the doctor.'

Belle had curled up on the sofa in the waiting room, trying to doze and after what seemed an eternity, the nurse came for her.

'Mr Harrison is out of surgery and the operation on his leg went well, but at the moment he's still in a coma.'

Belle felt sick. 'How serious is that?'

'We are trying to ascertain the seriousness of the head trauma,' she said. 'He's in intensive care at the moment. It's late. I suggest you go home, try and get some sleep and come back in the morning, then you can see the doctor after his rounds.'

Her face devoid of colour, Belle asked, 'Can I just take a quick look at him?'

The sister took pity on her. 'Come with me, but just for a moment now.'

Belle followed her into the ward and waited for the curtains round the bed to be opened for her. She looked down at the sleeping figure of the man who meant so much to her and smothered a cry. Her Tom, usually big and strong, lay pale and wan, on a ventilator, his leg in plaster, his ribcage bandaged, his shoulder in a sling. She saw there were cuts on the part of his face that she could see, probably from flying glass, she assumed. He looked battered, as if he'd been in a war zone.

Belle leant forward and kissed his forehead. 'I'll be back tomorrow, love,' she whispered.

The receptionist called a taxi for her and Belle waited outside, puffing on a cigarette to try and calm her inner turmoil. When she arrived home, she poured a stiff gin and tonic, and sipped it. She leant on the table, with her head in her hands and sobbed. Her cries of anguish, echoing round the kitchen.

Chapter Forty

Belle rushed around like a tornado the next morning, getting John organised with the butcher's shop, cooking the breakfast for a family who'd booked in for three days and prepping the vegetables for the evening meal, giving instructions to her help. Afterwards, she took a bath, changed her clothes and went along the road to the florist for some blooms to take to her man.

As she walked along the corridor of the hospital leading to the Intensive Care unit, her stomach tightened and her heart was beating that little bit faster as she approached the bed.

The sister spoke to her, 'He's still in a coma, Miss Newman, but do talk to him. It's said that the patient can hear sometimes.' She put a hand on Belle's shoulder. 'Try not to worry, he's being well cared for.'

Belle sat beside the bed and took Tom's hand. 'Bloody hell, Tom! If only you'd listened to me and now look at you. You have no idea how you've worried me. You daft bugger, don't you know I love you?' She caressed his face. 'We've had such good times together and no way is that going to change. Are you listening, Tom Harrison? You have to recover because I need you!'

She sat for a further hour talking about the things they'd done together, about her business, the latest news from Hildy and Cora until she was lost for words.

The sister came along with a cup of tea. 'Here, drink this and then I suggest you go home. There's nothing more you can do here today. Come back tomorrow and try and get some rest. When he recovers, Mr Harrison will need you and you need to be fit to look after him.'

Belle thanked her, drank her tea, kissed Tom and reluctantly made her way home.

For Belle, the following days were a nightmare. She visited Tom every day and talked to the comatose figure, trying to be cheerful when her heart was heavy, wondering what the outcome would be.

The next day, to stop her thinking, she cleaned the house from top to bottom, washed the linen that had been used by her guests, turned out cupboards, drank gallons of tea and walked along the beach, praying silently.

Eventually it was time to go to the hospital.

Just outside the ward the sister met her. 'I've some good news, Miss Newman. Mr Harrison has come round from the coma, but you'll find him slightly confused and his memory will probably be impaired. Don't worry about it, it's quite normal. Just try and keep him quiet.'

Belle walked to his bed. There was no ventilator she

was relieved to see. She took his hand. 'Hello Tom, how are you?'

He looked up at her and for one awful moment she thought he didn't know who she was and her heart sank – but then he smiled.

'Hello Belle.'

'How are you feeling?' She waited for his answer with some trepidation.

Tom frowned. 'I'm a bit sore and I've got a headache but I don't remember how I got here.'

'You had a car accident,' she told him.

'I did?' He looked at the sling on his arm. 'Well that explains it then. I only remember leaving the shop and climbing into the van.'

She squeezed his hand. 'Well don't you worry about it, at least you are in one piece even if a bit battered.'

The sister came along. 'I think you should leave Mr Harrison to rest now,' she said.

Belle rose from the chair. 'I'll be in tomorrow,' she told Tom. Looking at the sister, she said, 'I put some clean pyjamas and toiletries in the locker the other day.'

The sister smiled at her. 'Yes, we found them, thank you.'

Belle kissed Tom goodbye and left the ward.

It was a week later that the doctor decided that Tom could go home but a nurse would call every day to check on him for a while. Mentally he was getting better, but he still didn't remember having the accident and Belle thought that was probably just as well. He was now aware that

John was looking after the shop and was grateful.

She'd made a bed up for him in the dining room, having moved the furniture to another room. There was a downstairs toilet he could use so he didn't have to tackle the stairs with his broken leg. With the use of crutches he was able to move about. He still looked pale and drawn, but he had recovered his sense of humour.

'I can't see me chasing you round the bedroom for a while, Belle,' he said when she took him a cup of coffee.

She could see it took an effort for him to try and be light-hearted. 'I think I can wait for you, you daft bugger,' then she added, 'when you're better, you should think of taking on a helping hand and he could do the deliveries as well as help with the butchery side. I can't possibly have you wearing yourself out before your time.'

'You're right, of course, and I had meant to have someone in after Kev left – now I don't have a choice.' He closed his eyes for a moment.

She made him comfortable in a chair. 'You have a doze,' she said. 'I've things to do.' She walked quietly away.

Around noon the following day, hearing the slam of a car door, Belle rushed to greet her friends who had arrived by taxi. They had called the night before to ask if it was alright to come over and visit. Cora rushed forward and hugged her friend. Simon kissed her cheek and they all went into the kitchen.

'How's Tom?' asked Cora.

Belle gave them all the information she had. 'It will just take time for his recovery. He's having a nap now so I'll make you a cup of tea and you can tell me all your news.'

It was so good to be able to relax with friends and forget her troubles for a while and later when Tom woke, they all sat together and ate, then listened to the wireless until Belle could see that Tom was tiring and put him to bed.

The three of them sat in the living room until it was bedtime.

'Is there anything I can do in the morning?' asked Cora.

'If you could see to the breakfast for us all whilst I wash and dress Tom that would be a help,' Belle told her gratefully.

They were all sitting round the breakfast table together, chatting. Belle glanced at her patient, pleased to see that he had gained weight, his face had filled out and he'd lost that awful grey look. She breathed a sigh of relief.

After breakfast they took a gentle walk to the beach, wrapped up against the cold and sat watching the waves roll in and breathed in the salt air, before returning home, all with colour in their cheeks.

In the afternoon, Cora and Simon left to return to London.

'Well, they seem content with married life,' Tom remarked.

Belle smiled. 'Yes, they make a good couple. Simon is a lovely chap and they're deliriously happy.'

Tom looked at her and asked, 'What about you, Belle? Are you happy too?'

She looked at him with some surprise. 'What sort of a question is that?'

'Well look at me! You've been wonderful taking care of

me. After all, it's not as if you are duty-bound, like being married to me.'

'What's that got to do with anything?'

'I know my memory isn't great these days, but I do remember hearing you tell me that I had to get better because you needed me.'

She was floored for a moment. 'I said that to you when you were in a coma. I had no way of knowing if you could hear me.'

'Well I did.' He took her hand. 'Do you need me enough to marry me?'

She looked shocked, then she started laughing. 'Hoisted on my own petard, isn't that what they say?'

His eyes glistened. 'You haven't answered the question, Belle. Will you be my wife?' She sat gazing at the man sitting before her, remembering how she felt when she thought she might lose him. Leaning forward, she kissed him slowly.

'Yes, you old devil. I will marry you.'

'Really?'

'Really,' she replied. 'I love you, Tom. My life would be nothing if you were not in it.'

He drew her into his arms. 'My sentiments exactly!'

The wedding was a quiet affair in early March. They had waited until Tom had recovered and was able to go back to work. Simon and Cora acted as witnesses and they had the wedding breakfast at a local hotel.

Tom raised his glass and said, 'Never ever did I think I could persuade Belle to marry me and I had to have a car accident to do so. Well it was worth it! To Belle!'

'To Belle!' the other two said and drank to their friend.

Belle held out her left hand and looking at her new wedding ring said, 'Mrs Harrison! Who'd have thought it?'

'Are you having a honeymoon?' asked Cora.

'Not until the end of the year,' Belle told them. 'I'm fully booked and I can't turn business away. Then we'll go somewhere. Tom will be moving in permanently, of course, and his flat will be taken over by John, the butcher who helped out during Tom's recovery. He's staying on.'

'She'll need the money to keep me in my old age,' Tom teased.

'Wrong, darling! It's my fund for if you misbehave and I kick you out of the house!'

Simon laughed loudly. 'Now you know, Tom, so keep your nose clean.'

Later that night when they were in bed, Tom drew Belle into his arms. 'I can't tell you how happy I am and I bless the day you walked into my shop. I knew then you were the woman for me.'

'It took me a while,' she confessed. 'It was never in my mind to marry again, as you know, but I'm a lucky woman. I know how hard it was to face up to all the gossip after the court case.'

He stopped her. 'That is in the past, love, our future will be very different.'

It was a month later at Easter that Cora and Simon visited them again. Simon produced a bottle of champagne and asked for some glasses. He then opened the bottle.

'What are we celebrating?' asked Belle.

'I'm pregnant!' Cora said. 'The baby is due in November.'

Belle threw her arms around her friend. 'But how marvellous!' Then she kissed Simon.

Tom kissed Cora and shook Simon's hand. 'That's great news,' he said, 'children are a blessing. I'm so happy for you.'

They all went out to lunch to celebrate and as they ate, they discussed the trauma of the previous year.

Tom was delighted that he'd been working again since his accident.

He grinned broadly. 'I can't tell you how great it feels for me to pick up my meat cleaver again,' he said.

'There were times I think he'd have liked to use it on me,' Belle teased.

'Not really, love,' he replied. He looked at Simon. 'These two are a force to be reckoned with, you know.'

Simon burst out laughing. 'I knew that from the beginning, what took you so long?'

At the end of the day Belle and Tom waved their friends goodbye as the ferry left the dock and, as they walked away, Tom said wistfully, 'They'll make great parents.'

'Yes, they will,' she said quietly, knowing that Tom would have liked children of his own. But she had been adamant that she was in no way maternal. It was perhaps the only major thing that they disagreed about. She cast a glance in his direction. It was a great shame really because Tom would make a great father, she was sure of that.

That night in bed, curled up in Tom's arms, she tried to make sense of her own feelings about motherhood.

Throughout her life on the streets, the last thing any brass wanted was to fall pregnant. Some of the girls had and had to resort to back street abortionists, a thing she was terrified of. Was that at the root of her problem? Was it a problem? Not all women wanted children, did they? Was she unusual? Was there something wrong with her? So many questions filled her mind. At the same time she saw the joy that the news had given Cora, Simon . . . and Tom. But she was denying him the thing he really longed for.

Belle did not sleep well that night.

It was June and the government had declared that food rationing was to be cut. Tinned meat was cut to two pence worth a week, but thankfully the sweet ration was up five ounces from four and the extra sugar was to be allowed for jam-making. Belle found catering for her guests was a nightmare. She still kept chickens, one lot for the eggs and others for the table. Rabbit and fish made up the shortages.

Tom sympathised with his customers who complained bitterly, but he too was bearing the brunt of the shortages. It was a difficult time for everyone and they longed for the end to it all.

To add to all the problems, Belle was unwell. She thought she must have eaten something to upset her stomach as she was being sick and eventually Tom insisted she visit the doctor.

In the doctor's surgery she told him of her symptoms. He listened carefully.

'When did you last have your period, Mrs Harrison?' he asked.

'Well, they've never been regular,' then she thought and added, 'my last one was very light.'

The doctor then told her to lay on the couch and he would examine her. 'Remove your underwear,' he said.

When the examination was over, he left her to dress, then when she sat down before him, he smiled at her.

'I have some good news for you. You're pregnant! Congratulations!'

She looked shocked. 'But how can that be? I've had a show, a bit haphazardly it's true.'

'That's not unusual,' he said. 'Some women have a show all through their pregnancy.' Seeing the look of consternation on her face, he asked, 'Is this not good news?'

'I always said I didn't want children. I'm not a bit maternal!'

He chuckled. 'Women who have told me that have always turned out to be great mothers. Trust me, you'll feel differently when you first hold your baby in your arms. Sometime in January according to my calculations.'

Belle left the surgery in shock. She walked to the beach and sat on a bench listening to the waves sweep in. *Well Tom will be pleased*, she thought, but she was finding it hard to accept the fact that she was expecting. Tom had always taken precautions so how could this happen? Then she remembered when they'd been out for the evening and had quite a lot to drink and had gone to bed for a night of passion . . . that night Tom hadn't used precautions, she remembered now. She also remembered the joy on Cora's face when she told them she was pregnant. Why didn't she feel the same?

She rose from the bench and walked home.

* * *

That evening after she'd fed her guests and cleared away, she and Tom sat in the kitchen and had their meal, as was their habit.

'Did you go to the doctor?' he asked.

'Yes, I did.'

'What did he say was wrong with you?'

'He told me I was pregnant.'

Tom nearly choked on his coffee. 'He what?'

'You heard me. I'm expecting a baby, sometime in January, the doctor said.'

Tom got to his feet and walked round the table and put his arms around her.

'Oh Belle, that's wonderful news. We'll be a family.' Then he looked at her. 'Aren't you happy about this?'

She looked at the man she loved and saw how thrilled he was and felt ashamed that she couldn't feel the same. 'I don't know how I feel, to be honest. I'm in shock.'

He took her hands in his. 'What are you scared of, Belle?'

'I wish I knew.' Tears brimmed her eyes. 'I'm so sorry, Tom. I know how much you've longed for a child, well now you'll have one!'

'No, darling, *we'll* have one. Oh Belle, it's going to be alright, I promise. This child is born out of love. Maybe it wasn't planned, but you'll see you will learn that motherhood isn't something to be scared of. A child brings such joy with it, you will love it.'

'But, Tom . . . what if I don't?'

It was his turn to be shocked. 'I don't believe you just said that!'

'But it's a possibility. I've never wanted children. I don't mind other people's, but I don't have a maternal bone in my body!'

He was at a loss as to how to cope with her. 'But you care about people. Look how you gave Cora a wedding, taking her mother's place, now if that wasn't feeling maternal I don't know what is.'

'But she was my friend. I'm sorry, darling, I just have to get used to the idea, that's all. You will just have to give me time. Come on, I'm tired, let's go to bed.'

As she lay in Tom's arms that night, Belle tried to come to terms with her approaching motherhood. At least she'd be able to see the season through. Then she silently berated herself for putting her business before the child she was now carrying. But she *was* a business woman. She'd worked hard to get where she was and she had no intention of giving up her dream. How would a baby fit in with her life? Her thoughts were driving her crazy.

Eventually she slept but was beset with dreams. She was trying to serve her customers whilst pushing a pram and the child wouldn't stop crying.

Chapter Forty-One

Belle was fully booked all summer long and she was tired. Even with her help, by the end of the day she was shattered. It was now September and she was nearing the end of her bookings and for once she wasn't sorry. Six months pregnant, she was looking forward to a rest.

Tom was felicitous, worrying that she was doing too much, but she brushed his remarks aside. 'I have a business to run, the baby will just have to get used to it!' she snapped. He said nothing more.

During the intervening months, they hardly talked about the child. Tom had tried, but Belle didn't show any great interest. He'd been to see the doctor about it he'd been so concerned.

The doctor had listened and had said that somewhere in Belle's subconscious had to be the reason for her fears, but without sending her to a psychiatrist, they wouldn't be able to get to the bottom of it.

Tom knew that Belle would never agree to that and said so.

'Wait until she has the baby,' the doctor advised. 'If then she feels the same, we have a problem. Just be patient and don't push her.'

Tom then rang Cora.

She listened and said, 'I'll take a few days off and come over. Please stop worrying, Tom. We'll sort it out one way or another. Is there a room free? If not I'll book into a hotel.'

He assured her there was room and hung up. He felt more hopeful. Belle and Cora were so close and had been through so much together if anyone was able to get through to his wife it would be her friend.

When the phone rang that evening, Belle answered it.

'Hello Belle, it's Cora.'

'Hello love, how are you?'

'Feeling a bit tired and in need of a rest and friendly gossip. I have a few days off. Do you have a room free?'

Belle was delighted. 'I do, it's free now. When can you come?'

'How about tomorrow?'

'Great, I'll get it ready. Oh Cora, it'll be lovely to see you.' She put the phone down and went to find Tom.

'Tom, Cora's coming over tomorrow for a few days.'

He feigned surprise. 'That's great, it'll be so nice to see her again.' He was delighted to see Belle looking happy and silently prayed that this visit would help Belle to come to terms with having a baby.

Belle fussed around preparing a room for her friend. The two guests she had were leaving the next day so she'd be free to spend time with Cora and she was so looking forward to it.

* * *

373

Cora arrived the following afternoon. The journey had tired her so she settled in her room and took a nap after having a quick cup of tea. Belle was too excited and quickly made a few scones with some dried fruit she'd saved. She'd been surprised to see how much bigger Cora's bump was than hers but then, of course, she was two months further into her pregnancy than she was, but apart from looking tired from the journey, Cora looked blooming.

After Cora's nap, they drank tea in the kitchen and ate the freshly made scones.

'This reminds me of the old days, when I eventually came to work with you,' Cora said. 'They were good times, weren't they?'

Belle chortled. 'They were indeed.'

'And look at us now, Belle, both married, both pregnant, who'd have thought it?'

'Who indeed,' said Belle, the smile fading, which Cora ignored.

'Are you free tomorrow?'

'Yes, the last of my guests checked out this morning and the girls cleaned the room and washed the linen, so I can spend time with you.'

'Good. I'd like to go into Cowes if you don't mind, we can get a sandwich and a coffee somewhere, and I want to do some shopping.'

Belle grinned broadly. 'I don't remember when I last did that, I've been so busy since Easter.'

'Then you need the break more than me,' laughed her friend. 'Bring some money and we'll celebrate. Have you any clothing coupons, if so bring those, after all you never know what you'll see.'

When Tom came home at the end of the day he was delighted to see his Belle looking so cheerful and when he knew they were going shopping the next day, he gave Belle some money to treat herself.

It was the end of September and the sun was shining with a cool breeze off the sea, but the two women didn't seem to notice the chill. The bus dropped them off in Cowes and they stopped for a coffee before shopping.

'Gracious Belle, I'll be pleased when the baby is born and I get my figure back,' said Cora as she drank from her cup.

'That will be a bonus,' Belle agreed. 'I found my bump got in the way when I was working. I forgot to allow for it,' she laughed.

'Well thank goodness that baby clothes for those under four months don't need clothing coupons as I want to buy some more for junior,' she said patting her stomach. 'Have you had time to shop for your baby? I know you've been busy.'

'No, I haven't had the time,' Belle said dismissively.

'Well we'd better put that right today. Hurry up and drink up, we've got lots to do.'

Belle wasn't enthusiastic but finished her drink.

Cora had already checked out the baby shops before she came so she led Belle along the street to one and they stopped and looked at the display in the window.

'Oh, will you look at that,' she pointed to a dress and matinee set with bootees and bonnet to match. 'Isn't that adorable?'

Belle had to agree.

'Come on then, let's go inside. I refuse to buy blue or pink, it's bound to be the wrong colour. I'm sticking to white as that's safer.'

Egged on by her friend, Belle, despite her reticence, began sorting through the baby clothes that looked so small and delicate. She ended up buying several outfits and enjoying doing so to her great surprise. Then she purchased some vests and looking at them suddenly began to think that her baby would be small and vulnerable if she was to fit in them, then realised that she was referring to the baby as a she – in her mind. For the first time since she was told she was pregnant, she began to accept the reality of carrying a child. Before it was just a fact, like having to make the beds, order vegetables, something on a list of things to do . . . have a baby. The only concession she had made was to use her green ration book for pregnant women and take the free orange juice and extra pint of milk. Tom insisted she take the vitamin A and D tablets she'd been issued, which she'd done. But even when she had felt the baby move, it had been more of a nuisance than something to wonder at. But still deep inside she was terrified that when she eventually gave birth, she wouldn't be able to love the baby.

The women paid for their purchases then found a cafe and ordered a sandwich and coffee, piling their shopping bags on an empty chair beside them.

Cora removed her coat and sighed. 'Thank goodness for a seat!' She put her hand on her swollen stomach. 'I swear I'm carrying a footballer in here, because this baby won't keep still. What about yours?'

'It kicks Tom in the back when we're in bed,' she confessed. 'He thinks it's marvellous.'

'And you, Belle, what do you think?'

'I try not to,' she said, her voice trembling slightly.

'What's wrong, Belle?' Cora asked. 'What are you afraid of? I've never seen you like this in all the years I've known you, please tell me. I can't bear to see you like this – this isn't the woman I know at all.'

Taking a deep breath, Belle told her what was on her mind. 'I've never wanted children. I'm not like these women who coo over every baby they see in a pram. They have *never* featured in my dreams of a future. I have what I worked for – my business, now I'm married again, another thing I didn't imagine. I've no regrets about that – but a baby? I'm not sure I really want a child. Becoming pregnant was a mistake, it certainly wasn't planned for. But even worse . . . what if when it's born, I can't bond with it? That will break Tom's heart.'

Cora was lost for words. How could she help her friend, what could she say to allay her fears? Then she remembered Belle telling her a few years ago how she came to be on the game.

'Do you think it has anything to do with your mother kicking you out when you were a teenager, you know when she discovered that the vicar had seduced you? Could that be behind your fears?'

'I really don't know. She couldn't have loved me to do a thing like that, could she?'

'But you're not your mother, Belle! I've never known anyone with such a big heart. You *care* about people, look how you watched over me, how you mothered the younger prostitutes – the way you nursed Tom. How could you *not* love the baby you and Tom have created, even if it wasn't planned?'

Belle blinked away the tears in her eyes. 'I just hope you're right, Cora, I just hope you're right.'

During the following three days, Belle relaxed and enjoyed the company of her friend. She laughed as they reminisced about old times, walked on the beach, went to the pictures and she began to blossom. It was as if all restraints had been moved and she was her old self again.

She had shown Tom the baby clothes she'd bought and then put them away in a drawer. He'd admired them and, taking her into his arms, had held her close, without saying a word, but she knew he was pleased. Then after Cora had returned to London, Tom had taken her shopping for a cradle for the baby.

She was quiet when they were in the shop choosing, but Tom didn't push her, just let her choose the one she wanted, paid the bill and put the cradle into the back of the van. Then when they got home, he put it away until it was time to use it. They waited to buy a pram. Belle was insistent that it was unlucky to buy one until the baby had been born, so he said they'd wait.

In November, Cora gave birth to a son. Simon rang with the good news. He said, 'Cora said to tell you that she was right: she had that footballer after all.'

Belle smiled as she remembered their conversation.

* * *

At Christmas, Tom helped her do the cooking as he didn't want to tire her. There was just the two of them and Belle knew how much he was trying to help her cope with having his child and was grateful, but couldn't find the words to thank him.

Hildy had written enclosing photos of her, Milt and their child inside a Christmas card. She gazed at the pictures and was thrilled to see how happy they looked. Both her friends now had their family, it would soon be her turn and she was still uncertain.

It was in the middle of January, a few days before her due date that Belle's labour pains began in the small hours of the morning and she woke Tom, who rang the hospital. He helped Belle to dress, picked up the small suitcase that had been packed in readiness and drove his wife to the hospital. He waited until she was settled and was allowed to sit with her, to support her as the pains increased. He held her hand, talking softly, trying to sooth her, keep her calm until the nurse ushered him outside into the waiting room next door.

Before he left, he leant over and kissed Belle. 'I love you, darling, this will be over soon. I'll be waiting outside until then.'

During the following hours, Tom walked up and down, cringed as he could hear the cries of pain coming from his wife's room, then smiled as he heard her swear. He held his breath when things went quiet and stood rigid as he heard Belle being told to push.

At long last, he heard the cry of a baby. 'Thank God,' he murmured and wiped the sweat from his brow.

Shortly after, a nurse came out and said, 'You can come in now, Mr Harrison. You have a daughter. Congratulations.'

He took a deep breath as he walked into the room, his

emotions in turmoil. How would Belle react when she saw her baby? He paused in the doorway and looked towards the bed where he saw Belle holding a bundle in her arms, looking down at it and he waited to see the expression on her face. She looked up and smiled.

'Come and meet your daughter, Tom,' she said.

He walked over, kissed Belle and then looked at his baby. All his hidden emotions came to the surface as he looked at the perfect features of his child and tears streamed down his face. He had so longed for a family and now he was a father. He couldn't stop crying.

Belle reached out to him and took his hand. 'It's going to be alright, Tom, please don't cry. She looks just like you, isn't that marvellous?'

'She's beautiful and so are you,' he said and kissed her. 'What a very lucky man I am.'

'No, Tom. I'm the lucky one. I know how much you wanted children and I didn't. But you see, fate has a way of solving everything. Look what I would have missed. How could I not love this baby? I only wish I'd realised it sooner, I've missed so much joy.'

He sat on the bed and put his arms around her waist. 'But look how much more you have to look forward to.'

She looked slyly at him and whispered. 'I taught the nursing staff a few more swear words than they'd heard before, I'm afraid,' and she started laughing.

Tom laughed too. 'Oh Belle, I'm so happy to have you back to your old self. I have missed you!'

'Now we can go and buy the pram,' she said.

* * *

380

A few days later he took mother and child home. He'd put up the cradle in their bedroom and laid out some baby clothes in readiness, so thrilled he didn't know how to contain his happiness.

Belle settled in the living room and lay the baby safely on a chair and sat looking round at the familiar things, pleased to be home. Tom made a pot of tea and brought it in. He picked up the baby as Belle poured the tea into the cups. She watched her husband cooing and talking to his child, saw the joy and contentment of his face and gave a soft smile. He'd be a wonderful father of that she had no doubt.

After the pains of delivery, she had been taken by surprise when the nurse had placed the baby in her arms, and she felt the overwhelming feeling of love as she'd looked at her daughter for the first time. She'd never experience such a feeling before. It was all consuming. How could she have ever doubted herself?

She sat quietly drinking her tea. She thought back over her life on the streets of Southampton, of the years she'd spent as a prostitute, the time she'd left to work in the factory and eventually managing to buy this house and live her dream. Now she had a husband and a child. She felt truly blessed.

During those years she'd made friends with two other women who had all overcome their own problems and they'd all survived: Hildy with her scheming mother was now happily married in America with her family and Cora, her dearest friend, orphaned during the war, having to manage alone, was now happy with Simon and their son – and herself, with Tom, a man she adored and their child. Three strong women who'd overcome so much in their own way. It had been quite a journey and they'd all survived and triumphed.

Looking at her husband and child, she knew that the future ahead wouldn't be without its problems, but she'd never have to face them alone ever again. She would teach her daughter the difference between right and wrong, to be strong, give her the confidence to stand up to whatever she had to face but with the knowledge that she had parents who would stand by her always because they loved her. That was really all that anyone needed in this world – to be loved. After that you can overcome anything. She should know, she'd been there and survived. Her daughter would never ever have that struggle, she'd make sure of it, and she had vowed that the first moment she looked at her. Now she could relax and be a mother in the true sense of the word and it was her greatest achievement yet. The future was bright.

Acknowledgements

With thanks to my editor Sophie Robinson and the lovely staff at Allison & Busby.

As always, my love to my daughters, Beverley and Maxine.